Praise for THE

"I have read hundreds of books and it is extremely rare for me to be surprised or give 5 stars. I almost always anticipate the plot twists. I thought I had this one all figured out from the very beginning ... [I] couldn't have been more wrong! ... An exhilarating, emotional, fast paced read that I couldn't put down ... This story was utterly unique."

- Justine, Book Catharsis ★★★★★

"Gripping ... Lots of mystery and intrigue ... [Dystopian is] one of my favourite genres, but I haven't seen it written so well in a very long time ... I finished reading this book in awe."

- Carly, Goodreads ★★★★★

"I love dystopian novels, but I have to admit, after a while, they tend to follow the same plotline and twists. This is TOTALLY not the case here ... I was shocked."

- Gail, Goodreads ★★★★★

"Unique twist on the dystopian genre! ... Insanely thrilling!"
- Kelly, Twinsie Talk Book Reviews ★★★★★

"Lots of suspense, twists, and turns. I never saw the ending coming. It was a total surprise and explained everything!"

- Karon, Goodreads ★★★★★

THE UNKNOWN

J.W. LYNNE

ISBN 978-1082472978

To Angela, Ariana, Ashleigh, Avreigh, Brianna, Caren, Carly, Catharine, Chelsea, Davina, Donna, Doug, Gail, Hanna, Jennifer, Jenny, Jessica, Julie, Justine, Karon, Kathy, Kaye, Kelly, LA, Landen, Linzie, Lisa, Lois, Marc, Mark, Michelle, Peter, Sally, Sara, Shannon, Shaphir, Sherri, Siri, and Susan who were among the first to know …

Manifest:

Liam, male, age seventeen

Unpleasant, female, age seventeen

Harley, male, age fifteen

Lizard, female, age thirteen

Rain, female, age thirteen

Tiger, female, age twelve

Paris, female, age nine

Goat, male, age nine

GOAT

Screams. Screams. Everywhere. Everyone is scared. But I don't know who "everyone" is. Their voices sound young, so I guess they're kids, like me. I don't hear any older voices. So either the grownups aren't scared, or there aren't any grownups with us anymore.

I wish my dad were here to protect me, but he's not. He's hardly ever around when I need him. My mom isn't here either. The last time I saw her was about an hour ago, when two men who were wearing black masks came into my house and took me from her. The men put me inside the back of a van and drove me away. When the van stopped, they tied a ripped t-shirt over my eyes and moved me into this place that sounds like a helicopter.

I don't know why they covered up my eyes.

What is it that they don't want me to see?

Mom and Dad always tried to teach me to be brave. I know they'd tell me to be brave right now, because I am a man. But I'm *not* a man. I'm only nine years old. And I don't want to be brave. I want to go home. But I have a terrible feeling that I'm never going home again.

Somebody pulls my pajama shirt down over one of my shoulders. It's a grownup who is doing this—at least the hand feels grownup sized. I reach up to stop the hand, but it brushes me away. Something small and cold rubs against the skin on

1

my arm. All of a sudden, it smells like my doctor's office. And then there's a sharp poke into my skin. A needle.

And the screams fade away.

TUESDAY, MAY FIRST
0634

UNPLEASANT

Am I in a coffin? No, it's too big to be a coffin. But, whatever it is, it's extremely small. Too small. And it feels like it's getting smaller every second. *There isn't enough air in here.* The walls and ceiling are black. Even the light shining dimly above me seems to be tinged with black. *My eyes can't focus.* The pillow and sheets are white. Like the ones in a hospital. Am I in a hospital? *I can't breathe. I need air.* There's no sound in here except for my own raspy breaths. *I wonder if anyone outside my coffin will hear me if I scream.*

My head and neck feel strangely cold and bare. Something's missing from my body. I reach up anxiously, and my horrified fingers run panicked over the stubble on my scalp. Someone cut off my hair. It's like a boy's haircut. A really short one. There is less than half an inch left. Why did they cut off my hair? *Everything is getting blurry. Am I crying? No, I don't cry.*

I wonder if my mom finally made good on her threat to have me committed to a mental institution because she "can't control" me. I always thought it was stupid for her to say that. Just because I'm her daughter that doesn't give her the right to control me. I'm perfectly capable of making my own decisions. If I want to destroy my life, I should be allowed to do it.

But if she was going to have me committed, why now? In

3

less than two months, I will be an adult and my mom will be free of her legal obligation to me.

Maybe she thinks this is her last chance.

My heart is beating so hard it's going to give out. Is someone monitoring me? Can't they see that I'm freaking out in here?

This can't be a hospital. It's moving. The feeling is extremely subtle, but there is definitely some movement. Unless the movement is just an altered perception—a side effect from the drug that was injected into me last night to make me stop fighting.

Is anyone going to help me?

Maybe this whole thing is just one of my bad dreams.

Are they ever going to let me out of here?

This must be a dream. It has to be.

It's too bizarre to be real.

I don't want to die in here.

I'm losing my mind.

Please, someone, anyone, get me out of here.

TUESDAY, MAY FIRST
0702

TIGER

Last night, I was snatched from my family's house by masked men who didn't speak. I woke up here, inside this little black compartment that's only big enough for a tiny mattress. With my pretty hair all gone. I was alone until one of the compartment's walls slid away and a kid poked their upside-down face into my compartment—maybe from a compartment above mine.

The kid leaps down onto a floor that's below my compartment, and I see that she's a girl. She looks about a year or two older than me, maybe thirteen or fourteen years old. She's wearing white pajama shorts with purple dots all over them and a matching sleeveless top. Like me, her hair is almost nonexistent. Unlike me, her breasts have started to grow.

"Were you kidnapped too?" the girl asks me.

I nod, but I don't say anything.

I wonder if she knows that I'm a girl. I'm wearing my oldest brother's hand-me-down pajamas. With my hair now gone and my chest still flat, I could easily be mistaken for a boy. I guess it doesn't really matter right now.

"Come on," she says. "We need to find out what's going on here."

I climb out of my compartment, and the two of us search the space around us. It doesn't take long. The floor that we're standing on is only about two feet wide and six feet long.

There are two bed compartments—mine and this girl's—one on top of the other. Walls surround us on all sides, and there is a ladder leading up to a circular spot on the ceiling that looks like a covered manhole.

The girl points up at the manhole. "That must be the way out."

"It's probably locked," I say. "The kidnappers surely don't want us wandering about unsupervised."

"We might as well try it," the girl says.

She makes quick work of the ladder, and soon she's at the top. I watch as she touches a glowing red button on the ceiling. To my surprise, the button turns green and, silently, the manhole lifts open.

"I'm going up," the girl whispers to me. "Are you coming?"

"I'm right behind you," I say to her.

Barefoot, I climb up the cold metal rungs of the ladder, toward the exit.

TUESDAY, MAY FIRST
0713

GOAT

There's a girl staring at me. She's standing right outside the box that I slept in. I think she's close to my age, but she might be a little bit younger. Maybe she's eight years old. She's wearing a blue nightshirt with a black-and-white drawing of the Eiffel Tower on the front, and she's almost bald. I woke up almost bald too. I guess the men shaved off my hair after they gave me the medicine that made me go to sleep.

"Where are we?" I ask the girl.

"I don't know," she says very quietly, as if she's afraid that someone might overhear.

"How did you get here?" I ask, making my voice softer this time.

"Men came into my house and stole me from my bed …"

She stops talking and just looks at me with sad eyes.

"Where are the men now?" I ask her.

She shrugs. "I don't know."

UNPLEASANT

When my coffin opened, I found myself in a slightly-larger chamber that had a hatch on the floor. That hatch led me to a ladder, which deposited me in a place about half the size of my bedroom back home. The only way in or out of here seems to be via the hatches: four on the floor and two on the ceiling. On either side of this narrow space, there are four chairs and four small tables, all of them bolted down to the floor. Everything is pure white, except for a silver sink in one corner with eight silver cups set above it. Eight rectangular windows reveal that we are in some kind of aircraft, flying high above a body of water. An ocean, maybe. But which ocean?

There are three other kids in here. Two girls and one boy. All teenagers, but they're younger than me. The boy is probably the oldest of the three. He's maybe fifteen or sixteen. The girls look like they're twelve or thirteen. Everyone is wearing what appear to be their nightclothes, like I am, and they have ultra-short haircuts that match mine. The older-looking girl has reddened eyes, as if she's been crying. I haven't cried in a long time, and I don't plan to start now. Crying doesn't get you anywhere. I should know. I've cried more in my seventeen years than normal people do in an entire lifetime, and it has gotten me nowhere at all. Except maybe here.

Yesterday was an ordinary day. In the morning, my mom

dragged me out of bed twenty minutes before school started and left me lying on the cold tile floor of the bathroom. I forced myself to take a shower, so I didn't smell bad enough or look greasy enough to attract unwanted attention from people. I hate attention from people. Especially the people at school. After my shower, I toweled off, got dressed, and ducked out of the house before my mom could give me yet another one of her disappointed stares. I was halfway to the bus stop before I realized that I forgot to brush my teeth. That didn't matter though. No one sees your teeth if you never smile.

School was normal, and by "normal" I mean it sucked. I missed pointless homeroom, but I arrived before the bell for first period. The school and I have an understanding that if I arrive in time for *actual* classes, I won't be disciplined for being tardy. Despite the fact that I've missed every homeroom since the start of twelfth grade, they're still planning to let me graduate in June.

At least they *were*. Who knows what's going to happen now?

I'm pretty sure I'm not going to make it to school today.

Who knows if I'll ever make it to school again?

One more kid arrives. A girl, around thirteen years old. She looks bewildered, like the others, awkward and uncertain. She takes a seat on one of the chairs, probably because the rest of us are sitting, and she doesn't talk, probably because the rest of us aren't talking.

A few seconds later, a boy and a girl emerge together from one of the hatches on the floor. They can't be more than eight or nine years old. They're so little. Helpless. Frightened. But that isn't my problem. I need to focus on how to get out of here. Not that I really want to get back home. But I don't want to let anyone take control of my life ... end my life. Even though maybe they should.

The youngest boy and girl sit together on a chair. They're so small that they share it as though it's a diminutive couch. That brings the total number of kids here to seven, including me. Everyone except for me emerged from one of the hatches on the floor. I'm the only one who entered from a hatch on the ceiling. The other ceiling hatch is still closed tight. It could lead to anywhere. To another bedroom maybe. Or maybe it leads to our kidnappers.

Another minute passes before the remaining hatch on the ceiling finally opens. My body tenses as bare feet appear on the ladder that's below the hatch. The feet are big ones. Fully grown. Attached to muscular legs with hair growing on them. But I think he might be one of us, because he's wearing only boxers and a t-shirt. And then I see his face. Yes, he's a kid. About my age. Like all of the rest of us, his head has been shaved, rendering him nearly bald.

"Where the hell are we?" he says loudly.

I feel a shock inside me at the noise of his voice, disturbing the silence.

"Be quiet," the littlest girl says. Her tone is firm and gentle at the same time. "The bad men might hear you."

She's a bold little girl. The kind of little girl I used to be.

"I hope they *do* hear me," he responds. "I want them to come in here and tell me what the hell is going on."

I roll my eyes at his bravado. "And then what are you going to do?" I ask the boy.

His gaze locks with mine. "What do *you* propose?" he asks me, bristling.

I look at the faces of the other kids. They're scared. I doubt arguing with this boy will help calm their fears. He and I appear to be the oldest ones here. We need to take control. Or at least *I* do.

I inhale and address the group as a whole, "I take it that, last night, strangers wearing masks took each of you from your homes. And you were given an injection to make you sleep. And you woke up a little while ago in a coffin-bed. Is that right?"

Slowly, everyone nods.

"So we're all in the same boat." I'm really not sure where to go from here, so I buy myself some time, "Why don't we go around in a circle and introduce ourselves? Tell your age, a little about yourself, and what you're good at." That's something we did on the first day of a group therapy session I went to back in sixth grade. I got sent there because the useless school counselor said I had to attend at least one therapy session after I got beat up in the gym locker room. I went once, but I never went back because I was sure that it wouldn't help me. Even at that age, I already knew that nothing could help me.

And then I have a thought. "Maybe we shouldn't use our real names ... in case the kidnappers don't already know them," I say. "You can pick another name for us to call you. Whatever name you want."

The difficult boy slumps down into one of the two remaining empty seats. I guess he's done confronting me ... for the moment.

"You go first," the littlest girl says to me.

Maybe she should be the one in charge.

"Okay." I exhale. "I'm ... I'm seventeen years old," I say. "I'm good at swimming, which is pretty useless in our current situation. That's about it. Next."

"And what should we call you?" the little girl asks.

I haven't really considered what name I'd like to use here. I figured I'd go last, not first, so I'd have time to think. I despise my real name. This is my chance to pick a name that fits me. An honest name. We need to be honest with each other.

"You might as well call me what my mom calls me," I say. "'Unpleasant.' Because I'm generally unpleasant."

If I had said such a thing at school, everyone would have laughed at me. But no one here laughs. Not even the smallest of snickers. Not even from Difficult Boy. They all just turn to the kid to my left. The youngest boy. And focus their attention on him.

GOAT

"I'm nine years old," I say. "I'm good at tying knots, and I'm okay at sailing, although I haven't been sailing in a while. You can call me Goat." I feel my cheeks get hot. The "name" Goat sounded good in my head, but out loud it sounds … strange. I try to explain, "It's because … goats are good friends … and they make milk that can be turned into cheese … Anyway, goats are useful. I hope I can be useful someday."

That sounded completely stupid. I wish I could delete everything I said and start over. I stare down at the Han Solo picture on my pajamas, trying to stop tears from burning their way into my eyes.

The girl who is sharing my chair with me gently nudges my elbow. I look over at her, and she smiles in a way that makes me believe that she doesn't think I sounded stupid at all. It actually looks like she thinks the exact opposite.

"My name is … Paris," she says, looking only at me. "That's because it's my favorite place in the world, even though I've never been there. I'm nine years old. I'm good at spelling and math … pretty much anything at school, except for sports. I'm not good at sports."

Neither am I. So we have something in common.

Paris smiles at me again. It feels like she can hear my thoughts just by looking at my face.

"Next," Paris adds, and we move on to the person sitting next to us.

TUESDAY, MAY FIRST
0740

TIGER

It's almost my turn to introduce myself. There's only one person left before me. My heart is beating harder and harder every second. I don't want my turn to come. I hate speaking in front of people. I don't like people staring at me. I like to blend into walls. Usually I'm pretty good at that, but blending into walls is impossible here.

There's one person who is making me especially nervous about my turn. My brother. He's sitting in a chair just a few feet away from me. He must have noticed me here, but we haven't made eye contact, because we don't do that. Even though my brother and I have shared the same home ever since I was born, it's as if we don't share anything at all. He generally doesn't acknowledge my existence. Just like now.

It's my turn.

"You can call me Tiger," I say, staring at my feet. "I'm twelve years old. And I'm a girl. I'm good at … nothing much really."

I exhale, feeling frustrated with myself. That isn't what I rehearsed in my head. I was going to tell everyone why I chose the name Tiger. It's the name of the dog that my family adopted from the animal shelter on my tenth birthday. My parents said that Tiger was *my* dog. They said they got him for me because they felt I was mature enough to take on the

15

responsibility of caring for a pet. But, that night, when my dad was talking with my mom in their bedroom, I overhead him say the *true* reason that they adopted Tiger. They thought a dog would help bring me out of my shell. Apparently, someone told them that dogs were good for kids who have mild autism, like me. I wasn't going to tell everyone here that I have autism. I was just going to tell them the part about naming myself Tiger because of my dog.

I end up stopping where I did—with the statement that I'm not good at anything—and I nod at the girl who is sitting in the chair next to me, hoping that she will take over the spotlight.

Mercifully, she does.

TUESDAY, MAY FIRST
0742

UNPLEASANT

As I listen to the other kids introduce themselves, I start to feel like maybe my introduction wasn't as awful as it felt. It was truthful. Just like the other kids' introductions seem to be. If we were doing this in regular life, people would be saying things that they thought made them sound cool, or funny, or popular. But, here, people are talking the way they would to close friends, the kind of friends who you can discuss your true feelings with, even the ones that make you sound weird.

But we aren't friends. We barely know each other. I guess if we stay here long enough we will become friends ... or enemies. It's impossible to spend all of your time with someone without becoming one or the other.

As each kid introduces themselves, I try to remember what they say, but I can't seem to retain anything at all. My brain is painfully foggy. That's unfortunate because I need to be more alert than ever right now. Who knows what threat we are about to face?

Clearly, our kidnappers are carefully controlling things here. They opened the doors to our bedrooms and allowed us to gather. If we do anything that isn't to their liking, they will no doubt intervene. I saw last night *how* they intervene ... with gags and restraints and injections of powerful tranquilizers. I don't think it's wise to misbehave at this point. Eventually, I may need to take actions that could elicit punishment, but I won't do so until I believe that the risks are outweighed by the potential benefits.

For now, we are being allowed to sit and introduce ourselves without interruption. Maybe our captors are listening in, trying to collect information about us. Maybe they don't know much about the kids they've kidnapped, and they want to get some insight. Figure out our strengths and weaknesses.

It isn't until Difficult Boy speaks that I realize how far my thoughts have wandered. "I'm Liam," he says. "That's my real name. I'm seventeen. I can take apart just about anything and put it back together. When I turn eighteen, I'm going into the military." After he says that, Difficult Boy ... I mean, Liam ... looks at me. "Okay, we've all introduced ourselves. Now what?" It's clear by his tone that he's mocking me rather than considering me to be the one who's in charge.

The truth is, I have no idea what we should do now.

Maybe we should just sit here and wait.

But wait for what?

Something must be coming. Something nefarious. There would be no sense in kidnapping us and locking us up and leaving us until we die. The captors must have plans for us.

Suddenly, a bell dings. Two times. *A signal.*

An instant later, a long skinny portion of one of the walls slides up and eight transparent boxes are revealed. I can see what's inside. Food!

I am so hungry.

Everyone just stares at the boxes ... everyone except for Liam.

"Breakfast is served," he says, and he walks over to the boxes, as if there is nothing sinister to be considered.

"What if it's poisoned?" the littlest girl, Paris, says.

"If they wanted to kill us, they would have done it last

night," Liam replies.

"There could be some kind of tranquilizer in the food," I say.

"Why tranquilize us if we're being cooperative?" he counters.

"If you want to eat it, go ahead," I respond. "I'll wait and see what happens to you first."

Paris nods. "Me too."

The other kids nod as well.

"Suit yourselves." Liam selects one of the boxes and returns to his seat before opening it up. As soon as he does, the aroma of warm maple syrup wafts over to me, moistening my dry mouth. I watch as he pours fruit and nuts into some sort of hot cereal and then spoons the resulting concoction into his mouth. "Mmm, so good," he says, either truly relishing the food or mocking me again. Or maybe a little of both.

Liam's food is gone in minutes. He returns the empty container to its original location and obtains a cup of clear liquid from the nearby sink. He downs the liquid in seconds.

This boy has no fear, and maybe no common sense either.

"Anyone who wants to forgo their breakfast, let me know," Liam says. "I'll gladly eat it for you."

The other kids squirm as their resolve starts to weaken. Liam seems fine after eating and drinking what has been provided to us. After a few minutes, the others begin to collect their boxes of food and hesitantly eat.

I am no longer the leader. Liam is.

After about ten minutes, only one kid remains unfed other than me: Paris.

She stares—with a mixture of longing and worry—at Goat's food as he finishes it up.

"It's probably safe to go ahead and eat," I tell Paris.

"I'll wait a little longer," she says, giving me an uncertain smile.

I nod. "Suit yourself."

As everyone else finishes their meals and returns their empty food boxes to the wall, surprisingly-normal-sounding conversations begin. People are starting to let down their guard.

I won't let down my guard here. Not now. Not ever.

Suddenly, the bell sounds again. One … two … three times … And then, the wall slides closed, with all of the food boxes—two of them completely untouched—behind it.

My heart plummets into my aching empty stomach.

"Looks like breakfast is over," Liam says, in his mocking tone, looking directly at me.

Under different circumstances, I would punch him in the ribs. Liam needs to be put in his place, before his behavior escalates. But punching Liam will almost certainly get me punished by whoever brought us here. I highly doubt they want us beating each other up.

"I'm sorry about breakfast, Paris," I say loudly enough to make sure Liam hears me. I hope he feels ashamed of himself. By mocking me, he was also mocking that nine-year-old girl. *But maybe Liam doesn't feel bad about stuff like that.*

"I'm okay," Paris says quietly.

She isn't okay. She's hungry. Like I am. But she's little. She needs the food much more than I do. Guilt creeps up inside me. Paris didn't eat because I didn't. She was looking to me as a role model. But she deserves a better role model than me. Even back in my normal life I could barely take care of myself. But, in a way, life might be easier here. Here, everything is just about surviving.

And if I die here, maybe it doesn't really matter.

But I don't want to bring anyone else down with me.
Especially not that little girl.

TIGER

"I gotta pee," the youngest boy says. During the introductions, I think he said his name is Goat. After he speaks, Goat stays sitting, looking embarrassed by his need to carry out his bodily functions.

I have to pee too, but I didn't want to say so. I like to keep my bathroom needs private. For that reason, I drink as little as possible, especially on school days. Usually, if I go to the bathroom before school, I can hold my pee until I get home in the afternoon.

"Let's figure something out for you," Liam says hopping to his feet and looking around.

It surprises me to see Liam come so quickly to this kid's aid. It has been years since he has come to mine. But Liam and Unpleasant are the closest to adults that we have here. And since Goat is a boy and he needs a bathroom, I guess that's Liam's department.

I haven't seen any bathrooms here, but there must be bathrooms. This airplane is way too nice for the bad guys to allow us to soil it with our excrement. Besides, as far as I know, all airplanes, except for really small ones, have bathrooms.

One of the other boys—a fifteen-year-old named Harley, after the motorcycle—points to the shiny silver sink next to the spot where our breakfasts were delivered. "Boys can pee in there," he says.

Liam snaps around and glares at Harley. "And what about the girls?"

I wonder if he's thinking about me.

Harley tilts his head to the side. "The girls can pee there too."

I cringe at the thought of having to pee in front of everyone here, especially the boys, but even the other girls.

"I'm not going to pee in a sink," a thirteen-year-old girl, Lizard—because she loves reptiles of all kinds—protests.

"Enough!" Liam says so strongly that everyone stiffens. "There has to be a bathroom here somewhere."

I hear a sound behind me, and I spin around. There is an open doorway there. A doorway that wasn't there before.

I expect to see one of the bad men standing in the doorway. But no one is there. It seems the door opened by itself!

"Wait here," Liam says to us. Uneasily, he heads through the open doorway and into the hallway beyond it.

Liam is gone for just a minute or so before he returns.

"Come on, Goat," Liam says, and then he turns to the rest of us. "There are two bathrooms, so if anyone else needs one, go ahead."

Everyone heads toward the bathrooms.

"One bathroom is for the girls and one for the boys," Lizard calls out.

"But there are *three* boys and *five* girls," I argue.

"Girls are neater than boys," Lizard says.

"But that's not fair—" I start.

"Nothing here is going to be fair!" Unpleasant says in too loud a voice. "We've been *kidnapped*. Who knows if we'll make it out of this alive? Who cares who uses what bathroom?" She storms into one of the bathrooms, slams her fist on a button inside, and the door slides shut behind her.

Lizard looks at me as if I smell bad, and I feel my cheeks burn. I wish I knew what to say to make her stop looking at me like that.

Liam gestures to the other bathroom. "Go ahead, Goat." His voice is so calm that it is as if Unpleasant's tirade never happened.

Goat hurries into the empty bathroom and shuts the door.

"There are also showers," Liam says to the rest of us. He leads us to a room with two showerheads barely separated from each other by a translucent divider.

My heart thumps uncomfortably at the thought of having to take a shower right next to someone else, even another girl, but after Unpleasant's outburst, I don't say anything about that, and neither does anyone else, not even Lizard.

Liam continues down the skinny hallway to the final open doorway. "There's also a washer and dryer ... and clothes."

As Liam indicated, the final room in the hallway is home to a small washing machine and dryer. Stacked on top of the machines are dark-blue sweatpants and sweatshirts, white t-shirts, and two six-packs of white Fruit of the Loom socks. I do a quick count of the sweatclothes and t-shirts, and there are eight of each, one outfit for each of us.

Goat and Unpleasant reappear from the toilet rooms and others take their turns. Even though I really have to pee, I don't make any attempt to take a turn yet. If I wait until the others are done, maybe I can avoid further interpersonal conflict.

"I'm going to shower and change clothes," my roommate, Rain—because that's her favorite kind of weather—says. She's shivering. Her pajama shorts and top are very thin, and it's cold on this airplane. I'm glad that I'm wearing pajamas with long pants and long sleeves.

"I'm going to do some exploring," Liam says. "I suggest that everyone stay in groups, or at least in pairs. Just in case."

"Just in case what?" Paris asks, her voice anxious.

For the first time, I see Liam's ever-present confidence shake, but only a little. "We don't know what to expect here, so we need to stick together."

"But you went alone down this hallway, before you knew what was here," Paris says.

"I'm willing to put *myself* at risk," he says.

"Me too," Unpleasant says.

"Yeah," Harley says. "I don't need the buddy system."

"Okay." Liam exhales. "It was just a suggestion." He turns and starts back down the hallway. "I'm going exploring. Anyone who wants to come along can follow me. Or not."

No one follows Liam. Everyone is busy working out how they will take turns in the showers. I'm not sure what makes me do it, but I rush after my brother.

Liam glances back. And then … he stops.

"What do you need … Tiger?" His voice is gentle.

"Can … can I come with you?" I ask very softly.

My heart twists as he hesitates.

"Yeah," he finally says.

"But I also have to pee," I blurt out.

The door to one of the toilet rooms opens and Lizard emerges.

Liam gestures to the toilet room. "Go ahead," he says. "I'll wait for you."

"Thanks," I say and, without making eye contact—because it would be too hard right now with all the feelings I'm feeling—I rush into the toilet room and shut the door.

TUESDAY, MAY FIRST
0836

UNPLEASANT

Liam has gone off to explore the airplane. The second youngest girl, Tiger, went with him. I considered joining him, but I quickly nixed that idea. Although Liam and I obviously have the same goal of getting the hell out of here, I will do my investigating alone, which is my usual modus operandi.

Liam and Tiger headed down through the hatch that Rain and Tiger emerged from this morning, so I head up, climbing the ladder that leads to Liam's bedroom.

It feels strange to be in "Liam's room," even though it isn't exactly his. No part of this airplane belongs to any of us. For now, everyone and everything in here belongs to our captors. This airplane is our prison. And we might be serving a life sentence. A surge of anger raises the tension in my tight muscles. *How dare those men take us?* My dad must be beside himself. If he knows. If my mom was able to reach him. Or maybe he's not upset. Maybe he's glad to be rid of me.

Suddenly, I feel lightheaded. Maybe it's because I skipped breakfast. Maybe it's the stress. Maybe it's the after-effects of whatever drugs were injected into me last night.

I sit down on Liam's bed—so I don't faint—and try to distract myself with concrete thoughts. I focus on Liam's room. It is a mirror image of mine, and the color scheme is the same. The walls, ceiling, and floor are black, and the bedding is white. There are no cabinets or drawers or anything decorative. Like the rest of the airplane, Liam's room smells utterly clean, like a hospital, but I don't think this is some kind of airborne psychiatric ward. Now that I've met the others, I'm pretty sure I'm the only person here who merits hospitalization for mental reasons.

I decide to stand up again, taking it slowly, gripping onto the bottom of Liam's bed as I rise. As I do, I feel something shift beneath my hands. I lift the mattress and discover a handle. When I pull it, the base of the bed rises up about a foot in the air. Underneath is a hidden compartment with stuff inside it: notebooks ... pens ... board games ... books ... a deck of playing cards ... a toothbrush ... a full-sized tube of toothpaste ... a bath towel. Everything appears to be brand new. I check the notebooks and see that they are, as I'd suspected, devoid of any notes.

I wonder if there are similar items waiting for me below my mattress. Then it hits me like a punch in the stomach that, if all these things were placed here for us, then our kidnappers aren't planning to release us anytime soon. Based on the number of books and notebooks and games, they could be planning to keep us here for a very long time. However, if they bothered to provide all this, then maybe they aren't planning to kill us either. At least not right away.

"What'd you find?" a little voice asks from behind me.

I spin around and see Paris' head poking up through the open hatch.

"Are you trying to give me a heart attack or something?" I ask her.

"You're kind of young for a heart attack," she counters, as she climbs up into Liam's room.

"What are you doing, Paris?" I ask.

She peers into the hidden compartment under Liam's

mattress. "I'm going exploring with you."

"Why aren't you going exploring with your friend Goat?" I ask.

"He didn't want to go exploring," she says. "I thought it'd be safer to go with you than on my own, because of what Liam said about people sticking together. So is it okay if I stay with you?" She looks at me with hopeful eyes.

It would be cruel to say no to her.

"That's fine," I say, resigned. Eventually, Paris will realize that I'm not worth her time. That's how my life works. No one who has any real choice in the matter sticks around me for very long, and for good reason. Nothing good ever happens when I'm around. But it's probably better to let Paris figure that out on her own than to push her away when she thinks she needs me. It will be less painful that way ... at least for her.

Paris will figure out soon enough how worthless I really am.

TUESDAY, MAY FIRST
0842

TIGER

The two bed compartments in the room I share with Rain remind me of a bunk bed. When I was a little girl, I desperately wanted a bunk bed, even though that didn't really make any sense because I had no one to share it with. I had two brothers and no sisters, and my brothers and I each had our own separate bedrooms. I guess I thought I could use a bunk bed for sleepovers, like the ones I heard the other girls talking about at school. But, even if I'd had a bunk bed, I didn't have any friends who would have come to sleep over.

Liam is methodically checking every inch of the walls and ceiling. He has been doing that for a while now. I finally get up the courage to ask him, "What are you looking for?"

"I don't know," he says, without glancing away from his work. "Anything."

So I start looking too. I crawl into my bed compartment and check the walls in there, even though I know Liam will probably insist on checking them himself.

A few minutes later, I hear a strange creaking sound above my head. Hesitantly, I climb out of my compartment. When my head clears the bottom of Rain's bed, I see that Liam has lifted up her mattress. Hidden under there is a bunch of stuff. A couple of board games. A checkers game. Some pink and purple notebooks. Colored pencils and regular pencils. Pink towels. A toothbrush and toothpaste.

"I wonder if there's anything under my mattress," I say.

As I lean down to investigate, I realize something awful …

I run my fingers around my neck, and panic pounds into my heart. "No! No! No!"

"What's wrong?" Liam asks.

Frantic, I lift the door of the cabinet that's under my mattress. I see the same types of stuff that I saw under Rain's mattress. Different games. Different notebooks. But none of it is from back home. I sift through it anyway, searching for the only object I care anything about, but I can't find it. "It's gone!"

"What's gone?" Liam asks.

"Andrew's necklace!" Tears are spilling out of me now.

For almost four years, I've had that silver chain with the little frog pendant around my neck at all times. Our older brother, Andrew, bought that necklace with his own money when he was twelve years old and, from that moment on, it was his most prized possession. I was the only person who he ever allowed to wear it other than him. From the instant I was born, Andrew was my best friend. He was also my *only* friend, the only person in the whole world who ever really understood me. When Andrew enlisted in the military, it scared me to death. Being in the military is dangerous, but Andrew said it is important to serve our country. Before he left for boot camp, he asked me if I would do him a favor. He wanted me to wear his necklace for him, to keep it safe until he got back. Of course I told him I would. It made me feel special to know I had something of Andrew's with me all the time, especially something as important to him as that necklace. Every time he left for his deployments, he'd put it around my neck and, every time he returned, I'd give it back to him. We traded that necklace back and forth two times. But then, he put that necklace on me, and he never came home.

I check the bedclothes, hoping that maybe, somehow, the necklace is there.

"The kidnappers probably took the necklace," Liam says. "They took my chain too."

I steal a glimpse at Liam's neck and see that his cherished silver chain—the one he got from our grandpa a few years ago—is gone.

"Do you think they'll give them back?" I ask Liam, my voice shaking.

"Whether they do or not, it's okay," he says, as if he's trying to sound reassuring.

"No, it's not okay!" I shout, staring at Liam through blurry eyes. "I *promised* Andrew I'd take care of it for him!"

Liam grabs hold of both my arms. So tight that it hurts. "It isn't your fault," he says. "None of this is your fault."

I know that's true, but that doesn't make it any easier. "*Andrew* put that necklace around my neck. *No one* had the right to take it off."

"It doesn't matter," Liam says. "It's just a necklace."

I don't look at him. I can't. "How can you even think that? How can you not understand? Andrew was *your* brother too."

"What I mean is … *people* are what's important, not *things*," Liam says quietly.

I sit on my bed, trying to still the trembling that has taken over my body. "When all you have left of the people you love are *things*, then the *things* become really important."

My mind travels—the way it so often does—to my last moments with Andrew. He came into my bedroom after he'd said his private goodbyes to my mom and dad and to Liam. I'd asked to say goodbye last, because I wanted time to think of what to say to him, but when Andrew came into my room, I still hadn't figured out what to say. There was too much to tell him and, when I tried to figure out how to say it, I didn't know where to start. My thoughts were in a loop with no beginning and no end.

Andrew walked over to me and gave me a hug. I don't usually like hugging people, but Andrew knew how to hug me so it didn't feel overwhelming. As we hugged, he told me about a memory he had of the day when our family adopted Tiger from the animal shelter. When we got to our house with our new dog, Andrew and I took him into our backyard and the three of us played Frisbee for close to two hours. Tiger finally got tired and sat down next to me, and I sat down on the grass, and I rested my head against him. Andrew said it made him so happy to see the two of us sitting there like that.

Just when I was starting to feel happy, thinking about that day, Andrew said it was time for him to go. He put his necklace around my neck and then he said goodbye to me. I tried, but I couldn't say it back. I grabbed onto him, clinging to him like he was the edge of a cliff with a great chasm below. I couldn't let go of him. Not this time. I couldn't make myself release my grip.

My dad came into the room and he pried me away from my brother. I was screaming and crying. I felt like I couldn't breathe. Like I was going to die. I was shouting for my dad to let me go. And then, Andrew said, "Let her go."

My dad let go of me, but I just stayed where I was, in an inert puddle on my bed. Andrew took me back into his arms, and he held me really tight. He told me he loved me very much, and he didn't want to leave me. And in my crazy, desperate heart, I thought he was going to say that he wasn't going to leave. That he was going to stay.

But then he took my arms from around him, and he put my

arms around my dad. And he held them there for a moment. And then my dad held onto me very tight. So tight I couldn't breathe again. And Andrew walked away. Out the door of my bedroom. My heart broke, and my world shattered. I didn't think anything could hurt as bad as that.

Four weeks and one day later, I found out I was wrong. When they told us that Andrew died, every bit of happiness inside me died too. The only thing that kept me going was the need to protect his necklace. And now it's gone.

I lie down on my bed and cover my face with my hands. And then I listen to Liam quietly leave me alone. The way he always seems to do when I need him the most.

TUESDAY, MAY FIRST
0937

UNPLEASANT

When Paris and I return to the main cabin, after exploring the final bedroom, almost everyone is assembled there, including Liam. Some people appear freshly showered and are wearing the blue sweatsuits. Others are still in their pajamas. I'm starting to stink a little, so I ask, "Where are we in the queue for the showers?"

Lizard answers, "There's no more water."

"There's not even anything coming out of the faucets in the sinks," Rain adds.

"We're hoping it's temporary," Harley says. "A glitch in the system or something."

Paris goes over to share a chair with Goat again, seeming unconcerned about the loss of our showers. Nine-year-olds can go without bathing for a while without stinking too bad. But this prison is going to reek very soon if the rest of us can't bathe.

I sit down on the empty chair furthest away from the others. To my surprise, Liam gets up from his chair, walks over, and sits down in the chair next to mine. *I hope he can't smell my stench.*

"Did you discover anything during your exploring?" he asks me, keeping his voice low.

"There are compartments under each of the mattresses," I tell him, secretly hoping he'll be at least a little impressed, though I really shouldn't care what Liam thinks.

He nods. "Yeah, I found those too."

I try to hide my disappointment. "Other than that, I didn't find anything unanticipated," I say, feeling deflated. "There are two bedrooms above us, four bedrooms below us, the bathrooms, the showers, and the laundry room … and that's it."

"But, of course, there's something outside of all that," he says.

"Of course," I say. "And we'll have to figure out how to access it, but we can't just go banging down the walls."

"What's your plan then?" he asks in a way that makes me feel like he's testing me.

"I don't know," I say defensively. "What's yours?"

He exhales. "I don't know."

"I'm glad we're on the same page," I mutter bitterly.

Liam gives me half a smile. "You're funny," he says.

"Sorry," I say. "I just …"

He looks into my eyes, and I can't stop my heart from picking up speed. I feel a mix of fear and something else that I can't define.

"When you're talking to me, you don't have to censor yourself," he says. "You can tell me anything. Anything at all."

I can't believe Liam is suggesting that I drop my inhibitions with him, a stranger. A stranger who I don't even like. But it does seem that, despite our rocky start, he might actually be making an effort to connect with me now. If we want to have any hope of surviving this, being united is probably our best course of action.

I look down at my bubblegum-pink nightgown with a big cartoon cat stamped across the chest. "I think it's about time that I go change clothes. People have been subjected to my sexy Hello Kitty nightie far too much for one morning."

Liam lets out a self-conscious laugh. "It's good that you're a comedian. Comedy makes everything better. Even the end of the world."

That's a morbid thought, but maybe he's right. Laughing feels better than crying.

The thing is, I'm *not* a comedian. At least I never was before.

TUESDAY, MAY FIRST
1158

GOAT

Paris and I have been sitting together in a chair and looking out one of the airplane windows for a while now. All I can see out there is a cloudy sky and an ocean that looks like it goes on forever. That's all I've seen every time I've looked out any of the windows here.

"Why do you think those men took us from our families?" Paris asks me softly.

"I have a couple of ideas," I say, "but none of them really make sense."

She keeps her eyes fixed on the window. "Ideas? Like what?"

"They might want to get money from our parents," I suggest. "But my parents aren't rich. They're not poor either, but we really don't have a whole lot of money."

"I think my family is a little poor," Paris says. "My parents have trouble paying all the bills every month."

"So I guess we probably weren't kidnapped so they could get our parents' money," I say, feeling even more certain of it now.

"Probably not," Paris agrees.

I have another thought, but I don't even want to consider that it could be true. "I saw a video about a messed-up man who stole children so he could abuse them," I say as quietly as I can. "He hurt them really bad."

"Do you think these men are going to do that to us?" Paris asks.

"Maybe," I say. "But, last night, when they were tying me up, it felt like they were being careful not to hurt me."

"I think every one of us is important to them," Paris says, still staring out the window.

"Why do you think that?" I ask.

"They chose us specifically," she says. "You and I are from Virginia, but Tiger and Liam are from Washington, D.C., and Lizard said she's from New York. The bad guys went all over the place to get us. That's a lot of trouble to go through to get a couple of kids. If they just wanted to get some kids to abuse, they would have grabbed them all from one place. So there has to be a reason they took each of us."

"I can understand why they took *you*," I say.

She looks puzzled. "What do you mean?"

"You're smart and pretty and nice," I say. Paris' cheeks turn pink. I feel like mine are turning pink too. "But if they wanted *special* kids, then they wouldn't have taken me," I say. "The only people who think I'm special are my parents."

DING. DING.

There is a sliding sound on my right. The wall at the food spot has opened up again. Eight boxes are set out there, just like they were for breakfast.

"I guess it's lunch time," I say to Paris.

Everyone quickly gets up and grabs a lunch box. Paris and I take our boxes of food, and we bring them back to our chair. Paris must be starving, because she didn't eat any breakfast. She digs into this food immediately, without any signs of fear.

The food is brown and lumpy but, just like breakfast, it smells and tastes amazing. It's some kind of meat and potatoes in a sauce that's so good that I scrape up every last bit with my spoon and have to stop myself from trying to lick out the bowl. There's even a dessert: chunks of sweet apples wrapped up in a gooey cinnamon roll. This food is a hundred times better than any of our school lunches ever were. It's even better than the food my mom makes, and my mom's food is really good. I swallow my last bit of dessert, and I dig my teeth into my lip so I don't cry. *I miss my mom.*

"They're being nice to us," Paris says quietly. She doesn't sound comforted by that fact, instead she sounds worried. "Why would strangers kidnap children just so they could be nice to them?"

I have an answer, but it's an awful answer. Maybe I shouldn't say it, but I have a feeling we're both thinking it. "About two years ago, a hurricane passed right over my house," I say. "After all that terrible rain and wind, everything got calm and sunny. I wanted to go play in my treehouse, but my mom wouldn't let me. She said we were in 'the eye of the storm.' A while later, the wind and rain came back much worse than before. The storm smashed my treehouse into bits so small that my dad and I had to completely rebuild it from scratch."

Paris looks out the window again. "You think we're in the eye of the storm right now?"

"I think so," I say.

I get the feeling that something very bad is coming. A horrible storm even worse than the storm that brought us here. Something so strong that it will smash us into bits that might be too small to put back together again.

My only question is when it will come.

TUESDAY, MAY FIRST
2058

UNPLEASANT

A few hours ago, Liam went up to his bedroom and came back with the deck of playing cards from the compartment under his mattress. He and I have been using it to play War for a while now, interrupted only by dinner. War is pretty mindless, which is good because we need to use our mental energy to focus on coming up with an escape plan. As we play, Liam and I have been whispering escape plan suggestions to each other, but each suggestion has countless reasons why it isn't a good idea, at least not at this point. We've also entertained ideas from the other kids, who have quietly approached us with their thoughts on what we should do to get ourselves out of our predicament. It's clear that they consider Liam and me to be the leaders of the group. The both of us. The kids seem to address us as equally in charge.

After hours spent considering our options, our current plan is to lie low until we figure out what we're dealing with. So far today there haven't been a lot of clues. All of our basic needs have been met. We've been offered three meals. We've been provided with items to entertain us, comfortable clothing, toiletries, toilets, and showers. Our water supply was cut off for a few hours this morning, but it came back this afternoon. Lizard suggested that maybe the water was withheld as punishment for taking showers that were too long, so we all agreed to take the shortest showers possible from now on.

Since then, the water has remained flowing.

Outside the airplane, it is now dark, except for the stars in the sky. I can't see what is below us anymore. All day long we were flying over water. I would have thought we would have encountered land at some point, but maybe our captors were actively avoiding it for some reason. Maybe we're flying over land now.

DING. DING. DING. DING. DING. DING.

The bell just chimed more times in a row than it ever has before. When it chimed earlier today, it was associated with meal times. Two chimes for the arrival of food, and three chimes for the end of mealtime. Six times is new. Everyone is looking around, trying to figure out what the bell might signify, but nothing is happening.

And then the bell chimes again. DING. DING. DING. DING. DING. DING.

Six times again.

"The men want us to do something," Tiger suggests.

"What do you think they want us to do?" Paris asks.

"I don't know," Tiger says. "We've already taken showers and eaten three meals."

"Maybe it's time for bed," Goat offers.

That makes sense. But the thought of getting closed up in a coffin-bedroom again makes my stomach churn.

"We should go to our rooms and try to get some rest," Liam says to the group.

Most of the kids follow his suggestion without the slightest hesitation. They rise from their seats, collect their belongings, and murmur soft wishes of goodnight. It's remarkable how easily they follow Liam, but I guess for some people it's reassuring to have a leader. Unfortunately, I've never been a good follower. Or leader for that matter.

Within minutes, only Liam, Lizard, Harley, and I remain.

"You guys heading to bed?" Liam asks us.

Harley shakes his head. "There is no way I'm getting locked up in a box by choice."

"Yeah," Lizard says, crossing her arms in front of her. "If those dudes want me in there, they're gonna have to put me there themselves."

I can't help but be impressed by Lizard's fearlessness, especially considering that she's only thirteen-years-old. But taunting our kidnappers is probably not a good idea. At this point—trapped in an airplane flying over who knows what— we are completely at their mercy.

Liam looks at me. "Unpleasant?" It's the first time he has said my "name" out loud. I don't like the way it sounds when he says it. *Maybe I should have chosen a less honest name.*

"I'm going to sleep out here," I say. Unlike Lizard, I try to speak in a matter-of-fact manner, so it doesn't sound like I'm challenging our captors. "I need a little breathing room," I add to soften my statement further.

"Okay," Liam says, and he drops down into the chair next to me.

Why do I feel like he's staying here just because of me?

"Goodnight, everybody," Harley says as he and Lizard settle down as well.

A quiet chorus echoes his sentiment.

It has been a long time since I've had a good night's sleep. I'm certainly not going to have an easy time sleeping here. But for some extremely strange reason, I feel like I might rest a little better with Liam by my side.

TUESDAY, MAY FIRST
2132

GOAT

When Paris and I got to the bottom of the ladder in our room, I climbed into my bed right away. I figured Paris would go into hers and we'd both go to sleep, but she is still looking through the things that are in the hiding spot under her mattress.

"Maybe they won't close the bed walls tonight," she says so quietly that I'm not sure if she is talking to me or only to herself. I hear her lower her mattress and then she stands up, so I can see her. "What do you think?" she asks me.

"I don't think there's any reason to close them," I say. "Last night, they needed to keep us where we were until everything was ready for us. Now that everything's ready, why should they lock us up?"

Paris nods her head. "You're probably right."

Again, I expect her to climb into her bed, but she just stands there and looks at me.

I look back at her, not sure what I should say.

"When I woke up inside there this morning and couldn't get out, I thought I was going to die in there all alone," she whispers.

When I woke up this morning inside this little bedroom, I didn't think that I was going to die in here. Actually, I kind of felt safe, even though it's silly to feel that way. I think I felt that way because this bedroom reminds me of the cardboard refrigerator box that my dad put down in the basement for me, because I told him I wanted to use it as a hideout. It was a place where I could go to be alone when I was sad about all the bad things that happened to me at school. A place where no one would see me cry. I guess that's why being alone in this bedroom kind of made me feel safe.

But it isn't the same for Paris. I don't think she ever feels like she needs to be alone. I think being around people makes her feel safer. I bet people have always been kind to Paris. People have probably never hurt her. Until last night.

"May I sleep with you?" Paris asks me.

When I was younger and I woke up because of nightmares—which happened a lot—I used to go to my parents' bed, because it was the only place I'd be able to go back to sleep. Back then, I didn't want to be alone. Back then, being with people made me feel safe.

I say the same thing to Paris that my parents used to say to me, "Of course."

TUESDAY, MAY FIRST
2155

TIGER

Rain is crying.

She's inside her bed compartment, and I think she's trying to cry quietly, but I can hear her. My teacher says I have super-human hearing.

I wish I could help Rain feel better, but I'm not good at comforting people when they're upset. I never know what to say. Sometimes I say things that make people get *more* upset, even though I am trying to be helpful. Sometimes I even say things that make them get angry at me, which makes *me* upset because I was trying my best to make them feel better.

And so when someone is upset, I just stay nearby, out of the way, and watch over them to make sure they're okay, and I wait for someone else to come and comfort them.

But I doubt that anyone is going to come into our room now and comfort Rain.

I could go and get one of the other kids, but everyone is probably in bed already. They might even be asleep. Besides, I'm pretty sure that six dings of the bell meant that we are supposed to go to bed. And I definitely don't want to make the kidnappers angry.

I am staring at the ceiling of my bed compartment, trying to figure out what I should do, when Rain's face pops into view. Her eyes are slightly red, but she has wiped her tears away.

"What's up?" I ask her, which is stupid because I know

what's up. Rain is upset. Maybe, I should have asked if she wants to talk about what's bothering her. That's what my mom asks me when I'm upset.

"Are you having trouble sleeping?" she asks me.

"Yeah," I say. It's mostly because Rain's crying has kept me awake, but it would be unkind to say that, and so I don't mention it.

"At least you're not crying like a baby," she says.

"It's perfectly normal to cry," I say.

Rain smiles, but her smile seems sad. "Thanks, Tiger."

Her face disappears back into her bed compartment.

"Are tigers your favorite animals?" Rain asks me.

"My favorite animals are dogs," I say. "Although I like every kind of animal."

"Why did you choose Tiger as your name?" she asks.

"That's the name of my dog," I say. "Tiger is mine and Liam's, but he's mostly mine."

Rain's face reappears, looking bewildered. "What do you mean yours and *Liam's*?"

"Liam is my brother," I say.

Her eyes go wide. "The same Liam who's up there?" She points up at the ceiling.

"Yup," I say.

"That's cool," she says. "I wish I had a brother or sister."

"I don't know about sisters," I say, "but brothers are hit-or-miss."

She smiles. This time her smile doesn't look sad. "Is Liam a hit or a miss?"

"He's sort of a miss," I say.

"That's too bad." Rain plops back down on her bed.

"My other brother was a hit … but he's dead." I touch the bare spot on my neck where Andrew's necklace should be, and my eyes fill with tears.

"What did he die of?" Rain asks.

I've never really talked with anyone about Andrew's death, because it was too hard to talk about. I guess I shouldn't have brought it up. Now I have to say something …

But before I can decide to say anything at all, the door to my bedroom slides shut.

TUESDAY, MAY FIRST
2200

UNPLEASANT

The main cabin has suddenly gone dark. Not just a little dark, nearly pitch black. When my eyelids spring open, I see no light except for the stars visible through the airplane windows.

"What the heck?" Harley exclaims.

"I guess it's *literally* 'light's out,'" Liam says.

"That's fine," Lizard says. "We're supposed to be sleeping anyway."

Based on the rapid-fire succession of their responses, it appears that I'm not the only one who hasn't fallen asleep yet.

I close my eyes, trying yet again to see if I can relax enough to get some much-needed sleep. My stomach keeps asking for food. Usually, I get up at night somewhere between ten and two—after my mom has gone to bed—and indulge in things that I generally don't eat in front of other people, like cheese puffs and chocolate pudding and sugar wafer cookies. According to my stomach, it's time for a nighttime snack, but unless that little food cabinet in the wall decides to offer something up in the middle of the night, which I highly doubt, I'm not getting any food until morning.

BANG. The whole airplane vibrates. A disconcerting shudder passes from my flesh into the core of my body.

And then it happens again … and again … and again …

BANG … BANG … BANG …

"What the hell is that?" Harley asks, his voice drowned out by the incessant banging.

"How do we make it stop?" Lizard yells.

Nobody answers but the banging. BANG BANG BANG BANG BANG BANG …

The banging isn't showing any signs of stopping. If anything, it's getting more frequent.

And then, hundreds of pin-sized things begin to pelt us from above. They pass right through my clothes and impact my skin. It's almost like being showered by raindrops, except that they're painful—like shocks of electricity—and they're not wet.

"Let's go to our rooms," Liam suggests.

"Good idea," I agree.

It's difficult to get to my ladder in the darkness. I end up bumping both of my shins against a table and my left funnybone against the back of a chair. Finally, I find my ladder and start to climb, impeded by the "rain" that's making my body feel icy and slippery.

"It's locked!" Lizard shouts, sounding upset.

"Here too!" Harley calls out.

"What are you talking about?" Liam asks.

"The hatch that goes to my room," Lizard says. "I can't get it to open."

"Mine's locked too," Liam says a moment later.

I reach the top of my ladder, but I can't open my hatch either, no matter how hard I try, and so I head back down. By the time I make it to the bottom of the ladder, the air feels like it's getting colder, the banging is definitely getting steadier, and the "rain" is getting harder.

"It's freezing cold in here," Lizard says.

"We should stay close together," Harley suggests. "To keep

warm."

"He's right," Liam says. "Let's huddle up."

We decide to gather together in a corner, where it seems a bit less cold.

"Is everyone okay?" Liam asks as we finally settle down on the floor.

"I'm good," Harley says.

"Considering that we're trapped in a meat locker, being pelted by who knows what, I'm terrific," I say.

Liam kind of laughs and puts his arm around me. A pleasurable tingle begins where his body touches mine and travels straight into my chest, warming me from the inside. I've never had a boy put his arm around me, and I never dreamed it would feel in any way pleasant. I always thought it would be awkward and confining and incredibly annoying. But, right now, I don't feel any of that. Maybe it's just because it's so horribly cold here, that it feels good to have someone help keep me warm.

"Lizard, why aren't you over here with the rest of us?" Liam asks.

"I'm fine," she responds quickly.

"Come on, Lizard," Harley says. "You're going to freeze to death on your own."

"I'll be okay." Her teeth chatter as she speaks.

I feel Liam inhale. "Lizard—" he starts.

"I said, 'I'm fine!'" The shrillness of Lizard's voice pierces right through the banging.

I know that tone well. It's the same tone I use with my mom practically all the time. I used it most recently just last night, after she said possibly the last words she'll ever say to me—the same words she says to me every night before she goes to bed, even though it has been many years since I've said them back: *I love you*. That's the last thing my mom said to me. And, after she said it, I screamed with that same tone Lizard just used, "Go away!"

"Okay, got it," Liam says to Lizard, bringing me back to the present.

After a few minutes of silence, I realize that nobody's going to say anything else. And so, with Liam on one side of me and Harley on the other, and Lizard some distance away from all of us, I close my eyes and try to rest.

The "rain" picks up in intensity. I shiver from the coldness, and Liam pulls me closer. That stupid tingle of pleasure shoots into me again, forcing me to take a deep breath to slow the speeding of my heart. Although the tingling feels good, I don't like it. It makes me feel weak, and right now I need to be strong.

I try to bring my mind someplace else—someplace that I can deal with—but the disturbing physical sensations bombarding my body keep dragging me back to reality.

And so I resign myself to the fact that this is the way it's going to be.

I am going to be tortured.

All night long.

WEDNESDAY, MAY SECOND
0618

GOAT

When my bedroom wall closed last night, it was completely dark in here, but now it's light enough that I can see Paris in bed next to me. She's still asleep. Lying on her belly. The same way I like to sleep.

Paris' back moves up and down when she breathes, calmly and peacefully. Unlike most people, Paris is calm and peaceful not just when she's asleep, but all the time. Being around her makes me feel calmer. Not completely calm. But much calmer than I ever thought I would be in a situation like this.

Paris takes a few deeper breaths and then her eyes gently open. She glances around for a moment and then focuses on me. Her forehead wrinkles.

"Were you watching me sleep?" she asks.

My whole body burns with shame. *It's weird that I was watching Paris sleep.* I should have faced toward the wall and given her privacy. I wish I could be alone in my embarrassment, but the bedroom is still closed, and so I can't escape. I must stay here with Paris, even though she probably wishes I would leave.

"I'm sorry," I mumble.

"There's nothing to be sorry about," she says. "Watching someone sleep is really boring … unless they're talking in their sleep or something."

Relief cools my skin. *Paris isn't upset at me.*

"You weren't talking," I say. "You were just sleeping."

"Then it must have been extremely boring," she says.

"Kind of." I smile.

I like Paris. She makes me feel … normal. It's hard for me to find people who make good friends. Back home, out of my whole school of two hundred eighty-three people, I only have one friend: Antonio. He used to live in Puerto Rico, but his family moved to Virginia three months ago. We met in the school cafeteria. I was sitting at "the loser table" all alone, and Antonio came over and asked if he could sit with me. Of course I said yes, but I assumed that, after a while, he would make friends and go sit at their table. He never did. After hanging out with me for a few weeks, he told me that he hadn't had even one friend at his old school. Some of the kids there called him *"Flaco"* because he's kind of scrawny. *Flaco* is a Spanish word for skinny but, when those kids called him *Flaco*, they said it in a mean way, not a nice way. The other kids avoided him, because they didn't want to be friends with *Flaco*. And so Antonio understood what my life was like.

The three boys at my school who like to take turns humiliating me quickly added Antonio to their list of kids who should be made to regret ever being born. I don't know if they were mean to Antonio just because he was friends with me, but Antonio insisted that it would have happened anyway eventually, because "wherever you go, there you are." Antonio told me a school counselor said that to his parents when they met with him about his "difficulties assimilating" at our school. He said it basically means that, if everyone around you thinks you suck, and you move far away from all of the people who think you suck, once the people in the new place get to know you, they're going to realize that you suck. Because you do.

Paris probably had tons of friends back home. And no bullies.

Now, all of us have bullies: the men who stole us from our families.

But, here in this tiny room with Paris, I feel like the bullies can't hurt us.

Unfortunately, we won't be safe in here forever.

Eventually, the wall is going to open up.

WEDNESDAY, MAY SECOND
0630

UNPLEASANT

The main cabin lights just turned back on. And the banging stopped. My ears are ringing something awful though, and I still feel ghostly echoes of the banging in my head, back, butt, and feet—the parts of my body that have been pressed up all night against the vibrating wall and floor.

Liam takes his arm from around me, and Harley and I move apart. It didn't feel odd sitting so close together when it was dark, but it does now, in the cold morning light.

"I need to pee," Lizard says.

At first, I wonder why she's talking about it, rather than just going off to the restrooms, but then I notice that the hallway door is closed, just like it was yesterday morning. Actually, there's no sign that a door is even there.

Harley heads over to the place where the door used to be. "Open the door," he says, projecting his voice toward the ceiling.

"Who are you talking to?" Lizard asks.

"The guys who locked us up in here," Harley says. "They opened the door yesterday for Liam."

I think back to yesterday. I hadn't thought about it then, but the hallway door *did* suddenly appear when Liam started looking for a place for Goat to go to the bathroom.

But, today, there is no response to Harley's request.

"You need to be nicer about it," Lizard says.

"Go ahead. You do it," Harley says.

Lizard turns and addresses the wall, "Excuse me, sirs. We need to use the facilities, please."

Maybe it's because her tone is obviously sarcastic, but that has no effect either.

"I wonder if the hallway is off limits until the other kids arrive," I say. If our torture last night was punishment for not going to our bedrooms, maybe the punishment isn't over yet.

"So I just have to *wait*?" Lizard kicks the wall.

"Relax!" Liam says. "You're not the only one who needs to go to the bathroom."

Lizard's mouth begins to open but, before she gets out a word, the hallway door slides away.

"It's you!" Lizard says, pointing her index finger at Liam. "When you said you wanted a bathroom just now, the hallway opened, exactly like yesterday."

"It could be a coincidence," I say. "Why would the men care what *Liam* wants?"

"Maybe they want him to be in charge," Lizard says, as she heads toward the restrooms.

I cringe at the thought of Liam being the boss of us. Liam looks a bit uncomfortable with the thought as well.

"I'm going to use the bathroom now, in case they decide to close the door again," Harley says, then he looks at Liam and adds, "If that's okay with Your Highness."

Liam rolls his eyes. "Give it a rest, Harley."

Harley heads off down the hallway, followed by Liam and me. By the time I make it back to the main cabin, everyone else has taken a seat at one of the airplane windows. The sun is just barely starting to rise, and we're flying straight toward it. So we're still traveling east and, wherever we are, it's morning here. We are also still flying over a large body of water, with no land in sight.

"How long do you suppose we've been flying?" Harley asks.

"About twenty-four hours," I say, though I don't trust my own estimation. Our perception of time can easily be manipulated by our kidnappers. They fed us breakfast and we assumed it was morning. When the next meal came, we figured it was lunchtime. Then they fed us dinner. I watched the sun set not long after dinner but, depending on where in the world we are, the sun can set at any time.

"An airplane can't fly a whole day without refueling," Harley says.

"Maybe it landed in the middle of the night, while we were asleep," Lizard says.

I can't believe Lizard fell asleep in here last night.

"I didn't sleep," I say.

"Me neither," Harley says.

Liam doesn't say anything. I wonder if that means he slept.

"I guess they could have refueled us in midair," Harley says.

"You think our kidnappers are *that* sophisticated?" I ask.

"Yes," Lizard, Harley, and Liam answer in unison.

Maybe they're right. These aren't your typical throw-a-kid-in-the-back-of-a-van kidnappers. They were able to obtain a helicopter big enough to hold about a dozen people and an airplane with multiple bedrooms, showers, and a laundry room. Maybe they *do* have the ability to refuel in midair. But, whether we've refueled or not, no matter where in the world we're heading, we must be getting close.

This could be our last morning on this airplane.

WEDNESDAY, MAY SECOND
0700

TIGER

"He got shot," I say, when the wall of my bed compartment slides down.

Rain's face appears, hanging down from the compartment above mine. "Who got shot?"

"My brother Andrew." I take a deep breath, willing myself not to cry. "Last night, you asked what he died of. I couldn't answer you then, so I'm answering now."

Her face disappears from view. "How'd he get shot?"

"He was in the military," I say. "He and his buddies got attacked with grenades. Andrew was inside a truck when it happened, so he didn't get hurt much, but he saw his buddy Reese lying outside on the dirt, with both of his legs blown off and all of his blood coming out. Andrew got out of the truck and went and put tourniquets on Reese's legs, so he wouldn't die. Then he dragged Reese back to the truck, so they could take him to the field hospital. Andrew was about to close the truck door when the enemies started shooting ..." Tears flood my eyes. I force myself to continue, "Two bullets went right through Andrew's heart. There was nothing anyone could do to save him."

"What happened to Reese?" Rain asks.

"The doctors and nurses at the hospital did a bunch of surgeries on him, and he survived. He has two prosthetic legs now, but he's back to doing pretty much anything he could do before he got blown up." Reese and his wife and his two kids were at the ceremony where my mom and dad got Andrew's Purple Heart, the medal you get if you're in the military and you get wounded by the enemy ... or killed. My parents keep Andrew's medal in a safe deposit box, so nothing bad can happen to it. I wish I'd put his necklace in there too. Then it wouldn't be lost.

"Andrew was a hero," Rain says.

"Yeah, he was really brave and strong," I say, wiping away my tears. "Liam is too."

"What about you?" she asks.

"I'm not brave or strong," I say.

And, unfortunately, I think we're going to need to be both brave and strong to survive here.

"Maybe you can be," Rain says.

"I hope so." But I have my doubts. Being brave and strong just isn't in me. It never was, and I'm pretty sure it never will be.

"I hope so too," Rain says.

I'm not sure if she's talking about me or her, but I don't get to ask her, because after she says that, she leaps onto the ladder, climbs up to the hatch, and disappears into the space above us.

GOAT

When my bedroom opened up, there weren't any bad men waiting outside it, so Paris and I got out of bed and we climbed the ladder that goes upstairs. All of the other kids were already there. No one said anything to us, so Paris and I sat down quietly together in one of the seats by one of the airplane windows.

After a little while of looking out the window at the ocean and the clouds, I ask Paris if she wants to play Candy Land. That's one of the board games we found under Paris' mattress. At first I thought it was ridiculous that the kidnappers left that game for Paris. Nine-year-olds don't usually want to play games that are meant for little kids. But Paris wanted to play it. She said it used to be her favorite game in the whole world. We played Candy Land all afternoon yesterday, and it was actually kind of nice.

"I don't want to play any games right now," Paris says, answering my question without looking at me. She's staring out the window and, for the first time since I met her, she looks seriously upset.

"Are you okay?" I ask her.

"I'm okay," she says too fast.

Maybe she wants me to leave her alone.

Before I can figure out what to say or do next, Paris turns toward me. Her eyes are opened wide and her mouth hangs open.

And then she tells me something that changes everything.

WEDNESDAY, MAY SECOND
0740

UNPLEASANT

"Can I borrow that?" Paris asks Liam. She's pointing to the deck of playing cards on the table between Liam and me. Liam went up to his bedroom and got the cards a little while ago, but neither of us is really in the mood to play.

"Go ahead," Liam tells her.

Paris grabs the cards and rejoins Goat, but she doesn't climb into the chair with him again. Instead, she pulls a card from Liam's deck, steps up to one of the windows, and carefully slides the card into the gap between the airplane wall and the top of the window frame.

"Look!" Paris says.

She's holding onto the edge of the card. The rest of the card is no longer visible.

"Look at what?" Lizard asks.

"I put the card *inside* the window," Paris says. "And it disappeared."

"The card is bending *around* the window, inside the wall," Lizard says.

"It isn't bending," Paris argues. "It's disappearing."

"I think Paris is losing it," Lizard whispers.

Paris continues, "When I was looking out the window yesterday, I saw a cloud that looked like a bear and, today, I saw it again. I saw another cloud today that looked like an owl, and I saw the owl cloud yesterday too."

"Lots of clouds look alike," Lizard says.

Paris' face tightens. She pushes the card all the way under the window frame until it disappears from view completely.

"You lost Liam's card," Tiger says.

"It's not lost." Paris places her finger against the plexiglass at the center of the window, pointing at the clouds beyond it. "The card is right there!"

"Airplane windows don't work like that," Harley says.

"These aren't windows," Paris says. "The men are showing us a movie. It was the same one yesterday and it'll probably be the same one tomorrow, if we even get to have a tomorrow."

All of the other kids look alternately at Paris and me and Liam and the window. It seems that no one is sure what to believe. I'm not sure myself.

"Stand back," Rain says to Paris.

Maybe if I had gotten even a few minutes of sleep last night, I would have sensed what was about to happen but, before I can process anything, Rain, in one quick move, swings up her right foot and kicks hard against the window frame … *knocking the entire window to the floor.*

Liam's playing card flutters down and lands on top of a dark screen that, moments ago, showed views of water and sky and puffy clouds—one of which apparently looked like a bear and another, an owl. In the spot where the "window" once was, are a few stringy broken wires sticking out of an otherwise solid wall.

"No freaking way!" Harley says quietly.

Paris was right.

WEDNESDAY, MAY SECOND
0744

GOAT

Paris is standing next to me, frozen in place, staring down at the "window" that's lying on the floor. She looks so sad that you would think something died. I guess something kind of did. The window is dead. And even though the other "windows" still show clouds and sky and ocean, those "windows" are lies.

DING. DING.

It's breakfast time.

"We should eat something," I say to Paris.

At first I'm not sure if she heard me, but then she turns and starts walking toward the food spot. When we get there, only two boxes are left, mine and hers. I pick up both of them and find a chair that is as far away as possible from the dead "window."

Paris and I eat without talking, the way the other kids are. Then we put our empty food boxes back in the wall. And then we sit again.

No one is playing games or reading or drawing or writing. Everyone is just sitting. Their eyes stare at the "windows" or the floor or their laps.

"I knew the ride was too smooth," Harley says. "There's no way an airplane could fly for that many hours without any turbulence at all."

"If you thought something was wrong, why didn't you say

anything?" Lizard asks.

"I believed what I saw instead of what I felt," Harley says. "I shouldn't have."

"From now on, if anyone notices *anything* that seems strange or doesn't make sense, anything at all, I want you to come to Unpleasant or me, so we can talk about it," Liam says, then he turns in my direction. He seems to be looking at Rain or Paris, or maybe both of them. "We can't go taking actions on our own. That's too risky. We could end up damaging something important or causing the kidnappers to take action. Is everyone in agreement?"

Everyone nods or mumbles their agreement.

"So if this isn't an airplane, what is it?" Paris asks.

"It's moving a little, but not much, so I don't think we're traveling on land," Lizard says.

"Maybe we're on a space station or spaceship," I say.

"Doubtful," Lizard says. "Plus then we'd be weightless."

"It could have artificial gravity," I argue.

Lizard shakes her head. "Still pretty doubtful."

"Well, it's not a boat," Tiger says. "There'd be a lot more rocking around if it was."

Liam inhales. "What if we were underwater?"

"In a boat?" Lizard asks.

"In a submarine," Liam says.

Tiger's eyebrows rise up. "You think our kidnappers have access to an *actual* submarine?"

Liam sighs. "I guess that's a little far-fetched."

"We could just be in a room somewhere," Harley says.

"But it's *moving*," Tiger says.

"Maybe we're feeling the vibrations from some kind of power supply or generator," Harley says. "They took us here by helicopter, so our location could be pretty remote. We might be in the basement of an abandoned house somewhere. Or in some kind of bunker that they built in the middle of nowhere."

"Wherever we are, we need to come up with a plan to get us out of here," Unpleasant says impatiently.

Heads nod and other people offer quiet suggestions, but I stay silent. Maybe it's smart to make plans, but I don't think even the best plan is going to help us. The kidnappers are much more powerful than us, and they have us locked up somewhere that's probably far away from anyone who can help us. We are completely under their control.

And they're probably fairly unhappy with us right now.

WEDNESDAY, MAY SECOND
0925

UNPLEASANT

Liam and I are mindlessly playing War, because we needed something to do other than just sit and stare at the movie screens or each other. We've decided to hold off on making any escape attempts until we see how our kidnappers retaliate for this morning's destruction. Liam thinks that it's highly likely that they will do something and I guess I agree.

The common room seems to be getting warmer. Sweat is starting to materialize on my upper lip. I wish I could take off my sweatshirt, but all I'm wearing underneath is one of the white t-shirts that was provided to us, and the t-shirt material is pretty thin, and I'm not wearing a bra because I don't have one. My nightgown is thicker, but it needs to be washed because it smells like body odor. We didn't do any laundry yesterday because we were worried about the men shutting off our water again, like they did when we took showers that were too long. We're planning to do some laundry later today, after everyone gets their showers.

Suddenly, Liam smacks his cards down onto the table and pulls off his sweatshirt. As he does, his t-shirt rides up ever so slightly, and I unintentionally catch a glimpse of his muscular abdomen. My whole body flushes hot, making me even more uncomfortable in my sweatclothes.

Liam throws down his next card—a ten—and says, "Your move."

I put down one of my cards—a seven—and Liam collects them both.

"Aren't you hot in that sweatshirt?" he asks me.

"I'm all right," I say.

"You look hot," he says matter-of-factly.

I smirk at him. "You're just saying that because you want me to sleep with you again."

Liam's cheeks flush—probably as bright as mine—and his gaze falls to the table.

Words stumble out of my mouth, "I don't know why I said that … I was just …"

"You were finding the humor in our situation," he says.

"There is no humor in our situation," I say.

He exhales and looks deep into my eyes. "They've taken away our freedom, but we can't let them take away our spirit."

"*Humor* isn't in my spirit," I say. "I don't find the humor in situations. I focus on the worst-case scenario."

"Bad circumstances tend to bring out the *real* you," he says. "Maybe this is the real you."

"I wish," I say.

"So do I," he says.

My whole body flushes hot again. As much as I don't want to admit it, I'm starting to like Liam, and more disconcertingly, I'm starting to like him in a way that I've never liked anyone before. I actually like *myself* a little when I'm around him. I've never met anyone who made me feel that way.

But I can't let myself get attached to Liam or any of the kids here. If I do, it will hurt too much when we lose each other. And that is definitely going to happen. In one scenario, some of us, or all of us, will get out of here and go back home, and probably never see each other again. And in the other scenario—the much more likely scenario—some of us, or all of us, will die before that happens. So it's best if we don't get attached.

Unfortunately, despite my best intentions, it might be too late.

I'm already starting to like Liam.

And I feel like, for some completely inexplicable reason, he's starting to like me too.

WEDNESDAY, MAY SECOND
0930

TIGER

The bell happens again. DING. DING. DING. DING.

Four times. "Food is here" was two times. "Mealtime is over" was three times. "It's bedtime" was six times. Four times is new. And so is what happens next. A door opens up in the middle of a wall. A door that I didn't know was there until it opened. The place on the other side of the door is dark except for hundreds of tiny little lights that almost look like stars. It looks … dangerous.

"What the heck is in there?" Harley asks.

"It looks like outer space," Goat says, moving toward it.

Liam stands up. "Don't anyone go near it. I'll check it out."

Unpleasant stands too. "I'll come with you."

Liam says something to her that is too quiet for me to hear, and then Unpleasant sits back down. He probably told her that he thinks it could be unsafe. Liam likes to be brave and protect people. Andrew was the same way.

But being brave is why Andrew is dead.

My heart beats fast as Liam approaches the new doorway. Some of the other kids cautiously move a little closer to get a better look. I follow them. All of a sudden, Liam glances back. He looks directly at me, which makes me really uncomfortable, and says, "I told you to stay away from it."

The other kids back up, but I stay right where I am. Liam's glance has sucked away all of the energy from my body, rendering me unable to move. I am now certain that Liam believes this new place is dangerous. *Maybe he shouldn't investigate it. Maybe he should leave it alone.* But Liam can't hear my thoughts, and I can't make myself say them. And even if I asked him not to go, I don't think that would stop him.

Fear twists my stomach until it hurts as Liam passes through the doorway and moves toward the tiny stars. Suddenly, the stars go dark. I can't see anything beyond the doorway anymore, not even Liam. I start to run toward where I last saw him. But before I get there, the door slides shut … with Liam on the other side.

A horrified scream comes from deep inside me.

The star room swallowed Liam whole.

WEDNESDAY, MAY SECOND
0934

UNPLEASANT

Tiger lets out another pained yelp. I feel her distress in my own chest. *Liam is gone.*

"Is he going to come back?" Tiger's voice is high-pitched, bordering on panic. Her eyes are looking straight ahead, at the wall that used to be a door.

"I don't know," I answer honestly.

Tiger bangs on the wall. "Liam! Liam!" she shouts.

Some of the other kids follow her lead, banging on the wall and yelling, "Liam! Liam! Liam!"

Nothing happens in response. No doors open. No punishment is administered for being loud and banging on the walls. And there is no indication at all of whether or not Liam will return.

The frantic screaming of the kids echoes in my ears. I want to scream too, but I need to be strong. For the other kids, especially the little ones. I promised Liam I would be … if he didn't come back. He said they needed at least one of us. He said that's why we couldn't go through that door together. I didn't tell him that *I* needed him. *I need him to come back.*

I can't bear to listen to the kids' desperate cries anymore, not if I want to have any hope of staying strong.

"Stop shouting!" I bark out.

No one stops.

"It isn't doing any good!" I yell.

The kids don't seem to hear me.

"I SAID, 'STOP!'" I bellow in the strongest voice I've ever heard come through my lips.

Instantly, everyone freezes and silences themselves. Except for Tiger, who is still banging, and crying so plaintively that it breaks my heart, "Liam! Liam! Liam!"

"Tiger, stop," I say gently.

Something touches my arm. I spin around and find myself looking at Rain.

She says something in a whisper so soft that I don't hear her over Tiger's cries.

"What did you say?" I ask her.

She leans over and speaks directly into my ear, "I said, 'Liam is her brother.'"

WEDNESDAY, MAY SECOND
1022

GOAT

It's even quieter now than it was after Rain broke the "window."

Unpleasant is standing next to Tiger and talking very softly with her, comforting her. Looking at them makes me miss my mom even more than I already do, so I try not to look at them. I wish my mom was with me, but maybe it's better that she isn't. Even more than I wish I could be with my mom, I wish that she is somewhere safe.

Paris is right next to me, sitting in the same chair as me. Her eyes stare at the place where that door closed and trapped Liam on the other side, away from us.

"Do you think there's anything we can do to help Liam?" Paris asks me.

"No." I wish I had a different answer.

"How long do we wait before we give up hope?" she asks quietly.

Her question makes me flinch. "We *never* give up hope," I say.

Paris doesn't say anything after that.

Since there is nothing useful to do, and since Paris and I seem to have run out of talking, I ask her, "Do you want to play Candy Land now?"

"I guess so," she says.

Paris insists on going with me to get the game, which

makes me feel good because I like being with Paris, but it also feels bad because I think Paris is scared that she could lose me. The bad guys took Liam away. They could take any of us at any time.

Once we're back upstairs with the other kids, Paris and I get to work playing Candy Land. Like yesterday, when we play, it feels like we've gone back to being little kids. Back then, the only thing I was scared of was make-believe monsters that hid in the dark. I didn't know back then that there were *real* monsters waiting for me out in the world. Monsters who looked just like ordinary people. Now I know better.

When Paris' little blue plastic person and my little green plastic person are just a few spaces away from Peanut Brittle House, about halfway to Candy Castle, I hear Tiger shout, "Liam!"

By the time I look up, Liam has come out of the doorway that took him away. Behind him are the same stars that were there when the door first opened.

Harley starts walking toward the doorway. "So what's in there?" he asks Liam.

"I'm not allowed to talk about it," Liam says.

"Says who?" Lizard asks.

"The Room." Liam's answer sounds like a joke but, based on the tension in his eyes, I know he's not joking.

"All right then, I'll check it out myself." Harley takes a step into the starry room.

Liam grabs Harley's arm and pulls him back out. "Hold on."

"Why?" Harley asks.

"I think you should understand what you're getting into." Liam sounds very serious, the way my dad sounds when he's telling me something really important. "Once you go into that room, there's no getting out until it's done with you. Even if it hurts like hell, you have to deal with it."

"Fine." Harley yanks his arm from Liam's grip, but he doesn't have to yank hard. Liam is no longer trying to stop him.

Instead of heading through the doorway, Harley grabs a stack of playing cards and shuffles them up. "Anyone who wants to go into The Room can pick a card," he calls out. "Highest card goes in first. Ace is the highest. If there's a tie, we do a tiebreaker draw. Who wants to go?"

I've already decided that I don't want to go into the starry room. Liam seems troubled by it and that's enough to convince me to stay away. I look around to see if there's anyone other than Harley who wants to follow in Liam's footsteps, but I don't see any other volunteers. Only Harley has his hand raised.

"Okay, let's draw to see who goes first," Harley says, looking in my direction.

That doesn't make sense because I haven't raised my hand.

But then I look behind me and see that someone else has volunteered: Paris.

UNPLEASANT

Liam swallows hard when Paris draws an ace. Harley draws a five.

Goat grabs Paris' hand. "I'll go with you," he says.

Paris looks down at their joined hands, and then up at Goat. "You don't have to."

"I want to," he says.

Liam shakes his head. "I think it's only one person at time, Goat."

Goat turns to him. "But you don't know for sure?" he asks.

"No," Liam says. "I don't."

Goat shrugs awkwardly and looks at Paris. "We can try."

Paris nods. "Okay."

Seeing these two little kids about to face something that Liam indicated could be painful makes me sick to my stomach. "We can't let them go," I say quietly to Liam.

"It's not right for us to make their choices for them," he says. "Paris and Goat are in the same position as all of the rest of us. They should be allowed to make their own decisions."

"They're just nine years old," I whisper.

"Well, they're going to have to grow up real fast," he says. There is a coldness in his voice that I haven't heard before. I have to force myself not to shiver.

"Would you let Tiger go in there?" I ask him.

In his eyes, I see a moment of hesitation. "Yes," he says.

I haven't been inside The Room, and Liam has. If he would

let his little sister go in there, it can't really be that bad. And so, despite my unsettling reservations, I sit quietly and watch with an anxious heart as, together, Paris and Goat cross the threshold and step toward the stars. But, rather than going dark, the stars turn blood red, and then, slowly, they get brighter and brighter. If I didn't know any better, I would say that The Room itself is angry, and it's getting angrier by the second.

"It wants one person at a time." Liam's voice is tense.

Paris releases Goat's hand. "I'll be back soon," she says to him, attempting a smile that instead makes her look like she's fighting the urge to cry.

"You don't have to go," Goat says to Paris.

I see her strength rise to the surface. "I do," she says.

Reluctantly, Goat steps back into the common room and, instantly, the red stars surrounding Paris extinguish. She is embraced by total darkness, and the wall closes.

Liam looks down at the table.

"You think she's going to be all right in there?" I ask him, hoping for reassurance.

"It depends what happens," he says.

"What happened to you?" I ask.

He shakes his head. "I told you, I can't say."

Yes, that's what he said to the group, but I thought maybe it would be different when he was just talking to me. I guess I was mistaken.

I wish I knew what happened to Liam inside The Room. From the moment he emerged, he has appeared visibly shaken. Of course, the experience must have been disconcerting— being trapped inside a room, unsure if he'd ever be let out. Once the door reopened and he returned to us, I would have thought his unease would have faded, but it doesn't seem to have faded at all. If anything, it seems to be getting worse.

I try another conversation. "You didn't tell me Tiger was your sister."

"You didn't ask." He seems distracted. Maybe his mind is still in The Room.

"Do you have any other brothers or sisters?" I ask.

"No," he says. "Do you have any?"

"I'm an only child," I say. "I used to kind of want a little brother or sister, but my parents made it abundantly clear that was never going to happen. I guess once they rolled the dice and got me, they weren't going to roll the dice again."

Liam finally seems to pull his focus to the conversation at hand. "You sure don't think very highly of yourself," he says.

I give him a quick self-conscious smile. "You just now figured that out?"

"Maybe you should try to see yourself the way other people do," he says.

"Other people see me as a loser." That's the truth.

He looks forcefully into my eyes. "I don't."

"Give it some time." I'm not sure why I'm being so honest with this boy. I guess in part it's because I'm too tired to pretend to be something I'm not. But maybe it's also because I want to save myself from the pain of having him like me for a little while and then decide that he doesn't like me after all.

Liam glances uneasily at the place where The Room is hidden behind the wall, then he turns back to me. "Want to play War?" he asks.

We could probably both use a little time on autopilot, where we can focus our minds on a pointless card game instead of our sucky reality.

"Sure," I say.

WEDNESDAY, MAY SECOND
1156

GOAT

Candy Land is still set out on the table exactly the way it was when Paris left us. She will probably be upset when she gets out of the starry room, and it might make her feel better to play that game. So I'm keeping Candy Land waiting for her, ready for us to pick up with it where we left off. I hope she'll want to play.

It feels like forever before the starry room door opens again. Paris is standing in the doorway. She looks like she just woke up from a bad dream and doesn't realize yet that she's awake. I want to run to her, but I don't want to frighten her. So I walk to her slowly. When I finally arrive in front of her, I'm not sure what to do. She is looking at me, which I guess is a good sign, but she isn't saying anything or really responding to me in any other way.

"Are you okay, Paris?" Unpleasant asks.

"I'm okay," Paris says quietly.

She takes a step forward. Her body moves stiffly. It's kind of the way I walk when everyone is staring at me, the way everyone is staring at Paris now.

Harley is already heading toward the starry room. But before he reaches the doorway, the door closes.

He turns to Paris. "Did you upchuck in there or something?"

Paris shakes her head, still looking like she's in shock.

"She probably peed herself," Lizard says.

Liam slams his fist hard against a table. "Enough!"

"I'm sure they'll clean it up and open it again soon," Lizard says to Harley.

"It's not a ride at Disney World," Tiger says.

"If it was, they wouldn't have let Paris through the door," Harley says. "They don't let *babies* on the grown-up rides."

"I said, 'Enough'!" Liam says in a quiet voice.

Nobody says anything else after that.

I walk with Paris back to our seats, and we sit on either side of the table that has our game of Candy Land set up on it. Paris looks at the game.

"I kept everything exactly like we left it," I say to her. "Do you want to play?"

She nods a little.

When we left off, it was my turn, so I reach over and take a card from the pile. I get purple, so I move my green man to the next purple square, three spaces ahead. Paris draws a card and takes hold of her blue man. She doesn't move him though.

I want to ask her what happened to her in the starry room, but I know she's not supposed to tell, so I ask her something else, "How do you feel?"

"I don't know," she says, looking at her little blue man.

How can you not know how you feel?

Paris takes a really big breath, the way I do when I'm trying not to cry. "I don't want to talk right now, okay?"

"Okay," I say.

Maybe Paris will want to talk later. Maybe, when we're alone in our bedroom, she'll tell me what happened inside the starry room, even though she's not supposed to. Maybe she'll tell me everything ... But I'm not sure I really want to know.

DING. DING.

It's lunchtime.

UNPLEASANT

Some people eat more intensely after they are traumatized, and some people lose their appetite completely. I am in the former camp. Based on the way she is eating right now, I suspect Paris is in the former camp as well. Liam, it appears, is blessed to be in the latter. He barely touches his pasta with meat sauce.

"You need to eat, Liam," I say gently.

"Here, you can have it," he snaps, pushing his box in my direction.

"I don't want your food," I snap back.

"Sorry," he says. "That was uncalled for."

"I just want you to stay strong," I say.

He shakes his head. "I don't want to be strong."

His words scare me. I *need* Liam to be strong. I take a deep breath, hoping that I can keep my voice steady. "Okay, I'll be the strong one for a while." I cock my head and add, "I have to warn you, though, I *royally* suck at it."

Liam almost cracks a smile. "You should seriously consider a career in comedy."

"I never really considered a *career*," I admit. I kind of figured that, after high school, I'd just find whatever job I could. Just to make enough money to get myself a little apartment or something. Someplace where I could be alone.

"Well, when we get out of this mess, you might want to

look into it," he says.

Liam misspoke just now. It's not "*when* we get out of this mess," it's "*if.*" Normally, I would correct someone who made such a wildly-incorrect statement because—as my mom reminds me all the time—I tend to be contrary, always looking to find fault with everything. But maybe it's healthier to think the way Liam does, to think of a positive outcome as a *when* rather than an *if.* Maybe it is better to anticipate the good in life. I've never been very good at that.

I think that having Liam in my life is good, even though it will hurt when that time ends. Maybe I should focus on the good: Liam and I are becoming friends. We can support each other. We can help each other through this.

Right now, Liam needs someone to be strong.

I will be strong for him. Until I can't be strong anymore.

And then, maybe, Liam can be strong for me.

WEDNESDAY, MAY SECOND
1230

GOAT

DING. DING. DING.

The food hatch closes. Lunchtime is over.

Paris and I are sitting with our game of Candy Land. It's still Paris' turn, but she hasn't made her move yet. Suddenly, she startles, and her attention jumps to the wall behind me. When I turn to look, I see that the door to the starry room is open again.

"We're back in business!" Harley says, and he rushes toward the open doorway. In less than a second, he is inside the starry room. And the stars go dark. And the wall closes up again.

I can't imagine ever being as brave as Harley.

Paris looks back at the game board, but she still doesn't make a move.

"You want to … go downstairs?" I whisper to her.

She nods.

WEDNESDAY, MAY SECOND
1235

UNPLEASANT

Paris and Goat just went down to their bedroom together. They didn't say anything before they left. I can't help worrying about them.

"Maybe I should go check on Paris and Goat," I say to Liam.

His gaze goes to their hatch. "They'll be okay."

"How do you know?" I wish Liam would tell me something, anything, about what happened in The Room.

"Little kids are resilient," he says.

"Even so ..." I say.

"They've got each other," Liam says. "Everything is surmountable when you've got someone who cares about you."

Is Liam only talking about Paris and Goat, or is he talking about us too?

"Do you think she'll tell him what happened to her?" I ask Liam.

"No," he says, sounding absolutely certain.

"How can you be so sure?" I ask.

"The Room is very persuasive," Liam says. "You'd have to be stupid to go against it. And Paris isn't stupid." And with that, any hope that Liam will tell me what happened to him in The Room is ground into dust.

"I'm going in next," I say.

Liam looks into my eyes. "Why?"

"Because I need to know what happens in there," I say, holding his gaze.

"Why?" he asks again. He can't hide the concern in his eyes. A part of me likes seeing it there. Because it means he cares. But, unfortunately, it also means that, if anything bad happens to me, he will be hurt.

"I just ... need to know," I say. "So unless you'll tell me ..."

I can't read the expression on Liam's face. Sadness? Frustration? Pain? Fear? Maybe all of those.

He shakes his head. "I can't."

WEDNESDAY, MAY SECOND
1240

GOAT

When we got to our bedroom, Paris sat down on her bed and I sat next to her, and then she started crying. I wasn't sure what to do then.

Of course I know the kinds of things people say when other people are crying, but most of those things wouldn't be right.

I won't say, "Don't cry." Paris probably needs to cry. Sometimes I need to cry and, because enough people have told me not to cry, including my mom and dad, I've started hiding it. Now, I only cry when I'm alone. I don't want Paris to have to cry all alone.

I won't say, "Things could be worse." Our current situation is fairly bad. And I don't know what happened to Paris inside the starry room. It's true that, whatever happened, it didn't kill her, but there are some things that are worse than dying. I certainly can't say for sure that things could be worse.

I won't say, "It's going to be okay." Things might not turn out okay for us.

I won't say, "I'm here." That's something my dad used to say to me when I was a little kid, and it used to make me feel better, but it turns out that was the worst thing ever to say, because there were so many times after that when I needed him and he *wasn't* there. And all I could think was, *My dad isn't here.* And that just made me more upset. I guess my dad never considered that, someday, I might need him—*really* need him—and he might not be there. Like right now.

There's really nothing *right* that I can think of to say to Paris. And so, without saying anything, I put my hand on Paris' hand. Paris reaches over and hugs me tight, and I feel her shaky breathing and her tears and her pain. And I feel my own shaky breathing and tears and pain too. It's the first time I've cried in front of anyone in a very long time.

"I'm scared," Paris whispers to me.

"I'm scared too." I'm scared that I'm never going to see my mom and dad again. Or my goats. Or my other animals. Or my friend Antonio. Or my teacher, Mrs. Dockery. I'm scared that the bad men are going to kill us. I'm scared that it will hurt when I die.

"Did they hurt you in that room?" I ask Paris.

Slowly, she nods her head.

Anger burns inside me. It makes me so angry that someone hurt Paris, but it makes me angry at Paris too. Liam told us that we might get hurt in that room, but Paris went in anyway.

"*Why* did you go in there?" I ask her.

"I think the bad guys opened that doorway because they wanted to see if we would go through it," she says. "I wanted them to know that I was strong enough to go through it. I wanted them to know that they can't hurt me … But I was wrong. They *can* hurt me."

"They can hurt you, but they can only break you if you let them." Those words come out of me without me thinking them first. And then I realize where I heard them before. My dad said them to me once, just once. He was talking to me about the boys who bully me at school. My dad said we can choose to stay strong no matter what happens to us. We can stay strong up until our very last breath. And, when he said that, it made me feel powerful. It made me believe that I could make my life better … just by refusing to be broken. "Don't let them break you, Paris," I say. "I won't let them break *me* either."

And then I decide: *I'm going into the room with the stars.*

WEDNESDAY, MAY SECOND
1315

UNPLEASANT

The Room opens and Harley emerges. Unlike Liam and Paris, he looks completely unruffled. *That kid must have nerves of steel.*

"Who's next?" Harley asks the rest of us.

"Me," I say, being careful to keep my voice steady. I don't want Liam, or anyone else, to worry about me. I want them to believe that, whatever happens to me in there, I can handle it.

I stand and walk toward The Room, keeping my focus on the mesmerizing stars. I don't look back because I don't want to see the expression on Liam's face. If he looks upset, that would make me upset. If he looks unaffected, that would make me upset too. It's best to focus on the stars. I keep walking toward them … until they disappear.

I hear the door close quietly behind me. I am now surrounded by complete and utter darkness. Even as time passes, my eyes can't seem to adjust to it. I don't like this at all. Anyone or anything could be coming toward me right now, and I can't see them or it. I pull back my shoulders and try to stand strong. *Liam survived this. And Harley. And even little Paris.* But I'm not as strong as Liam or Harley, or even Paris. I'm pretty sure Paris has more guts in her little body than I ever will.

"Remove your clothes."

It's a woman's voice. Pleasant-sounding, but it makes my

skin prickle with unease. My eyes search the darkness for the woman, but I see nothing.

Are the men who brought us here watching me now? I guess they can watch us whenever they please. I haven't seen any cameras, but that doesn't mean they aren't all around: in the common room, inside the showers, all over the bedrooms, above my bed. Besides, if the men wanted to see me naked … if they wanted to do anything at all to me … they could have done it that first night, after they drugged me to make me sleep. They could drug me again right now if they wanted.

"REMOVE YOUR CLOTHES!" the woman shouts.

My body stiffens at the intensity of her voice. I don't like being spoken to the way the woman is speaking to me now.

But I made a choice to come in here. And now I must choose whether or not to do as The Room asks. A positive relationship involves give and take. If I want that kind of relationship with The Room, I must give something. It wants me to remove my clothes. And so I reach for the hem of my sweatshirt.

One piece at a time, I remove every single bit of my clothing. I fold each item carefully and place them in an orderly pile inside the dimly-lit locker that has appeared beside me. It makes me feel a little more in control to fold my clothes and arrange them neatly like that. Besides, The Room can't get angry with me for folding my clothes, can it?

Once my clothes are in the locker, it closes on its own. I'm not sure how it knew that I was through with it, but I suppose the answer is obvious: the woman is watching me. And I highly doubt she is alone. I stand up tall again with my arms at my sides, trying to look strong, but feeling horribly exposed.

"Have a seat," the woman says.

A few feet away from me, a ray of light illuminates a lone

chair that reminds me of the one at the dentist's office. This one is thicker than a dentist's chair though. And plain white. Instead of resting on the floor, it seems to hover in midair. I don't like the looks of it. Maybe it's the circumstances. I've never been asked to sit on a dentist's chair naked.

I scan the darkness, looking for the woman who offered the seat to me, but she is still nowhere to be seen. "I'd rather stand," I say to the nothingness that surrounds me.

"HAVE A SEAT!" the woman bellows.

I guess her words weren't a request, they were a command. I look back toward the door that leads to the common room, and I see nothing there. It is entirely possible that, as Liam said to us, I must satisfy The Room before it will release me. It is also possible that it can choose not to release me at all, or to release me somewhere different … somewhere less desirable.

I step up to the chair and ease myself onto it. It's strangely soft. Too soft. Without warning, the chair begins to recline. It tilts back more and more, until I am lying completely flat on what is no longer a chair, but a table. The table begins to embrace my body. My hips, back, neck, head, legs, arms. It conforms to me, finding every bulge and curve and crevice. I feel like it is *merging* with me. My heart quickens with sickening anxiety, but I don't fight. I don't think it wants me to fight.

Something appears above me. The shape of a human.

"Remain still," the woman says.

It is impossible not to follow her instructions. The table now has a tight grip on every inch of me. My entire body is being held firmly in place, unable to move at all.

The thing that emerged from the ceiling continues its descent. As it moves closer, away from the light shining above, I see that it is pure white in color, just like the table. The thing comes right down on top of me, joining with me and then the table. I feel it snap into place, as if it has snapped right into my body.

"Sit up now," the woman says.

Just after she finishes speaking, the table returns to its original semi-sitting position. I no longer feel attached to it. Now I am sitting *on* it rather than *in* it.

I am almost completely covered from head to toe in some kind of bodysuit. A layer of the table has become a part of my clothing, forming the suit that envelops me. The only part left open is an area around my mouth and nose, just below a transparent piece that covers my eyes.

"Stand by for calibration," the woman says.

The bodysuit begins to squeeze me, rhythmically, like I am inside a beating heart. Maybe my own heart. Or the woman's. The squeezes come fast and strong.

"You will now be exposed to a series of stimuli," the woman goes on. "Your responses will be monitored. Try to react naturally. This is very important. We need to ensure that your shield suit will protect you properly. During the testing, I will take the opportunity to get to know you."

I've heard about shield suits, but I've never worn one before. After the Third World War, large areas of the Earth became unsafe for humans to inhabit. People still live there, for various reasons, but they must wear specially-designed suits for protection. *Does this mean we've been brought to an uninhabitable place?*

My suit—and my heart—pump faster.

"To begin, please say, 'Shield up,'" the woman says.

I take a deep breath, not feeling ready for this. "Shield up," I say.

Something slides over the bottom half of my face and snaps

into place with a stomach-turning click … and then thick black restraints emerge from the table and wrap across my arms, chest, abdomen, and legs. And I am thrust into terrifying darkness.

WEDNESDAY, MAY SECOND
1340

GOAT

Paris and I lie side by side on her bed, getting ready to face the other kids. We need to go back upstairs, or at least I do, because I'm going to go into the room with the stars.

"Are you ready?" I ask Paris quietly.

"I'm ready," she says.

I'm ready too, not only to face the other kids, but to face the starry room.

Paris starts up the ladder first, and I follow her. A few people glance at us as we climb into the main room, but no one says anything.

The door to the starry room is closed, so going straight in there isn't an option. I don't feel any relief though. Now that I've decided to go in, waiting only makes my fear get worse.

Harley isn't in the starry room anymore. He's here, playing chess with Lizard. He seems to be acting the same as he was before he went in the starry room. Maybe the room didn't hurt him. Or maybe it *did* hurt him, but Harley didn't let it break him … not even a little.

Unpleasant is the only one of us who isn't here.

"Is Unpleasant in the starry room?" I ask Liam.

He nods, barely looking at me.

"I want to go in next," I say, loud enough so that everyone can hear me.

Liam's eyes widen a little. "Are you sure?" he asks me.

"Yes," I say, trying to sound confident.

He looks at Paris, and then he looks back at me. "Okay," he says.

No one else says anything. So I'm next, I guess.

WEDNESDAY, MAY SECOND
1352

UNPLEASANT

My body throbs and aches and burns like hell.

I'm not sure how long I've been in here, but The Room has asked me so many questions that I've lost count. Each question brings on another round of torture. If my answer doesn't come fast enough, I am tortured. If my answer isn't to The Room's liking, I am tortured. If I refuse to answer, I am tortured.

The torture comes in the form of 'stimuli.' Each time, it's a different stimulus. I am not warned as to what kind of stimulus it will be. I can't see them coming, because the room remains completely dark. I'm not sure anymore whether it is *worse* to experience this in the dark, or *better*.

"Next question." The woman's voice echoes in the pitch blackness.

I brace for what is to come.

"What are you most afraid of?" the woman asks.

My heart beats faster. The rhythmic squeezing of my shield suit quickens.

"Death," I say.

Seconds after the word leaves my lips, hundreds of dull, scratchy needles emerge from the table, stabbing into my shield suit. It is possible that the suit is protecting my body from puncture, but it doesn't protect me from the pain. The shield suit continues its rhythmic squeezing, scraping my flesh across the jagged tips of the abrasive needles, over and over.

I bite back an "Oww!"

"What are you most afraid of?" the woman asks again, more insistently this time.

"Pain," I say.

The needles press deeper into me. I want to cry. I want to scream. I'm not sure how much more of this I can handle. I've passed out before from pain—when my arm got broken in sixth grade, and again last year when I cut myself on the leg with a knife. If I pass out now, who knows what The Room will do to me?

"WHAT ARE YOU MOST AFRAID OF?" the woman growls.

My heart accelerates to a panic. Every other time the woman asked a question, it was only asked twice before she moved on to the next one. But this is the third time she has asked this question. If I can't give her the answer she wants, will she refuse to release me from The Room? Will she torture me here until I die?

"You!" I shout out. "I'm afraid of you."

My restraints tighten, pressing the needles even deeper into me. Down into my muscles. The torture is unbearable. It is the worst pain I've been subjected to so far. The worst pain in my life.

"BE HONEST!" the woman's voice booms.

"I am trying to be honest!" I say with a trembling voice that I can't steady. The shield suit is squeezing so fast now. Each squeeze brings more pain. I just want this to end. But I don't know how to make it end. Frantically, I search my brain for an answer that will satisfy The Room, but my thoughts jumble up. "What do you want me to say?" I plead.

The needles suddenly retract. The suit continues to squeeze me, hard and fast, but I don't hurt as much anymore.

"I want you to tell me the truth." The woman's voice is gentle.

I close my eyes and try to think, but it hurts to think. I don't want to think anymore. I just want The Room to take what it wants from me—whatever it wants—and let me go. I just want this to be over. I just want to be left alone.

"What are you most afraid of?" the woman asks quietly.

"I'm most afraid of …" I start, bracing myself for The Room's wrath. The squeezing is getting faster and faster. "I'm most afraid of … the unknown."

That's the truth. That is what scares me the most. The unknown is why I haven't slept well in years. And why I sometimes eat more than I should. And why I don't have any *real* friendships with anyone back home. The unknown terrifies me, because it has the potential to destroy me.

The unknown is why this place is my worst nightmare. I've been forced into close quarters with a bunch of strangers who I know almost nothing about. Our fates ultimately rest in the hands of our captors. I don't know whether they are planning to release us or keep us here until we die. Or what will happen to us in the next hour or minute or second.

Suddenly, the squeezing stops. I see, hear, and feel absolutely nothing, except the absence of everything. It's as if I'm floating on air in the middle of a dark, empty room. All of the pain I've experienced here fades away, at least the physical pain.

"You're afraid of the unknown?" the woman asks.

I take a deep breath, trying to slow my racing heart. "Yes."

"Tell me more," the woman says.

WEDNESDAY, MAY SECOND
1403

TIGER

Rain and I are playing gin rummy with her deck of cards. We haven't been talking, which is good. I've been busy thinking about the star room. I don't think Liam wants me to go in there. I don't think I want to go in there either. But part of me feels like I *should* go in there. I'm not sure what to do.

"What are you thinking about?" Rain asks me.

I hate it when people ask me that question, because I like to keep my thoughts private. But maybe it would be good to talk to Rain about this.

"I was thinking about the star room," I say to her.

She nods her head. Maybe that means she's been thinking about the star room too.

"What do you think happens in there?" she asks me.

"I think someone hurts us." Basically that's what Liam said.

"Harley didn't look hurt," Rain says softly.

"Yeah, well, Harley is Harley," I say quietly.

"You're right." Rain smiles, but then her face goes serious again. "I'm gonna volunteer to go in after Goat."

I can't believe that Rain wants to go into the star room. She doesn't seem like the kind of person who likes to face scary things. But Rain also doesn't seem like the kind of person who can knock a big heavy movie screen "window" off the wall with a single kick.

"Why do you want to go in there?" I ask her.

"I don't *want* to," she says. "But sometimes it's better to take action instead of waiting for action to be taken on you."

"Is that why you knocked the movie screen off the wall?" I ask.

"I guess," she says.

"Where'd you learn to kick like that?" I ask her.

"My dad taught me," she says. "He thinks it's important for a person to be able to defend themselves. He said it would make me feel safer."

"Did it?" I ask.

"Yeah … up until recently."

Rain's self-defense lessons didn't stop the bad men from kidnapping her.

"I can teach you if you want," she offers.

Rain looks kind of excited about teaching me, and it might be good to know how to defend myself, even if it can't stop bad people from hurting me.

"Okay," I say.

WEDNESDAY, MAY SECOND
1420

UNPLEASANT

I don't think I've ever felt this spent in my entire life. I am completely drained. Both emotionally and physically.

The woman hasn't said anything for a few minutes. I wonder if she's conferring with someone else. The men, maybe. Trying to figure out what to do to me next.

Without warning, the table reclines until I am flat on my back, facing a starry ceiling. My heart beats wildly in my chest. I feel like I am being prepared for execution. I imagine the sharp silver blade of a guillotine falling out from among the stars.

Suddenly, my black restraints release me and retract into the table. I feel a pop that seems to come from deep within me and then the top half of my shield suit lifts away from my body and ascends into the stars, where it disappears. The bottom half of the shield suit gently pulls itself away from my skin. Then I lie naked on the table. Motionless. Unsure if my body is still capable of movement.

"That's all for today," the woman says. "Please get dressed."

Shooting stars appear across my vision as I sit up. I feel dizzy and sick to my stomach. I should probably lie down again, but I force myself to stay sitting until the flittering stars disappear. I find my clothes in the locker, in the neat little pile that I made when I placed them there. I gracelessly pull them on, and then I stumble over to the now-illuminated door.

"Will you come back tomorrow?" the woman asks as if she didn't just finish inflicting a torture session on me so severe that I can now barely hold myself upright.

There is no way in hell I'm ever coming back here, I think to myself. But there is no way I would say that right now—even though I'm no longer strapped to the "torture table."

I place one hand against the door to steady myself, take a deep breath, force my bitterness down, and then I speak as calmly as I can, "Why do you want me to come back here?"

"Remember what you said when I asked what you wanted most of all?" she asks me very softly. The way she speaks, I wonder if she's afraid someone will overhear her.

"Of course, I do." I think it was the only time she accepted my first answer to one of her questions, without subjecting me to any torture.

"I can help you," she says in a hushed voice. "But when you leave this room, it is absolutely essential that you do not discuss what happened in here with anyone at any time. Do we have a deal?"

I stare at the closed door, considering her proposal. If I refuse, will she let me go without further punishment? Or is her proposal not an offer but a command, one that I will be forced to obey? The answer to that question isn't essential for me to know, I suppose. If there's a chance, any chance at all, that the woman will make good on her promise, then I need to come back here. Even if it hurts. Even if it kills me. Although it seems unlikely, it *is* possible that this woman holds the key to what I told her I want most of all … to go home.

I swallow and force my answer from my lips, "We have a deal."

WEDNESDAY, MAY SECOND
1428

GOAT

My little green plastic man is in Peppermint Forest and Paris' little blue plastic man is just a few spaces away from Candy Castle when the starry room opens again. Unpleasant almost trips over her own feet when she walks out of it. Liam goes over to her and holds out his hand, but Unpleasant doesn't let him help her. She says something to him, and then she walks shakily down the hallway that goes to the bathrooms.

It's my turn to go in the starry room now. I stand up and try to make myself feel brave.

"Do whatever she says," Paris whispers to me.

"Whatever *who* says?" I ask, confused.

"The lady in the room," Paris answers quietly.

There's a *lady* in the room? Is *the lady* going to hurt me?

"Promise you'll do what she says," Paris insists.

Years ago, I decided that I would never make a promise that I wasn't sure I was going to be able to keep. So I can't promise what Paris is asking.

"I promise I won't let anyone break me," I say to her instead. And I repeat that to myself over and over as I take one step and then another and then another and then one last step right into the room full of stars and darkness.

The door shuts behind me.

The stars are gone now. All that's left is the darkness.

"Remove your clothes." It's a lady who is talking. *The lady.*

Why does the lady want me to take off my clothes?

My mom told me nobody is supposed to see me naked unless she says it's okay. But my mom isn't here to ask. And Paris wants me to do what the lady says. And so I take off my clothes and put them into a little cupboard.

"Have a seat," the lady says.

Her big white chair is kind of high up off the ground and it's slippery, but I'm good at climbing, and so I get in it pretty fast. When I sit properly on the chair, I sink down into the cushion, and the chair reclines so that I'm looking straight up at the light that's shining down on me. Suddenly, something white comes out of the light, heading straight toward me. I try to lift my hands to protect my face, but my hands are stuck to the chair ... or *inside* it.

"Let me go!" I shout, trying to sound strong.

"Remain still," the lady says.

I close my eyes and wait for the hurt that Liam and Paris told me would come.

I won't let anyone break me ... I won't let anyone break me ...

Something touches me from above, but the touch doesn't hurt. Actually, it feels ... good. Like a soft blanket that covers me perfectly. A gentle snap happens inside my bones.

"Sit up now," the lady says.

The chair helps me get into a sitting position.

"Stand by for calibration," the lady says.

And then my whole body is squeezed tight, again and again, over and over, but not hard enough to hurt. The squeezes get a little faster and then a little slower, faster and slower, every time I breathe.

"You will now be exposed to a series of stimuli," the lady says. "Your responses will be monitored. Try to react naturally. This is very important. We need to ensure that your shield suit will protect you properly. During the testing, I will take the opportunity to get to know you."

It's strange, but I'm starting to feel kind of ... a little bit ... almost ... safe. The lady is scary, because she does things to me that I don't expect but, so far, she hasn't hurt me.

"To begin, please say, 'Shield up,'" the lady says.

"Shield up," I say.

Something slides over my mouth and nose and snaps shut.

And the room goes black.

WEDNESDAY, MAY SECOND
1438

TIGER

Rain's self-defense lesson involves touching, which I don't like. When someone touches me, my natural instinct is to push the touch away. But the ultimate goal in self-defense is to make other people's touch go away, so I guess it's a good skill to have.

After a little while of Rain teaching me self-defense in our room, she says, "We should probably head back upstairs."

"Yeah," I agree.

She spins around and starts toward the ladder.

"Thanks for teaching me," I say.

She turns and smiles. "That's what friends are for."

Is it possible that something can be one of the worst things that has ever happened to you, but also one of the best things that has ever happened to you? Being taken away from my parents is one of the most terrible things that has happened in my life. But having a friend is something I've wanted ... something I've needed ... ever since Andrew died.

When Rain and I make it back upstairs, the door to the star room is closed.

"Who's in the star room?" Rain asks Harley softly.

"Goat," he answers.

"I'm going in after Goat," Rain says.

Against my better judgment, I add, "I'm after Rain."

We look at Lizard. She's the only person who hasn't either

gone into the star room or volunteered to go, so Lizard will be last. I guess you don't have to volunteer if you're last, but I think everyone expects her to make it official.

Finally, just as I expected, Lizard opens her mouth, but she says something I didn't expect, "I'm not going in there. Not ever."

WEDNESDAY, MAY SECOND
1443

UNPLEASANT

My mouth still tastes of vomit when I finally make my way back to the common room. I glance toward The Room and see that the door is once again closed. When I came out of there a little while ago, I couldn't see straight. I didn't notice whether the door closed behind me or if someone else went in. I take a look around the common room, and my stomach sinks. There is one person who is missing: Goat.

"Is Goat in The Room?" I ask Liam, bracing for the answer. He nods.

I curse under my breath. Now that I know what happens inside The Room, I can't bear to see others endure it. Especially Goat.

"You *know* what happens in there. How could you let him go?" I seethe at Liam. "And Paris …"

"Going into The Room can't possibly be optional," Liam says.

As much as I don't want to agree with him, I think that is probably true.

"So we should just march in there and let them hurt us?" I ask angrily.

"It should be up to each of us to decide," Liam says. "*You* chose to go in there. If *you* don't want to go back, then don't go."

"I'm going back," I say, half-hoping that upsets him.

"I'm going back too," he says, staring hard at me. "So who are we to say that the others shouldn't have that choice?"

I don't know what the right thing to do is. Trying to prevent the other kids from going into The Room could cause the kidnappers to unleash something far worse than anything we've experienced so far. The kidnappers have already demonstrated that they aren't afraid to drug us and to torture us. Fighting back when we are so utterly at their mercy will probably only serve to get us tortured even more severely than what I experienced just now ... or killed. It could be that the only reason I was released from The Room alive was that I finally acquiesced to its demands. Maybe it's better to comply with the kidnappers' terms until the sacrifice is too great. Then it will be time to fight. But, if so, where do we draw the line?

I wish I could have prevented Goat from going into The Room, but it's too late now. I try to tell myself that he will be okay in there, because he's just a little kid. Who would torture a little kid? But when I see the worry in Paris' eyes, any slight feeling of reassurance vanishes.

The Room obviously punished Paris, and she's just as little as Goat.

The Room will punish Goat ... unless he gives it what it wants.

WEDNESDAY, MAY SECOND
1450

GOAT

The lady asks a lot of questions, but they are easy to answer. They're mostly about back home, which makes me sad to think about, because I miss home very much. Even though her questions make me sad, the lady has been nice and gentle to me. She hasn't hurt me at all.

"I want you to imagine that you're floating on your back in a swimming pool," the lady says. "The sun is shining down on you."

I guess I have a good imagination, because I feel the chair below me get bigger and fill up with water.

"Do you feel the water?" the lady asks me.

"Yes, ma'am," I say. "I feel it."

"And the sun?" she asks.

I close my eyes and try to make this dark place disappear in my mind. I imagine that I can feel the heat of the sun on my face and my body.

"Yes, ma'am," I say. "I feel the sun."

"Good," the lady says. "Now I want you to imagine your best friend is floating in the pool next to you. What is the name of the person floating next to you?"

The answer should be Antonio. He has been my best friend for more than two months, but when the lady told me to imagine my best friend next to me, I saw *Paris*.

"Is something troubling you?" the lady asks.

"Do I have to pick only *one* best friend, ma'am?"

"Yes," she says. "I want you to choose the person to whom you would tell your deepest secret."

I wouldn't tell my deepest secret to anyone, especially not Antonio or Paris. But the lady isn't asking me to tell anyone a secret. She just wants me to choose someone to have in my imagination when I face whatever is going to happen next. I don't know what is going to happen next, but it might hurt. I need to pick someone who—

"Make a choice!" the lady says.

I feel ice cold water gush into my make-believe pool. I try to sit up to get away from it, but I sink down into the water, as if I'm *really* in a pool. I take a big breath and try to get my body floating on the water again. Water that I'd thought wasn't really here, but maybe it is.

"I choose Paris!" I shout through shivering teeth.

Suddenly, something that I can't see grabs me and pulls me underwater. My heart races. The water underneath me is definitely real. I'm not imagining it. The chair has become a swimming pool. I kick a foot down to try to find the bottom of the pool, but I can't reach it.

"Breathe," the lady says.

Does the shield suit allow me to breathe underwater? The lady hasn't told me that, and I can't ask her any questions because I'm holding my breath. If I breathe and the shield suit doesn't protect me, I'll suck water into my mask, like I did when I tried snorkeling in my bathtub back home. If I get water into my mask now, I'll drown.

"Breathe," the lady says again.

Maybe she's saying that because it's safe for me to breathe.

Or maybe she's trying to drown me.

"Breathe!" the lady says, louder.

Something tugs me deeper under the water.

The lady is not going to let me free.

"BREATHE!" she shouts.

My body is begging for air. I'm going to have to breathe or at least try. I let in the tiniest bit of air, even though my body wants a lot more. No water enters my mask. I let a little air out, and then a little in. Again no water comes into my mask. I try a small breath. And then one that's a little bigger. Bigger. Bigger. Each time I breathe, the shield suit gives me fresh air. The shield suit *is* protecting me. In this suit, I can breathe under the water.

I don't relax though. I'm still in a pitch-black pool with something holding me underwater. I have air, but maybe the lady can control that. Maybe she can control whether I live or die.

"I want you to tell me about the time when you felt the most trapped," the lady says.

"I feel trapped right now, ma'am," I say.

"Is this the most trapped you've ever felt?" she asks.

The answer is no. I've felt trapped even worse than I do right now. But I don't want to tell the lady about that. I don't want to tell anyone.

Hot water bubbles into the pool. *The lady is making the water hot.*

"The water's too hot," I say.

"Tell me about the time when you felt more trapped than this," the lady says.

The water gets hotter.

"The water's hurting me!" I shout. "The shield suit isn't protecting me!"

"Tell me about the time when you felt more trapped than this," the lady says again.

The lady knows the water is too hot. She knows the shield suit isn't protecting me.

The sweat on my face mixes with my tears. If I don't answer her question, will the lady let the water burn me? Will the lady *kill* me?

"My goat, Mary, had two kids ..." I start.

Cooler water instantly flushes the hot water away. Tears still run from my eyes though. Those tears won't stop, because I know I have to keep talking, or else the lady will punish me.

"When my teacher found out that my goat had babies, she told the whole class," I say. "One of the boys said he wanted to come over and see them, but I didn't want him to because he liked to call me names and poke me with pencils and stuff. I told him my mom said I couldn't bring anyone over but, after school, he followed me to my house anyway. My mom wasn't home, because she was still at work. When he realized my mom wasn't there, he searched for the goats, which wasn't hard because they're kind of noisy. I thought maybe he would just look at them and leave, but he sat down with them, like he was going to stay for a long time. Mary seemed to sense that something was wrong, but she didn't do anything about it. I was there and she trusted me.

"He picked up one of the babies—the boy one—and started petting him. He was actually being nice. I worried that he was going to take the little goat home, but then he put the baby in my lap and said, 'Kill it.' He wanted me to kill Mary's baby.

"Up until then, I never imagined that anyone, even that boy, would want to do something that awful to something so innocent. I tried to think of what I could do. I could scream, but our neighbors lived far enough away that they'd never hear me. I could grab the kids and run, but then he might hurt Mary or our other animals. I could fight him, but I'd never win. He was almost twice as big as me. There was no good choice.

"And then everything got worse. He told me, 'If you kill one, I'll let the other one live. If not, I'll kill them both.'

"And so I fought him, even though I knew I couldn't win. It took only a few seconds for him to pin me down and tie me up. And then he killed Mary's baby boy. And then her baby girl. He told me if I ever ratted on him, he would come back in the middle of the night and kill Mary too.

"I slept with Mary every night until that boy burned down his family's house, and the police took him to a place that my mom said was kind of like jail. My mom said I'd never see him again.

"But I still see him every night, when I close my eyes. Every night, I'm in that barn again, with those baby goats dying because I couldn't protect them. Every night, I see their small lifeless bodies. Their mama nudging them with her nose, trying to get them to wake up."

"Next question." The lady's voice is completely calm. She doesn't sound at all shocked or upset by what I've told her.

I guess that's because what I said doesn't surprise her. The lady already knows there are monsters in the world.

The lady is one of them.

WEDNESDAY, MAY SECOND
1524

UNPLEASANT

The Room opens and Goat walks out. He's holding his head high, trying to look brave, but the rest of his appearance betrays him. His clothes are disheveled, he's trembling, and his eyes are red and wet. Rage burns inside me. *We shouldn't have let him go in there.*

Rain gets up from her seat and heads toward the doorway of the deceptively-beautiful room. I put myself between her and The Room, blocking her path.

"No one else is going in," I say.

"Why not?" Rain asks.

I wish I could tell her exactly why I don't want her going in there, but I made a pact with The Room that I wouldn't share its secrets, and I need The Room to make good on its promise.

"I can't say," I tell Rain.

"I'm not blind," she says. "I've watched other people come out of that room. I know I'm probably going to get hurt in there. But I need to do this."

I feel everything inside me deflate. Rain hasn't told me her reasons for wanting to go into The Room, but I have no business asking them. She understands the risks, and she's willing to take them.

Rain inhales as I step aside.

And then she allows The Room to take her.

When I turn back toward the common room, everyone is

looking at me, but their gazes quickly settle elsewhere.

By the time I return to my seat, Liam is focused on Tiger, who is sitting alone, staring blankly at a table.

"I guess you think I shouldn't have tried to stop Rain," I say to Liam.

His gaze remains fixed on his sister. "You had a right to try, and she had a right to continue on," he says.

"Are you worried about Tiger?" I ask.

"There's stuff she doesn't handle well," he says under his breath.

"What do you mean?" I ask.

"She's …. sensitive."

"Sensitive how?" I ask, trying to understand.

He shakes his head. There's something that he's not saying.

"Why don't you give her some advice?" I suggest.

"Like what?" he asks.

I try to think of what advice I would give her, but I come up empty. "I don't know," I say. "But you know her better than I do."

"I've never been able to help her," Liam says.

Tiger squints her eyes shut very tightly, like she's trying not to cry.

"Maybe she could use a hug," I offer.

Liam shakes his head again. "She doesn't like hugs."

"I don't like hugs either," I say.

Liam finally looks at me. "If *you* had an older brother here, and you were about to go in that room for the first time, what would you want him to do?"

I can't even imagine what it would be like to have a brother who was looking out for me.

"I don't think I'd want him to *do* anything," I say. "It would be enough just to know he cares about me."

Liam looks back at Tiger, and then, without a word, he rises to his feet.

WEDNESDAY, MAY SECOND
1530

TIGER

Liam startles me. It seems like he magically appeared beside me.

"Sorry, I didn't mean to surprise you," he apologizes.

"I was kind of in my own world," I say.

"Right." He fidgets a little with his feet. I've never seen Liam fidget before.

"Are you okay?" I ask him.

He sits down in the chair that's next to me. "I'm as okay as I can be. How are you?"

"I'm all right, I guess," I say.

His eyebrows move closer together, like he's worried about something. "You know … if you decide not to go in The Room, that's okay."

"Is it bad in there?" I ask him.

He nods his head.

My heart beats harder. *If it was bad for Liam, how am I going to handle it?*

"That which doesn't kill you makes you stronger," I say. It was Andrew's motto.

Liam fidgets again. "I guess."

"I thought you believed that," I say to him.

"I don't know what I believe anymore." He reaches out, like he's going to touch my arm, but then his hand moves away, as if some invisible force pulled it back. "I just want you to know that, whether you go in that room or not, I care about you …" he says. "I love you."

The shock of hearing him say those last three words makes me look at him, but I quickly look away. Andrew used to say "I love you" to me all the time. My mom and dad said it too, and I know they meant it, even though they got frustrated with me a lot. But Liam never said he loved me, at least not as far back as I can remember. I knew that *technically* he loved me, because I was his sister, but I never thought he *actually* loved me.

"I love you too, Liam." I force my eyes to lock with his, so he knows I mean it, and then I let myself look away again.

Liam stays put in that chair next to me. For the first time in a long time, we sit together. We stay quiet, but that's okay. I like quiet better than words.

Liam is still with me when the star room opens again, and Rain comes out. I don't go in after her, because the door closes right behind her. The dinner bell rings a few minutes later. Liam and I eat together in silence. After everyone's empty food boxes are inside the wall, the star room door reopens. I rise to my feet, ready to do what I said I would do.

"You don't have to go in there," Liam says softly to me.

"I know," I say. But I also know that I won't turn back now.

Andrew always used to say, "Never go back on your word."

As I walk toward the star room, Rain runs over to me and grabs my hand too tightly. "Remember all that stuff I taught you in our room today?" she asks.

I nod, and my heart heaves in my chest. I was hoping to have a lot more practice before I had to put Rain's self-defense lessons to use.

"Sometimes it's better not to fight," she says.

"What?" I ask, unsure if I heard her correctly.

"Give them what they want," she says.

My heart pounds even harder. I'm not good at giving people what they want. Most of the time, I have no idea what people want. And most of the rest of the time, I have no idea how to give it to them.

Apparently that is the only advice Rain has to offer, because she releases my hand. I continue toward the stars, feeling even more nervous than I did before. From my vantage point, it looks like I'm about to walk out the door of a spaceship. And I feel no less anxious about what I'm doing. To walk out the door of a spaceship without a spacesuit would result in a very painful death. But what is inside the star room might hurt even worse.

The stars blink away. And the door slides closed behind me.

I am surrounded by darkness. And silence. Silence. Silence.

"Remove your clothes."

A woman is speaking to me. That's strange. I expected that the men would be in here. But it's very dark and I can't see anyone at all. The men are probably here as well. I don't think the woman is the only one. Or maybe there isn't even a woman here. With technology today, the voice that I hear might not belong to a woman. It might actually be one of the men who is speaking to me.

"Remove your clothes," the female voice repeats.

"I don't want people seeing me naked," I say.

"REMOVE YOUR CLOTHES!" the voice shouts.

I plug my ears with my fingers. "Stop shouting!" I yell.

"REMOVE YOUR CLOTHES!"

"No!" I scream.

"REMOVE YOUR CLOTHES!"

The room is too hot.

"REMOVE YOUR CLOTHES!"

There isn't enough air here.

"REMOVE YOUR CLOTHES!"

The voice keeps shouting the same thing over and over again. Every word goes right through my fingers and into my ears, where it hurts my brain. The voice shouts and shouts until I can't think any thoughts. Sweat drips down my face and chest. My heart is beating too fast. I feel too weak to stand ... too weak to do anything at all.

And then, my whole body goes ice cold.

Like death.

WEDNESDAY, MAY SECOND
1734

UNPLEASANT

Tiger emerges from The Room much sooner than I expected. Despite her relatively-brief visit, she looks extremely affected by what happened behind the closed door. It appears as if The Room sucked out everything from inside her and left just a vacant shell of a person, one that still walks, but is otherwise not even living.

"Are you all right, Tiger?" Rain asks.

Tiger doesn't even glance in Rain's direction. She just walks over to the hatch that leads to their bedroom and descends.

Rain hesitates, but only for a split second, then she descends after Tiger.

WEDNESDAY, MAY SECOND
1745

TIGER

Rain is sitting on my bed next to me, talking to me in a soft voice. I know she is trying to be kind to me, but I don't need kindness right now. I need to be by myself.

How do you make people who care about you go away? I guess you have to let them give up on you. The way Liam did back home. The way he is doing now. Liam's not here with me. But that's okay. I don't want him here. I don't want anyone.

It takes a while, but Rain finally leaves.

Weirdly, once I am all by myself, I feel worse instead of better. Being alone usually makes me calmer, but now it makes me more nervous. I guess that's because, in the star room, I was alone, and I was hurt.

Maybe it's safer to be with the other kids.

And so I force myself to stand up and climb the ladder.

So I won't be alone.

WEDNESDAY, MAY SECOND
1957

UNPLEASANT

Almost every one of us has gone into The Room today.
Liam, Paris, Harley, me, Goat, Rain, and Tiger have all been
in. But The Room remains open, waiting for its final victim.

Everyone seems to be ignoring that fact, until Harley asks
Lizard, "Did you change your mind about going in The
Room?"

"Why would I change my mind?" she responds coolly.

"Everyone else survived it," Rain says.

"So what?" Lizard replies.

"Aren't you curious?" Harley asks.

"The only thing I'm curious about is why the rest of you
went in there," Lizard says. "I kind of understand why the first
person—Liam—went in. What if that doorway was a way out?
But Liam came back, so obviously it wasn't. And, based on
what he told us, it sounded pretty awful in there. But, okay,
maybe you didn't believe Liam. Maybe you thought he was
pretending it was bad, so he'd look courageous. So I
understand why the second person—Paris—went in. But then
Paris came out, and she looked like her soul had been ripped
out of her and stuffed back in. But she's just a little kid, so
maybe you thought, *I can handle it*. So I understand why
Harley went in. And, when he came out, he looked all right, so
I can understand why Unpleasant was willing to give it a try.
But then Unpleasant came out, and then Goat, and Rain, and

Tiger. And each one of those people looked like they'd visited hell. And, no, I'm not curious to know what *hell* is like."

Liam rises to his feet. "I'm going back in."

It takes all of my self-control not to reach out for him as he walks toward the menacing stars. I hold my breath as he steps into The Room and waits for the stars to extinguish. But they don't. Instead, they glow red.

"Let me try," I say. I jump to my feet and start toward The Room. I've already decided that I'm going back in there eventually. I might as well go now. I need to find out if the woman can do as she promised, and the sooner the better.

With a deep inhale, Liam moves back into the common room, so that I can enter The Room. I step toward the white stars and brace myself for the darkness, but no darkness comes. Instead, the stars glow red, just as they did for Liam. As I step out of The Room, the stars rapidly turn back to white.

"We'll try again tomorrow," I say to Liam.

"Right," he says.

Together, Liam and I walk back to our seats. A few minutes later, we've returned to our card game, but I think both of our minds are far away.

"The Room wants Lizard," Rain whispers.

"I'm not going in there," Lizard mutters.

"I think we all need to have a turn before anyone gets another chance," Rain says, insistent.

Liam shakes his head. "Whether or not Lizard goes in there is up to Lizard," he says.

"That's right," Lizard says. "And I'm not going into that room. Not today. Not tomorrow. Not ever."

Without warning, Rain leaps to her feet and grabs hold of Lizard.

"What the hell are you doing?" Lizard shouts at Rain.

It's clear what Rain is doing.

Liam and I race toward The Room.

But before we can get there, Rain shoves Lizard into the stars.

And the door to The Room closes.

WEDNESDAY, MAY SECOND
2003

TIGER

"What did I say about taking action on your own?" Liam says to Rain in a low voice.

"Sometimes the ends justify the means," Rain says.

"We all need to work together," Liam says. "That is the only way we're going to survive this."

"You don't know that," Rain says. "You don't know *anything*. You act all big and strong, but people much bigger and stronger than you brought us here. And you were no match for them, were you? You were kidnapped just the same as the rest of us, so why should you get to tell us what we can and can't do?"

"I won't stand by and watch you sacrifice anyone," Liam growls.

"I didn't sacrifice Lizard," Rain argues. "She'll be all right."

"You don't know that," I say.

Rain glares into my eyes. And then she goes to our hatch, and down into our room.

I don't follow her.

Rain is … was … my friend, but what she did wasn't right. She doesn't know what's going to happen to Lizard in the star room. She only knows what happened to her. And I only know what happened to me. Actually, I only know *some* of what happened to me. I remember a female voice shouting and shouting. And then I think I passed out. When I woke up, I was lying on a white table. Completely undressed. And I felt like my body had been touched. All over.

The night we were kidnapped, someone might have touched me too, after they gave me the medicine that put me to sleep. But, this time, I *know* I was touched. I could still feel it when I woke up. I can still feel it now.

But I volunteered to go in that room. It was my decision. It wouldn't have been fair for Rain, or anyone else, to force me into it.

The kidnappers have taken away most of our power of choice.

We can't start doing that to each other. No matter what.

WEDNESDAY, MAY SECOND
2055

GOAT

A while after Lizard was pushed into the starry room, the door opens again, but there aren't any stars in there. It is only dark. Lizard steps out of the dark, and then the door closes behind her. Maybe just for a little while. Maybe for the rest of the day. Maybe forever.

Unpleasant goes over to Lizard, and the two of them talk very quietly. Then Lizard waves Unpleasant away, and she sits down all alone.

DING. DING. DING. DING. DING. DING.

It's bedtime.

Paris and I put the Candy Land game into its box and take it to our room. Paris puts the game into the hidden space under her mattress, then she stands up and looks at me.

"Can we sleep together again?" she asks.

"Of course," I say, and she climbs into my bed.

I'm glad Paris wants us to sleep in the same bed again tonight. I want that too. It's not for the same reason that I wanted to sleep with my mom and dad back when I was a little kid. Back then, I thought my mom and dad could protect me from all the scary dangers of the dark. I thought nothing could hurt me when I was in their bed. But I don't think Paris can protect me from danger, and I don't think I can protect her. The bad men are stronger than both of us put together.

I want Paris to be in bed next to me because I want to be

sure that I won't wake up in the morning and find out that she was taken away in the middle of the night.

I wish Paris and I could be friends forever and ever. But Paris and I probably won't get to have a very long forever.

When our forever is about to end, I at least want to be able to say goodbye.

WEDNESDAY, MAY SECOND
2114

UNPLEASANT

Everyone has gone to their bedrooms, except for Liam and me. Even Harley and Lizard have decided that they'd rather endure being locked inside their minuscule rooms than remain here in the common room and be tortured all night.

"Are you going to stay out here tonight?" Liam asks me.

It's not clear from his tone whether he'll be staying out here or not.

I'm not sure what to do. I don't want to spend another sleepless night in the common room. But I don't think I can bear to be locked up in my coffin.

"I don't want to be alone," I blurt out.

"I can stay with you," he offers.

"You're willing to stay out here again?" I ask.

"We don't have to stay here," he says. "We can stay wherever you want."

My heart accelerates. Did Liam just offer to spend the night with me … *wherever* I want?

"I'd like to be somewhere quiet," I admit.

"The bedrooms are quiet," Liam says.

"I know …" I start, but I don't know how to finish.

It frightens me to say yes to sleeping with Liam in one of the bedrooms. It's true that Liam and I spent last night cuddled together, but we were in a freezing-cold room with two other people. Tonight, it looks like it will be just the two of us.

But I desperately need to get some sleep and, to do that, I need to be somewhere quiet and torture-free. And I want to be with someone … I want to be with *Liam*.

"Your bedroom or mine?" I ask him reluctantly.

"How about yours?" he suggests.

I take a deep breath, trying to slow my heart. Liam takes a deep breath too.

"Okay," I say.

"I'll get my mattress," he says.

Liam returns from his room a few minutes later, dragging his mattress, bed sheets, and pillow. He gestures to my ladder. "Lead the way."

My hands tremble as I move up the ladder. But maybe there's no need to be nervous. Even though I've known Liam for less than two days, I feel like I know him much better than that. Sometimes, when I look into his eyes, I see the kinds of feelings most people try to hide from others: Worry. Fear. Loss. Pain. At those times, I feel like I know him more intimately than anyone I've ever known. But, at other times, I feel like he is a complete stranger, which is what he pretty much is.

I help pull Liam's mattress and bedclothes into my room. Once everything is inside, Liam shuts the hatch, adjusts his mattress on the floor, and starts making up his bed.

I sit inside my coffin, remembering the intense feeling of panic that I had when I woke up in this tiny place with no way out.

"I can't sleep in here," I say.

"Would you rather sleep out here?" Liam asks, gesturing to his mattress.

The prospect of sharing a bed with Liam seems a lot less undesirable from my vantage point inside my coffin.

"I guess so," I say.

"All right," Liam says.

I climb out of my bed and into Liam's. At the same time, he climbs out of his bed and into mine.

"Better?" he asks.

I look at the doorway to my coffin—which is now the doorway to Liam's coffin. It is almost certainly going to close soon, and then it won't open again until morning.

"I wish that wall wouldn't close," I say softly.

"Maybe we can get it to stay open," Liam says.

"How?" I ask.

He slides his pillow toward me, so it rests between us, in the threshold. "If the pillow's there, the wall can't close all the way. We can talk to each other through the opening."

We are both quiet for an awkward moment, and then I lie down on Liam's mattress and he lies down on mine.

"What do you want to talk about?" I ask him.

"What did you say to Lizard after she got out of The Room?" he asks.

"I asked if she was okay, and then I told her that you talked to Rain, and that behavior like Rain's won't be tolerated here."

"And what'd she say?" he asks.

"At first, she said she'd make Rain regret it," I say. "But then she said she was better than that."

"I hope she meant it," he says.

"I do too," I say.

"Is it just me, or do you feel like we've suddenly become parents?" he asks.

"I never wanted to be a parent," I admit.

"Me neither," he says. "I'm not even getting married."

That surprises me. Liam seems like the kind of person who has solid, healthy relationships. I pictured him married with at least a kid or two someday.

"Why don't you want to get married?" I ask.

"Because I'm going into the military," he says, as if that answers my question.

"A lot of people in the military get married," I say.

"My older brother, Andrew, was in the military. He was engaged. He had twin boys on the way ..."

My throat tightens. I sense an unhappy ending to Liam's story.

"What happened?" I ask.

"He was hit by enemy gunfire ... and he died," Liam says. "Now his fiancé is raising their boys on her own. She's never going to marry anyone else. She said she's going to be engaged to Andrew forever, even though their marriage can never happen." He shakes his head. "*I'm* never going to leave a wife and kids behind, because I won't have any to leave."

"I'd rather have you in my life for a little while, than to never have you in it at all," I say.

"You don't know me well enough to say that," he says.

"You're right," I say.

And then the wall between us starts to slide shut. Liam and I grab hold of his pillow, securing it in place so it doesn't slip. The wall comes down on the pillow, compressing the pillow. And then ... the wall reverses direction, opening back up completely.

I smile. "It worked."

And then, the lights go out, plunging us into complete darkness.

"Liam," I say softly.

"Yes," he says.

"I ... just wanted to make sure you're still here," I say.

"I'm still here," he says.

"Good," I say.

But nothing about this is good.

I am locked up with a boy who I barely know, in a pitch-black, sound-proof room.

That thought should be absolutely terrifying.

So how is it possible that I feel ... safe?

THURSDAY, MAY THIRD
0700

TIGER

My bed compartment just opened up for the morning. I'm not sure if I should hurry and climb up the ladder now, before Rain, or wait for her to leave our bedroom first. I think, since she is in the compartment above mine, we'll have less chance of interacting if I wait for her to go up the ladder before me, as long as she doesn't come down here looking for me, which I don't think she will.

I'm pretty sure Rain isn't going to go out of her way to interact with me. I don't think she wants to be my friend anymore. I think she expected me to stand by her yesterday with that fierce loyalty that friends are supposed to have for each other. But Rain was willing to sacrifice another person. I can't stand by somebody who would do that.

So I don't have a friend anymore. And, even though I know I'm doing what's right, that doesn't stop it from hurting my heart.

THURSDAY, MAY THIRD
0701

UNPLEASANT

I awaken to a gentle touch on my shoulder.

"I heard something click," Liam says. "I think the hatch is open."

I rub my eyes, feeling disoriented. I can't believe I actually slept last night.

"We should try to get to the common room before the other kids do," Liam says.

"Right," I agree. It might be best if the other kids don't see Liam and me emerging from the same bedroom. I don't want them to think something non-platonic is happening between us—because *that* isn't happening between us.

I sit up and lift Liam's mattress away from the hatch. Liam opens the hatch slightly, but then he promptly closes it.

"Too late," he tells me. "Harley and Lizard are already there."

I cringe at the rumors that are going to start, if not aloud, at least in people's heads.

"We're going to have to go down there eventually," I say.

Liam nods. "That's true."

He inhales, opens the hatch again, and begins his descent. As I climb down after him, I notice that Harley and Lizard are distracted by something other than us. They're facing the closed door to the bathroom hallway, taking turns saying different things in an attempt to get the men to open the door.

"Open sesame," Harley tries.

"Please," Lizard adds.

Nothing happens.

"Come on, give us a break," Harley says to the wall. "Liam isn't here, and we need to use the bathroom."

The door slides open.

"Still think Liam's so special?" Harley asks Lizard.

And then Lizard sees us. Harley must notice her gaze, because he spins around and gives us a forced smile.

"Hey, Liam, Unpleasant," Harley says. "I got the door open."

Liam nods. "I saw that."

Harley's cheeks flush ever-so-slightly pink.

"Did you two spend the night together?" Lizard asks us.

"Yes," Liam says. "We did."

"Oh," Lizard says.

Surprisingly, that's all either of them says about it.

Not long after the other kids emerge from their bedrooms, breakfast is served. The food has barely settled in my stomach when The Room opens again.

Liam jumps up from his seat and makes his way toward it.

Harley blocks his path. "Who says *you* get to go first?"

Liam stops. "We don't know what's going to happen in there today."

"I'm assuming it'll be fairly similar to yesterday," Harley says.

Liam shakes his head. "I don't think so."

I kind of don't think so either.

"Well, I want to go first," Harley says.

"Let's draw cards then," Liam says.

"That's fair." Harley retrieves his deck and then holds it up in the air. "Anyone who wants to go in The Room first can draw a card."

As I head toward Harley, I am shocked to see that almost everyone lines up to pick a card. Even Lizard wants to go back in The Room. Tiger is the only person who remains seated.

We draw: Jack. Ten. Seven. Six. Queen. Jack. Jack.

Harley sighs. "Unpleasant wins fair and square."

I take a deep breath and head toward The Room. Liam moves with me.

"Do you want to trade?" he asks.

I shake my head. "I won fair and square … or I lost, if you want to be honest about it."

"That doesn't matter," he says.

"I promised I'd be the strong one for a while," I say under my breath.

But that's not the reason why I want to go first. The reason I want to go in The Room before Liam is because, last night, lying in that dark bedroom with him, listening to his steady breaths, I concluded that I'm not as valuable to the other kids as Liam is. He is much stronger than me. I'm not talking about physical strength. That kind of strength might not really be important here. Liam is stronger than me mentally. I'm pretty certain he won't crack, no matter how bad things get. The kids need someone like that.

Liam looks hard into my eyes. "I don't want you to do this for me."

"I want to do this *for me*," I say and, before he can try to persuade me otherwise, I turn away from Liam and march into the stars.

The darkness comes quickly. In the silence that follows, I try to prepare myself for whatever torture lies ahead.

"Remove your clothes," the woman finally says.

Is it crazy to willingly remove my clothes, knowing that I

am shedding my only pitiful protection against danger? If it is, then I'm crazy, because I strip off everything … socks, sweatshirt, sweatpants, underwear, t-shirt.

I'm ready to be your victim, Room.

"Lie down," the woman says.

A thick black bed appears, bathed in the glow of red light. Apparently, this time *will* be different than last time. And I have a terrible feeling that it won't be better.

The bed that awaits me is long enough for even the tallest adult and wide enough to accommodate two people comfortably. There are no bedclothes on it and no pillows, but I suppose bedclothes and pillows are unnecessary. I'm sure I won't be sleeping here.

I walk over to the bed and lie down, unable to slow my accelerating heart. In an instant, the bed conforms to my body, like the chair did yesterday, except this time it feels like it was expecting me. Like it *knows* me.

Something emerges from the red light above: a second bed that matches the bed that I occupy. It falls toward me. It's going to crush me. I fight to free myself, but I am unable to move. The first bed has already taken hold of me.

I feel the impact of the second bed throughout my entire body. But I am not crushed. Instead, I am trapped between two beds, inside a space barely large enough for my body. I suck in a terrified breath and find that, somehow, there's air here. *But for how long?*

Just before I descend into a spiral of panic, the suffocating bed above me lifts away and ascends back into the light, and the first bed releases its grip on me.

"Sit up," the woman says.

As I get into a sitting position, I notice that I am now wearing a shield suit similar to the one I wore yesterday, except this one is inky black with little silver details here and there, and it isn't contracting with every beat of my heart. In fact, this suit isn't contracting at all.

"Stand," the woman says.

I stand, and The Room floods with bright white light. Through squinted eyes, I see the black walls surrounding me for the first time. The Room is bigger than I thought it was—almost four times as large as the common room. On the wall to my left, I see the common room door. To my right, about twenty feet away, I see another door. A larger one. Before I can take in any further details, there is a strange whirring noise, and The Room thrusts me into darkness once more.

I hear a sliding sound in the direction of the large door.

"Come with me!" a male voice says.

I spin toward the voice, expecting only darkness, but there is a little bit of light. It's enough to see that the large door is now open. Beyond it is a closed door with translucent panes. The light coming through the panes outlines a male silhouette. He appears to be wearing a shield suit like mine.

I think he expected me to follow his instructions immediately. When I don't, he steps toward me, giving me a better look at his face. He can't be more than eighteen or nineteen years old.

"Nevah sent me," he says so softly that I can barely hear him. "She said you need my help."

"Who's Nevah?" I whisper.

The boy looks puzzled, seeming confused by my lack of understanding. And then he inhales sharply and his eyes widen, as if he suddenly became aware of something disconcerting.

"We have to go right now," he says, speeding toward the open door. "Put your shield up and follow me.'"

Who is this boy? Is he really here to help me or is he actually here to hurt me?

I suppose either way I should put up my shield.

I take a shaky breath and say, "Shield up."

My face shield pops into place.

"Run!" the boy says. "This way!"

"Why?" I ask.

"No questions," he says. "Run!"

I don't have a good feeling about this, but I run anyway. If Nevah is the name of the woman who speaks to me here in The Room, maybe she sent this boy to help me escape. But if this is the right thing to do, why do I feel like I'm running toward my doom?

As soon as the boy and I are past the threshold of the open door, he slams his hand against a red button on the wall. The door behind me slides shut. Closing me off from The Room.

The two of us are now trapped in a room about the size of a bathroom. This small room begins to fill with white smoke that rains down on us from above.

"Where are you taking me?" I ask the boy.

"No questions," he says. "When the door opens, be ready to run."

Before I can ask another unwelcome question, the translucent door slides open, and the boy darts left into a barely-lit corridor.

"Come on!" he calls back to me in a hushed voice.

Against my better judgment, I run after him, still wondering what we are running from or to. The answer to the latter question turns out to be … the blind end of a corridor. Before I can ask where we go from here, the boy pulls open a small square door on the wall, just below our knees. Hot air pours out from the opening.

He turns to me. "Get in here."

"You go first," I say.

He glances at me. "Do you want me to help you or not?"

"It feels like an oven in there," I argue. "I'm not going to just—"

I'm interrupted by the sound of something large and loud and metallic behind me. The sound is distant, but it seems to be approaching fast.

"What's that sound?" I ask.

The boy's eyes dilate wide. "Go now!" he hisses.

Without waiting for me to respond, he shoves me toward the tiny opening in the wall and pushes me inside it. He crawls in after me and shuts the door behind us. Although there seems to be no light source in here, I can see that we are surrounded by the smooth black walls of a long narrow tunnel. Apparently the shield suit gives me the ability to see in total darkness.

"Don't you ever push me anywhere again!" I growl at the boy who is now pressed up next to me in this too-small space.

"Even if your life depends on it?" he asks.

"Does it?" I ask.

"I told you, no questions," he says.

"Why the hell not?" I ask.

He looks deep into my eyes, so deep it scares me more than anything else so far. "Just ... let me help you. Okay?"

It goes against every ounce of sense inside me, but I say, "Okay."

"Good," he says. "Start crawling."

I crawl forward a little and, when I glance back, I see that the boy is crawling after me—which I guess would be somewhat reassuring if it weren't for the fact that this tunnel is incredibly tiny, and the heat makes it feel like it's even tinier. I'm trying to keep my breathing slow and steady, but it's proving impossible. *I need to get out of here. Now!*

"It's too hot," I say, breathless.

"Tell your suit to cool you down," the boy says matter-of-factly.

"Tell it to cool me down?" I ask him. Just as the last word leaves my mouth, the shield suit floods with wonderful coolness. "Whoa! That's amazing!"

"Sorry, I forgot that you're not familiar with these suits," the boy says.

"I'm not familiar with *anything* here," I say.

"So what's your name, new kid?" he asks me.

I really don't want to talk right now. Even with the soothing coolness that's now bathing my body, I need all of my mental energy to keep at bay that horrible feeling that I am going to die in this stupid tunnel. But if I want this boy to help me, I'm going to have to be civil to him. Besides, I guess he needs to have something to call me.

I've already decided that I hate the "name" Unpleasant. I definitely don't want this boy to call me that. But I hate my real name too. I don't want anyone here to know it. Maybe I can choose another name. I brace for pain—in case The Room still has control over me here—because the answer I am about to give is an outright lie.

"My name's Terra," I say.

No pain comes.

But even though no punishment has been inflicted on me for my lie, I wonder if using that name is a mistake. Terra is the name of the most popular girl in my school. A girl whose life is the complete opposite of mine. Perfect and stable. So unlike my life which, even back home, was completely out of my control. So many times, I've wished my life could be like Terra's.

146

"How are you doing, Terra?" the boy asks me.

"I'm fine," I say, even though that is a lie.

Apparently, lies are allowed here. It seems that I've left the torture of The Room behind. Even so, every second that goes by, I like this situation less and less. This little tunnel seems to go on forever. Every once in a while there are branches. I try to imagine that every branch leads to a wide-open exit. *We're heading out of here,* I tell myself. *It won't be much longer.*

After a while, the boy says, just as we arrive at a branch, "To the right, I think."

"You *think*!" I squeak.

I'd assumed that he knew exactly which way to go. I *need* him to know the right way to go.

"I'm not sure," he says.

I curse in my head and make the right turn. We crawl for what feels like half an hour, until we reach … a solid wall of stone.

"Sorry, this isn't the right way," the boy says.

"I can see that," I seethe. The overwhelming fear that I've somehow kept under control for however long we've been crawling around in here starts to get the best of me.

"We'll have to backtrack," the boy says calmly.

He maneuvers himself around and starts crawling back the way we came. I follow him, but I feel like I'm not moving forward at all. I feel as if I'm backing deeper and deeper into this tiny tunnel. A tunnel that has no exit. I'm breathing so fast that the darkness around me is getting darker. *I'm going to pass out.*

"I need more air," I whisper.

My mask instantly flushes with cool, fresh air but, even so, my fear continues to grow.

"You doing okay back there, Terra?" the boy asks.

"I'm good," I tell him.

"You seem upset," he says.

"Listen, whatever-your-name is …" I start.

I can't believe I don't know the name of the person who is leading me to my death.

"My name's Kev," he says.

"Listen, Kev," I start again. "I am seriously claustrophobic. I have nightmares like this. Actually, my nightmares aren't as bad as this, because they're not real, and I think that, on some level, we know our dreams aren't real. But my nightmares are still bad enough that I wake up wanting to crawl out of my own skin. Two nights ago, I got kidnapped, and I woke up locked in a bedroom that felt like a coffin. I nearly lost my mind in there. I'm pretty sure I would have if it didn't open up when it did."

"But you survived," he says.

"I'm still kidnapped," I counter.

"But you're alive," he says.

"For the moment," I grumble.

"Then keep crawling," he says.

I don't like Kev. I *really* don't like him. And I'm pretty sure he dislikes me too. But I keep crawling. The only other choice is to stop moving and stay here until I die, and I don't plan to die without putting up a fight.

Suddenly, something about the size of my thumb skitters past me. I startle, hitting my head on the roof of the tunnel. The shield suit cushions the blow a little, but it still hurts enough that tears spring to my eyes.

"I forgot to warn you about the cockroaches," Kev says. "Don't worry. They're harmless."

Just as I start to wonder how much more of this I can take, we make it back to the branch point, and Kev makes a turn into the main tunnel.

"It's probably the next right," he says, sounding more than a little uncertain.

If I were to say anything in response, I'm sure I'd regret it. So I keep my mouth shut and crawl to the next branch point and make a right.

After a while, up ahead of Kev, I see a wall. Another dead end.

So why is Kev still crawling forward?

And then I see something more. There is another branch to this tunnel, but this branch, unlike all the others I've seen here, goes up.

Kev reaches the end of our tunnel and stands up into the new one.

"I have to warn you, Terra, it's going to be a bit of a climb," Kev says.

"That's all right," I say. *Anything would be better than crawling.*

Kev steps onto the thin metal bars that stick out of the wall and, within moments, he climbs completely out of view. I crawl to the end of the tunnel and stand. It feels like it has been hours since I've last stood up. Blood rushes out of my head and shooting stars flitter across the dark tunnel wall. I grip onto a metal bar to steady myself, and I look up. Kev is already about thirty feet above me. I can't see where this tunnel ends, but it's probably best at this point to just focus on what's in front of me. And so I start to climb.

The metal bars that form the ladder are skinny, but the hands and feet of my shield suit have incredible grip. It would be hard to slip in this suit. However, as I climb, and the ground gets further and further away, my palms and soles tingle with fear, so much so that slipping feels like a real possibility. But escaping from our kidnappers is going to involve risk.

I wonder if Kev was kidnapped too. Maybe that's why he's helping me. Maybe he figured out how to escape and he wants to help others do the same. I wish I could get more information from him, but he has told me repeatedly that he doesn't want me to ask any questions.

I look up and notice that Kev is gone.

"Kev?" I whisper.

There is no answer.

A jolt of anxiety grips me. *Kev left me.*

Of course he did. I wasn't being very pleasant to him, especially if he was actually trying to help me. I chased Kev away, like I've done with practically everyone else in my life. Now, I've probably lost my only hope of escape. Without anyone to guide me, I'll be lucky if I can find my way back to the other kids.

"Hey," Kev says from just above me.

I nearly lose my grip on the ladder. I bite back the urge to scold him for startling me, and I climb up to meet him. He's standing just inside a tunnel that branches off at a right angle to this one.

Kev extends a hand to help me into the new tunnel, but I say, "I'm good."

"Have it your way," he says.

He steps back to give me some room to make the jump from the ladder into his tunnel, about three feet away. I take a breath and take a leap and land successfully but, when I see where I've landed, my heart nearly stops from terror. I am now perched precariously on a long narrow platform that's barely wide enough for one person. Aside from the platform, this tunnel has no floor. Whatever ground there is below it is too far away to see.

"Next time, will you please warn me if I'm jumping into a tunnel that doesn't have a *normal* floor?" I demand.

"Sure thing," Kev says.

I really dislike this boy.

Kev starts walking along the platform, and I follow him. My hands and feet sting with slippery fear. There is nothing to hold onto—except maybe Kev—and I've already rejected that possibility. At the end of the tunnel, Kev pushes a black button beside a tall door, and the door slides open. He peeks out and then exits through the doorway.

Cautiously, I look at what's outside the tunnel. It's an open space. A rooftop, I think. Opaque walls encircle the rooftop completely, blocking any view of our surroundings.

Strangely, the sky is dark. As if it's nighttime.

It isn't remotely possible that I've been gone from the other kids long enough that morning has become night, so I know for sure now that what we've been told inside our little prison isn't true. The kidnappers have manipulated our sense of day and night. Either we traveled far enough away from home that we're in a whole new time zone, or our days and nights inside the common room have been shortened or lengthened or reversed altogether.

"The sky's really clear tonight," Kev says.

I take a good look at the sky. There are so many stars there. More stars than I ever saw in the sky back home. More stars than I ever knew existed.

"I wonder if that's the Milky Way," I breathe, staring in awe at a band of ethereal light directly above us.

"It is," Kev says quietly. "It's incredible, isn't it?"

Maybe he's finally ready for my questions.

"Where in the world are we?" I ask.

Kev shakes his head. "I can't answer any questions."

"Why not?" I ask, frustrated.

"I just … can't." He exhales. "It would be easier if you don't ask them."

"So you just want me to follow you blindly, and answer your questions, and not ask any of my own?" I ask, and then I add, "I know that I just asked you another question, but that one was rhetorical."

"Then you already know my answer," he says.

"Unfortunately, I do."

After that, the two of us just stand in silence, staring up at the stars. I'm not sure what to say. All I can think of are questions, and Kev can't … or won't … answer them.

Suddenly, a horrible siren blasts through the air.

I don't bother asking Kev what it means, and I suppose I don't need to, because he murmurs an expletive, and then he says, "Follow me!"

He races straight across the rooftop and yanks a lever that opens a door. Once we're both through the doorway, Kev uses another lever to shut the door behind us. We run at least thirty flights down a wide staircase and enter an indoor courtyard. It's dark like night here, but there is a small amount of light emanating from lamps near the ceiling.

"Stay in the shadows," Kev whispers.

If I didn't know better—and I guess I don't—I would say that he thinks we're being hunted.

We dart in and out of shadows cast by protrusions high above us, until Kev points to an unremarkable grey hatch on the ground.

"In there," he says. "Go! Quick!"

I open the hatch and start to climb down the ladder below it. When I look up, I see that Kev hasn't climbed in after me. Instead, he's looking down at me from above.

He gazes into my eyes. "It's essential that you don't tell anyone about me or *anything* here."

"Okay," I say. Because *why not* is a question.

He smiles. "You'll be safe now," he says.

Safe? Have I escaped the confines of this prison? But what is outside it? Is someone waiting there to rescue me? And what about the other kids? Is Kev going to help them escape too?

"Wait!" I call up to him.

Kev reaches to the leg of his shield suit and pulls out … *a gun.* My heart leaps into my throat. With one hand, Kev aims his gun toward something or someone I can't see and, with the other hand, he shuts the hatch.

I am now locked inside a closet-sized room with no apparent safe exit. The room floods with thick smoke. This could be an airlock. But, if so, where's the other exit? Is there another exit?

As if to answer my unasked questions, a ring of golden light illuminates a hatch below me. I pull the lever to open it and look down at what is below.

And my heart plummets into my stomach.

THURSDAY, MAY THIRD
0946

TIGER

"Unpleasant should be coming out soon," Harley says to Liam.

"Right," Liam says, without looking up from his game of solitaire.

"We should probably break our three-way tie, so we know who's going in The Room next," Lizard says.

Liam looks at her. "Fine."

Harley shuffles his deck of cards, and he, Lizard, and Liam draw.

Three. Four. Ace.

Liam won, Lizard will be third, and Harley will be fourth to go in the star room today.

"That sucks," Harley says.

"You want to switch places?" Liam offers.

"I thought you wanted to go first," Harley says, sounding suspicious.

"I did," Liam says, "but that ship has sailed, so you can go next."

"All right," Harley says. "We'll switch."

I think Liam wanted to switch even more than Harley did. I don't think Liam wants to go into the star room right after Unpleasant, because he wants to be here for her.

Back home, I never saw Liam spend one-on-one time with a girl. He never went on a date, even though I'm sure tons of girls would want to go on a date with him. He didn't hang out with girls at all. It seemed like he actively avoided them.

But here … Liam is different.

THURSDAY, MAY THIRD
0951

UNPLEASANT

Every rung of the ladder brings me closer and closer to The Room. The black bed is just below me, bathed in red light. Waiting for me.

And so Kev didn't rescue me. He took me away, nearly got me killed, and then he brought me back to exactly where I was before. What was the point of all that? Maybe Kev was planning to rescue me, but his mission was cut short by some kind of emergency.

I jump from the bottom of the ladder and land on the floor. And I wait.

And wait.

"Lie down," the woman says.

I shiver, even though I'm not the least bit cold. Hearing the woman's voice is both reassuring and terrifying. If she is Nevah, and she arranged for Kev to come for me, maybe she will explain what went wrong and what the plan will be going forward. But if my excursion with Kev was discovered by those who did not authorize it, then I will most certainly be tortured now for my misbehavior.

I lie down on the bed, take a deep breath, close my eyes, and await my fate.

The bed takes hold of me, and something forcefully, but gently, impacts me.

And then the bed releases my naked body.

I open my eyes and see the locker presenting my clothes to me.

"Please get dressed," the woman says.

I don't ask any questions, because I have no way of knowing who might overhear what I say. I dress in my sweatclothes and then stand facing the common room door, waiting for it to open.

"Will you come back tomorrow?" the woman asks.

"Why do you want me to come back?" I test her.

"Because I want to help you," she says quietly.

"Why didn't that happen today?" I ask, choosing my words carefully in case someone else is listening.

"These things take time," she says very gently.

For the first time, she reminds me of someone. *My mom.*

The thought of my mom forces a painful lump into my throat. I swallow hard, trying to make it go away, but it persists, and the pain makes tears pool in my eyes.

I used to think that I would be better off without my mom in my life. But I'm *not* better off without her. Even though she is far from a perfect mother, I want her in my life. I wish I'd told her that. Instead, I told her to go away. And now she has.

Tears fall down my cheeks. I wipe them away furiously, but new tears quickly take their place. I shake my head in frustration.

"Will you come back tomorrow?" the woman asks me again.

"Yes," I say to the woman.

And the common room door slides open.

THURSDAY, MAY THIRD
1001

TIGER

From the looks of it, the star room hurt Unpleasant even worse than it did yesterday. Her face is scrunched up with pain and her reddened eyes are soaked with tears. Harley goes right past Unpleasant to take his turn in the star room, and the door slides shut behind him.

Back when we were friends, Rain told me that she thinks Harley is really brave. I nodded my head in response, but I actually don't know whether Harley is brave or not.

Andrew used to say, "You're only being brave if you're doing something you're afraid to do." Before he left for his last deployment, I asked him if he was afraid to go back to the war. He told me that fighting in the war was the scariest thing he'd ever done in his entire life.

But he went anyway.

I watch Liam lead Unpleasant to a chair by one of the "windows." After they sit down, Liam looks at her and exhales. And then he says very softly, so soft that I can barely hear it, "I get to be the strong one now."

Unpleasant is brave. And so is Liam.

I'm not sure if Harley is brave or fearless.

I will never be fearless.

I wonder if I'll ever be strong enough to be brave.

GOAT

Lizard has been pacing back and forth for a while. I guess she's getting antsy because she's next to go in the starry room.

All of a sudden, the starry room door slides open. Harley is sitting cross-legged on the floor, just inside the doorway, staring straight ahead with a look on his face that's like something out of one of the horror movies that my mom won't let me watch but my dad lets me watch anyway. Harley looks like he just saw his best friend get chopped into bloody bits.

Liam walks over to him and stops just outside the starry room doorway. Even though Liam is standing right in front of him, Harley doesn't look up.

Liam sits down on the floor, and then he says to Harley, "It's over now."

Harley shakes his head.

"You need to walk away from it," Liam says.

Harley shakes his head again.

I'm sure there is a look of shock on my face. I thought Harley was a rock. I was sure he couldn't be broken. But it looks like he almost was. I wonder what the lady did to him. Or maybe it was the men this time.

Lizard goes over to Harley and Liam.

"Harley, you need to get out of there," she says.

He doesn't look at her. "Why?"

"I need to go in," she answers.

He finally looks at her. "You're going in?"

"Yes," she says. "And I need you to get out of the way."

Harley shakes his head again and, with a lot of effort, he crawls out of the starry room.

And then Lizard walks right into the stars.

UNPLEASANT

When Lizard is released from The Room, she looks almost as disturbed as Harley did when he emerged. As soon as she is clear of the doorway, The Room closes. A few minutes later, the lunch bell rings. After we have eaten a silent meal, The Room reopens.

"I'll see you soon," Liam whispers to me.

My heart sinks. I was hoping Liam had changed his mind about going in The Room today. But the woman in The Room probably promised Liam the same thing she promised me. I assume she offered that same incentive to everyone. That would explain why everyone is so willing to go back in there.

So far today, everyone who has gone into The Room has returned. No one has escaped our prison. But if anyone can succeed on the first try, it's Liam. That is my greatest hope right now ... and my greatest fear. If Liam succeeds, I might never see him again. I might never know whether he is alive or dead.

"Be careful," I say to Liam.

"I'll be okay," he says.

Everything inside me tenses with worry anyway.

Once Liam is gone, I go grab my towel from under my mattress, and then I head to the showers to get washed up. I need to do something to pass the time while Liam is in The Room ... other than worry about him.

When I get to the shower room, I push the button to open the door and—

A girl screams. *Lizard.*

"What the hell?" she yells at me from inside one of the showers.

"I didn't know anyone was in here," I say.

Lizard curses at me, reaches out of the shower, and slams the button to shut the door.

I should have closed the door myself. I didn't because I was in shock.

I wasn't shocked by seeing Lizard undressed. I've seen plenty of girls undressed in the showers at school and, although I wouldn't dare to let anyone see *my* ugly body naked, it doesn't bother me to see other people undressed.

I was in shock from seeing what was *on* Lizard's body.

There were bruises … all over her back and legs and arms and butt. She was beaten up mercilessly. But by who?

Did the men beat her that first night? That would explain why she was afraid to go in The Room yesterday. She didn't want to risk facing them again. But I don't have any bruises from the night we were kidnapped. I didn't think any of the kids did. But no one has talked about exactly what happened to them that night. Maybe, like Lizard, they've been hiding their injuries. Maybe they assume that we all have them.

Based on Lizard's willingness to go in The Room today, I don't think she was beaten up in there yesterday. But was she beaten in The Room *today*? When she came out, she was obviously traumatized. She sat alone and picked at her food at lunchtime, and then she quietly slipped off to take a shower. I don't think Kev would beat anyone up, but maybe Lizard and Kev encountered whoever it was that he seemed to want to protect me from. Maybe that's who hurt Lizard.

Or maybe Lizard tried to make Rain pay for forcing her into The Room that first time. Maybe the two of them fought last night after Liam and I went up to my bedroom together.

Whatever the cause, I need to find out how Lizard got her bruises. Based on what I saw, whoever beat up Lizard is seriously deranged. The next time they act, their actions could be even worse. They could be deadly.

THURSDAY, MAY THIRD
1241

TIGER

Rain is looking at me, but she isn't saying anything. That makes me nervous because I can't tell what she's thinking, and I don't trust what she's thinking.

This morning, after my bed compartment opened, I waited for Rain to leave our bedroom. But instead of leaving, she *arrived*. She fumbled around under her mattress for a while, and then she left again.

When I thought about it, I remembered that, last night, after I was in bed, Rain opened our hatch. A minute later, she closed it. After that, I thought I heard her plop down onto her bed, but I guess I was wrong.

Last night, Rain left our room, and she didn't come back until morning.

But I have no idea why.

THURSDAY, MAY THIRD
1247

UNPLEASANT

When Lizard exits the shower room, I am waiting for her.

"Can we talk?" I ask.

Lizard walks into the laundry room. I follow her, even though I'm not sure she wants me to.

"What do you want?" Lizard asks me brusquely.

"I saw your bruises," I say. "Who did that to you?"

"If I needed your help, I'd ask for it." She starts out of the room.

"Please ..." I start.

Lizard stops walking, but she doesn't turn back toward me.

"Please tell me what happened," I say.

"Why do you care?" she asks.

"Whoever did that is dangerous," I say. "The next time they act, it could be worse."

She spins around to face me. "How do *you* know?"

"I don't," I say. But that's not the truth. I *do* know. I know that, even when you think it's as bad as it can possibly get, it still gets worse.

"Mind your own business," Lizard says.

"This is my business," I say. "We're on the same team."

She stares into my eyes, like a wild animal ready to attack. "If you want to be a team player, the next time you're going to barge into anyplace with a closed door, you'd better knock first."

I feel the hair on the back of my neck stand on end. "Was that a threat?"

"It was a polite request." Lizard spins back around and walks out of the room.

I exhale, defeated.

Back home, there were people who hurt me. No one ever really tried to stop them. I told myself that no one cared, but I don't think that's true. I don't think anyone knew how badly I needed help. Over the years, I built a wall around me that was too thick for anyone to get through. I quietly dealt with my suffering in the same unhealthy way that my mom deals with hers. I hid my pain so well that no one ever saw it.

I have a feeling that Lizard's wall is just as thick as mine. Walls like that can't be broken through by force. Lizard knows now that I'm aware that she's suffering. She knows that I want to help. Maybe, eventually, she'll open up her wall enough to let me in.

Until then, I need to figure out how to protect her and the others.

I guess the first step is to find out if anyone else is being hurt.

The problem is, the hardest time to admit you need help is when you need it the most.

THURSDAY, MAY THIRD
1335

GOAT

I stare at the open door of the starry room. Liam just came out of there, and it's my turn to go in. Just like everyone else so far, the starry room seems to have upset Liam much more today than yesterday. I try not to think about what could happen to me in there. I just say goodbye to Paris and walk into the stars, trying to be brave.

The stars disappear, and the door closes, and I wait in the dark.

My heart beats hard.

I won't let anyone break me ... I won't let anyone break me ...

"Remove your clothes," Monster Lady says.

I don't want to do what she says but, yesterday, she told me she can help me, and I think she might be the only one here who can. So I do what she asks.

Once I'm not wearing anything, Monster Lady tells me to lie down on a big black cushion that has a red light shining on it. It looks like the open mouth of a demon, but I push that thought away and lie down. The cushion grabs on tight to me, and then a large black block comes down from the ceiling and presses itself onto me. It leaves me dressed in a shield suit, like last time, except this suit is black instead of white.

"Sit up," Monster Lady says.

I sit and look around the room, but it's too dark to see

anything.

"Stand," Monster Lady says.

I stand and the lights in the room flicker, on and then off again. And then a big thick door slides open. Someone is standing in the doorway. Someone small, like me, wearing a black shield suit, like mine.

"My name's Nym," the someone says. "What's yours?"

I'm not sure if I should say my real name or my here name.

I decide to say, "Goat."

"Come with me, Goat," Nym says.

I'm not sure whether to go with her or not.

"Where are we going?" I ask, without going anywhere.

"The Plant," she says.

"Is it dangerous?" I ask.

"There was some trouble there last night, but things are better now," she says, and then she whispers, "Come on, Goat. I'm going to help you."

I still feel unsure, but I go to her. Once I'm through the doorway, Nym presses a button and the big door closes behind me. Cold white smoke falls out of the ceiling, making it impossible to see anything, even Nym.

"Why is there smoke here?" I ask.

"It's the Decon," Nym says. "It prevents contamination from The Plant from entering your living quarters and vice versa."

"Where we live is *contaminated*?" I ask her.

"Only a little. The Plant is much more contaminated. That's why we have to wear shield suits there," she says. "Unless we're in a Safe Room, like my treehouse."

"You have a treehouse?" I feel myself smile, but then sadness breaks my smile. I miss my treehouse back home.

Nym tilts her head. "I can take you to my treehouse if you

want."

"Okay," I say, but I don't think Nym hears me over the sound of the door ahead of us opening up.

Nym starts walking down the dark hallway and starts talking fast, "The most important thing about being in The Plant is you need to act like you belong here. Don't let anyone know that you're different. Don't let anyone notice you. Walk with your head high and your shoulders back, like you know exactly where you're going, even when you don't. Keep your face brave, even when you don't feel brave. Don't ever show any fear."

Her instructions sound impossible to follow.

"Why do I need to do all that?" I ask.

Nym steps up to a tall black door and pushes a button.

"So the Predators don't hurt you," she says.

I'm starting to think that maybe it wasn't a good idea to go with Nym, but it's too late to change my mind. I follow her into a wide hallway with white walls. We make a right turn and then a left one and then …

It feels like the whole world has expanded. We are now inside a gigantic room with a sparkling glass ceiling very high above us. Through the ceiling, I see a slightly-cloudy sky. The room is filled with people who are dressed the same way we are. There are grown-ups and kids, and even little babies. The people go this way and that way. None of them seems interested in us, and I am careful not to bring attention to myself.

Nym walks me past waterfalls made of glittery stones that look like diamonds, and blue-green glass sculptures that remind me of ocean waves, and walls decorated with colorful silvery metal seashells. We walk across bridges and we ride escalators that carry us so smoothly that I almost feel like I'm flying. I try not to react to what I'm seeing and feeling because no one else is reacting. Everyone here seems completely unimpressed by the magnificence all around them.

Suddenly, Nym says in an anxious whisper, "Predators!"

In the direction Nym is looking, I see three large men coming our way holding silver guns. The men are wearing shield suits like ours, but otherwise they look very much like the men who stole me from my house.

"Hide!" Nym says to me.

I follow her to a row of hollow benches that no one is sitting on. Nym and I are both small enough to fit inside. She crawls in first and I crawl in after her.

"Cover your eyes," she says.

I do as Nym tells me.

Once my eyes are covered, I try to imagine that I'm closed up inside my cardboard box in the basement of my family's house, where no one comes looking for me.

And then I hear screams.

Suddenly, I am plunged into a different memory: the memory of the night I was kidnapped. I remember hearing kids around me screaming in fear. I couldn't see why the other kids were screaming, because my eyes were blindfolded. I thought about taking off my blindfold, but I was too scared to try. I was scared of what the men would do to me if I misbehaved, but I was also scared of what I might see. Maybe it would have been better if I'd seen what was happening. Sometimes, what you imagine is worse than what is real.

Now, my eyes are not blindfolded. My own hands are covering them. I'm free to see what is happening, if I want to. The only thing stopping me are Nym's instructions.

Cautiously, I uncover my eyes. The Predators are close. They're searching the faces of panicked people. There is a terrible tension, as if something horrible is about to happen. And then, it does. A Predator grabs a girl who looks a little younger than me and points a gun at her head. The girl goes limp. The Predator tosses her over his shoulder and heads back the way he came. The other Predators go with him.

I'm not sure what I just saw. Why did the Predator choose that girl? Where is he taking her? What will he do with her when he gets there? Was his gun a stunner gun, like the police use back home? Or was it a killer gun, like bad guys use?

I can't ask Nym any of that. She would be angry with me for not following her instructions. And so I cover my eyes again and wait for her to tell me that it's safe to leave our hiding spot.

It seems like forever before she does.

THURSDAY, MAY THIRD
1359

UNPLEASANT

I ask Liam to meet me at the shower room. His expression tells me that he thinks my request is odd, but he nods anyway. I go down the hallway and wait outside the shower room. A few minutes later, Liam meets me there. I open the door and urge him inside.

"What's going on?" he asks as I close the door behind him.

"While you were in The Room, I went to take a shower," I say. "When I opened the door, Lizard was already in here. I saw bruises all over her body. Someone beat her up real bad ... someone without a soul."

"Did she tell you what happened?" Liam asks me.

"No," I say. "I don't think she trusts me enough to tell me anything. I was planning to talk with the other kids, one at a time, to see if they've been hurt too."

He nods. "Tell me what you find out."

I'm about to open the door when Liam takes hold of my arm, stopping me.

"Have you told anyone else about Lizard?" he asks.

"No," I say. "I think it's probably better not to worry the other kids about this ... until we know what we're dealing with."

He thinks for a moment, and then he says, "You're probably right."

I let Liam out of the shower room and take a few minutes to

mentally prepare myself for what I'm about to do. Then I go back to the common room and choose the first kid to question.

I decide to start with the youngest.

THURSDAY, MAY THIRD
1408

TIGER

Liam is sitting alone. I go over and sit down in the chair next to him.

"What's going on, Tiger?" he asks in a quiet voice.

"Will you be disappointed if I don't go back in the star room?" I ask.

"I told you yesterday—" he starts.

"I know you love me whether I go in or not," I say. "But do you *want* me to go back in there?"

"No," he says.

"Why not?" I ask.

"You're my little sister," he says. "I don't want you to get hurt."

"So I shouldn't go in then?" I ask.

He shakes his head. "You need to make your own decision."

"I made my own decision yesterday, and I failed," I say.

"What are you talking about?" he asks.

"The voice told me to take off my clothes," I say. "And I didn't."

Liam turns abruptly toward me, looking concerned. "What happened then?" he asks.

"The voice shouted and shouted until I guess I passed out." I decide not to tell Liam that I woke up naked on a table. I don't want to upset him too much. "I failed, Liam."

"You don't fail unless you don't try," he says.

"Andrew tried ... and he died," I say.

"Our brother died a hero," Liam says. His voice almost breaks apart as he says that. I look at him and I see that there are tears in his eyes, but they don't leave his eyes. Liam takes a deep breath and continues, "If something is worth fighting for, you can't give up just because you're afraid of what might happen if you fight."

I stare at the floor, trying to process our conversation. As I go over and over it, Liam's message becomes clear. I think I missed it the first time, because I didn't want to hear it. I still don't want to hear it, but Liam is the only person I trust here to give me advice. And he just gave me the most disturbing advice anyone has ever given me: If you decide to fight, you need to be prepared to die.

THURSDAY, MAY THIRD
1416

UNPLEASANT

"Go fish," Paris says to me.

I choose a card from the small pile on her bed and add it to the cards in my hand.

Paris looks up from her cards and presses her lips together. "You didn't ask me to come down here just to play Go Fish, did you?"

I guess I might as well get to the point of our visit.

"There *is* something I wanted to talk with you about," I say.

"Go ahead," she says, sounding wary.

"Sometimes people ... hurt other people ..." I start.

Paris' expression turns serious, and a little scared.

I force myself to keep talking, "Paris, has anyone hurt you?"

She looks down at her cards, even though I have a feeling that our game is over.

I continue, "Did anyone hurt you on the night we were kidnapped, or in The Room, or anywhere at all?"

"I can't talk about what happens in the starry room," Paris says.

I try to gather strength to ask what I need to ask next. "Do you have any cuts or scrapes ... or bruises?"

"I don't think so," she says.

"How about on your back?" I ask.

"Do you want to look?" she asks.

I nod, even though I don't think I can handle seeing the kinds of bruises that I saw on Lizard on someone so little. I lift the back of her sweatshirt and her t-shirt, exposing her skin, and then I exhale and adjust her clothing back into position.

"There aren't any marks there," I tell her.

Paris turns to face me. "Do you think the lady's going to hurt me worse today?" she asks, her frightened eyes searching mine.

"I don't know," I say, because Paris deserves an honest answer. "But I didn't get hurt today as bad as yesterday."

"Then why were you crying?" she asks.

Her words bring on instant embarrassment. I guess somehow I convinced myself that my crying was just in my mind. But it wasn't. Paris saw it. All the other kids did too, I guess.

"I was crying because I want to go home," I tell her.

"I want to go home too," she says.

Tears come to Paris' eyes. She places her cards on the bed and climbs into my arms, as if she's much younger than nine years old. I think I know how she feels. I wish I could crawl into my mom's arms right now and have her hold me. But my mom isn't here, and neither is Paris'.

And so I put my arms around Paris and hold her while she cries.

THURSDAY, MAY THIRD
1421

GOAT

Nym hasn't said anything since we left our hiding spot inside the hollow bench. Not that I really expected her to. There are lots of people around us, and Nym told me at the very beginning that we needed to try not to call attention to ourselves. Talking would certainly cause other people to notice us, because no one else is talking. Not at all. Even the babies are quiet.

We've ridden escalator after escalator, and now we're nearly at the top of the gigantic room, thirty levels high, very close to the glass ceiling. When we get to the end of the final escalator, Nym darts into a silvery passageway and starts up a tall set of silver stairs. Our reflections in the walls and stairs chase us to the top where there is a very small door that looks like it's meant for someone only half as tall as we are. Nym opens the door, and we squeeze into a silver room that is only large enough to sit in. She closes the door behind us, and the room fills up with Decon smoke.

After the smoke goes away, Nym opens another door, and my mouth drops open. We crawl into a slightly-bigger room that sticks out over the gigantic room. The walls, ceiling, and floor are made of glass so, when I look down, I can see all the way to the ground. My first look makes me so dizzy that I don't dare to look down again.

"Welcome to my treehouse!" Nym says.

I look through each of the four glass walls of the room, searching for any sign of a tree, but I don't see one. In fact, I haven't seen any trees or plants or flowers or anything living here in The Plant, except for people. Maybe they don't have trees here. Maybe Nym doesn't know what a tree is. But then, why would she call this a treehouse? Was Nym stolen from her family too? Does she know about trees from back home?

Suddenly, through one of the walls, I spot a group of people riding up the highest escalator. I stay very still, so I don't catch their attention.

"Are we allowed to be in here?" I ask Nym.

"No," she says. "If anyone found out, I'd get in big trouble."

"Don't people see you through the glass?" I ask.

"It's one-way glass," Nym says. "The other side looks like a mirror so, from the outside, the only thing people see is themselves." She looks into my eyes. "No one can see us or hear us, so the treehouse is a good place for secrets."

"Secrets like what?" I ask, feeling uneasy.

"Secrets like you have."

THURSDAY, MAY THIRD
1429

UNPLEASANT

Rain sits beside me on her bed, staring at the wall, her shoulders tense.

"Are you still mad at me because of what I did yesterday?" she asks me.

"I'm not mad at you," I say. "I think what you did was wrong, but being mad gets everyone nowhere."

Rain drops her gaze to the floor. "So you're going to lecture me."

"No." I inhale, trying to collect my scattered thoughts, and then I start speaking, even though I'm not certain how to get where I'm trying to go, "Sometimes people hurt other people …"

Rain looks at me. "I thought you weren't going to lecture me."

What I just said *did* sound like the beginning of a lecture. I'm starting to realize that I'm not very good at getting people to talk with me about their problems.

"I didn't mean it like that," I say, feeling flustered. "I'm just trying to find out … if someone hurt you."

Rain's eyes narrow. "The answer to your question is no."

She jumps off the bed and starts up the ladder. I don't try to prevent her from leaving. If she doesn't want to talk to me, that is her choice.

When Rain gets to the top of the ladder, she stops. "I don't kick things off walls and push people into rooms because somebody hurt me. No one ever hurt me. Nobody caused me to be this way. There is nothing that can explain my behavior. This is just the messed-up way that I am." In a very subtle move, she wipes her eyes, and then she opens the hatch and disappears into the common room.

"You're not messed up," I say, but it's too late for her to hear me.

THURSDAY, MAY THIRD
1433

GOAT

After Nym said that I have secrets, she stopped talking. Since then, we've just been sitting here quietly in her treehouse, looking at the view. Maybe she's waiting for me to tell her a secret, but I only have one secret that has anything to do with her: that I peeked at the Predators while we were hiding, even though she told me not to. It's probably best that I keep that secret from her for now.

Suddenly, Nym says, "It's time to go back."

"But I thought you were going to help me," I say.

She leans against one of the glass walls. "First, I need to make sure I can trust you."

"How are you going to do that?" I ask.

"I don't know yet." Nym looks just as disappointed with her answer as it makes me feel.

"Can you help me get home?" I ask. It's the most important question I've asked her so far.

"Yes," Nym says.

Hope builds up inside me. More hope than I ever thought I could feel.

"Will you come again tomorrow?" Nym asks.

"Yes," I say. "I will."

"Good," Nym says.

We leave Nym's treehouse and ride a glass-walled elevator all the way down to the bottom of the gigantic room. Then we go down a white hallway, and through a black hallway, and into a black room that is just as tall as the gigantic room, but much skinnier, with walls that go all the way up to a dark ceiling that doesn't let us see the sky.

Nym opens a hatch on the floor, and she says, "Everything we said and did and saw today … *everything* … needs to be our secret."

"I'm good at keeping secrets," I say.

She points down at the open hatch. "After you go through Decon, the hatch on the floor will unlock, and you'll be back where I found you."

Nym shuts me inside the little Decon room. After the smoke comes and goes, I open the hatch on the floor and see the starry room, right below me. I climb down a ladder, and then I lie on the big black cushion and wait for my shield suit to be removed, so I can go back to the other kids.

I wish I could tell them everything Nym told me, but I need to keep her secrets. Maybe keeping her secrets is how I can earn her trust. And I need to earn her trust.

It might be the only way I can go home.

THURSDAY, MAY THIRD
1935

TIGER

Everyone went in the star room today. Except for me.

Nobody asks if I am going to go in. They all pretend to be occupied with their games or quiet conversations, but I can feel them looking at me out of the corners of their eyes.

Finally, Liam gets up from his seat.

"I'm going back in The Room," he says, and then he adds, in Harley's general direction, "Unless anyone has any objections."

Nobody says anything in response, so Liam walks toward the star room. He steps inside … And the stars turn red.

"Everybody has to have a turn before anyone can go back," Rain says under her breath, but loud enough that I think everyone heard her.

"It could be that we're only allowed in once per day," I say.

"Tiger might be right," Paris agrees.

"But if she's not, and Tiger doesn't go in there, then none of us get to go back. Ever," Rain says. "That's not fair."

"*This situation* isn't fair," Liam says, giving Rain a hard stare. "And it's never going to be."

"We can make *this decision* fair," I say.

"How?" Lizard asks.

"We can take a vote on whether or not I go in the star room," I offer. "If the majority of people vote that I go in, I'll go in there right now. If the majority votes that I don't, then no one gets to say or do anything to try to get me to go in there ever again."

"Tiger, stop," Liam says, but I don't let him stop me.

"Raise your hand if you think I shouldn't go in the star room tonight," I say to the group.

Liam raises his hand ... And Unpleasant raises hers.

Two out of seven.

Then Paris raises her hand. "It isn't right to make anyone go in there."

Three out of seven.

"Everyone should get to make their own choice," Goat says, and he raises his hand.

Four out of seven.

Lizard raises her hand. "People should decide for themselves."

Five out of seven.

Slowly, Harley raises his hand. "I respect Tiger's wishes."

Six out of seven.

Everyone looks at Rain. Maybe they're expecting her to raise her hand too.

She doesn't though.

I look directly at her. "Who thinks I *should* go in?"

"It doesn't matter," Rain says. "It's already decided."

And then she goes down to our bedroom.

After a minute, everyone else returns to their games and quiet conversations. I keep my eyes fixed on the door to the star room, as if I'm waiting for it to cast its vote. The door stays open for a while. And then, finally, it closes. A while later, the bell sounds.

DING. DING. DING. DING. DING. DING.

It's bedtime.

THURSDAY, MAY THIRD
2118

UNPLEASANT

Liam is lying in his makeshift bed on the floor of my bedroom, staring up at the ceiling. I'm in my coffin, but I folded my shower towel and placed it across the coffin threshold, so the wall can't close tonight.

Liam has been very quiet all day, even before his visit to The Room. Aside from our brief conversation in the shower room, we haven't talked today about anything of any real importance. I thought maybe it was because he was reluctant to talk about important things in the common room, where others could overhear, but he's still quiet now, even though the two of us are alone.

Finally he asks me, "Did you find out anything when you talked to the other kids?"

"Everyone denied being injured, but I think a few of them were holding something back." And then I ask, "Do *you* have any injuries like Lizard's?"

His gaze meets mine, unafraid.

"No," he says, and then he asks, "Do *you*?"

"No," I say, my gaze falling from his. I don't tell him that I've had injuries like Lizard's in the past. That I know what it feels like to be hurt like that.

"If you ever want to talk … about anything …" Liam says.

"Thanks," I say. And then I close my eyes.

Strangely, I feel like it might be okay to talk to Liam about things that I've never been brave enough to tell anyone else. Of course, right now, it's too soon to tell him my secrets. But maybe … someday.

THURSDAY, MAY THIRD
2129

TIGER

I'm lying in my bed, pretending to be asleep, but I'm fully awake and aware. I have my eyes open a little, so I can try to see what Rain is up to.

In the faint light of our bedroom, I see her standing at her bedside, fumbling with the things under her mattress. She tucks something into the waistband of her sweatpants, but I can't tell what it is. And then she lightly walks to the ladder and goes back up into the common room.

I guess Rain won't be spending tonight in our bedroom.

I wish I knew what she will be doing instead.

THURSDAY, MAY THIRD
2137

GOAT

Paris didn't ask if she could sleep in my bed with me again tonight. I made room in it for her and, without talking about it, she climbed in. She closed her eyes right away, so I guess she doesn't want to talk tonight.

I don't think she's upset about what happened to her in the starry room today. When Paris came out of it, she looked ... okay. That's how everyone looked today, except for Harley, Lizard, and Unpleasant. I guess I probably looked that way too.

But nobody here is okay.

Even though Paris has been quiet for a while now, I'm fairly sure that she's still awake, because even though her eyes are closed, there are wet tears on her lashes.

I don't think people cry when they're asleep.

FRIDAY, MAY FOURTH
0819

TIGER

Ever since I came up to the common room this morning, and all through breakfast, the other kids have been watching me. I'm pretty sure every single one of them wants me to go into the star room today, even Liam.

When they voted yesterday for me not to go in, their reasons—if they gave a reason—were that I shouldn't have to go against my wishes. I think that means, if it weren't for my wishes, they would want me to go.

But maybe I won't have to decide whether or not to go in there. Maybe the star room won't open ever again. Maybe yesterday was our last chance to go in.

I have a feeling that's unlikely.

And then my feeling becomes a certainty. Because the star room door slides open.

"Who wants to try?" Lizard asks.

Liam stands. "I will."

No one voices any objections. I guess they're confident that it won't matter which one of them tries, because no one will be allowed to enter until I go back in.

Liam steps into the star room … And the stars glow red.

He returns to his seat, and everybody returns to what they were doing before the star room opened. They are keeping their side of the deal. No one is trying to convince me to go into that room. Except for me.

I can't help feeling that going into the star room could benefit us. The star room might bring us closer to our captors. The closer we are to our captors, the closer we are to escape. To going back home to our families. *That* is worth fighting for.

I take a deep breath and stand up. Some of the kids glance in my direction, but they quickly avert their eyes. *They're still keeping their side of the deal.*

My heart beats hard and fast from fear. But I start walking, and I don't stop until I'm standing among the stars. And then the stars disappear, and I am plunged into dizzying darkness.

Weirdly, nothing happens after that, except for the frantic pounding of my heart. The female voice doesn't speak to me. The air in the room remains cool and comfortable. There is nothing to see. Nothing to hear. My vision and hearing and all of my senses grow blurry.

I think I hear a hatch open above me. My heart pounds even harder. My eyes search for the hatch, but they see nothing. And then something heavy drops down onto the floor in front of me. I step back blindly, too disoriented to figure out what else to do. Unsure of how to escape.

A voice brings everything into focus.

It's not the voice that I heard last time. This is the voice of a boy.

"You're the last one, right?" he asks.

I squint my eyes, looking for him, but it's still too dark to distinguish anything at all.

Something is pushed into my hands.

"Put those on," the boy says.

It feels like I'm holding some kind of swim goggles but, when I put them on, the darkness lifts away, and everything in the room instantly comes into view. Standing directly in front of me is a boy who is just a little taller than I am. He's wearing a black flight suit and helmet. Behind him is a ladder that leads to a hatch on the ceiling. A few feet away from us is a big thick bed. I lift the goggles from my face, and everything disappears again into the darkness. Then I put them back into position.

"They're night-vision goggles," the boy explains. "My name's Pax. What's yours?"

"It's ... Tiger," I say, and then I ask, "Where'd you come from?"

He gestures to the ladder. "The Plant," he says. "I need to take you there for our mission."

"What mission?" I ask.

Pax squirms a little in his flight suit. "I'm not allowed to talk about it."

"Then how am I supposed to know if I want to go on your mission?" I ask.

"It's not *my* mission. It's *our* mission." Pax leans closer to me. "I'm going to help you," he says in a soft voice.

"How are you going to do that?" I ask.

"I can't say," he says. "You'll just have to trust me."

Something about Pax makes me want to trust him, but it's not smart to trust a stranger. Especially here.

"I wish we could get to know each other first," I say.

Pax shrugs and plops down on the bed. "As you wish."

FRIDAY, MAY FOURTH
0840

UNPLEASANT

Liam rubs his forehead with his hand. "We forced Tiger to go in there."

"No one forced her," I try to reassure him.

"She knew we all wanted her to go," he says. "She knew *I* wanted her to go."

"Did you tell her that?" I ask.

"Actually, I told her I *didn't* want her to go," he says, "but actions speak louder than words."

"I'm sure Kev will take care of her," I say.

Liam's eyes search mine. "Who's Kev?"

"The boy we met in The Room yesterday," I say.

"What boy?" he asks.

I assumed that all of us met Kev. But apparently Liam didn't.

"I guess I shouldn't have said that," I say. I didn't think there was any reason to withhold it. All I said was a name. A name that I figured Liam already knew.

But if Liam didn't meet Kev, then did he meet someone else?

And why does that question unnerve me so much?

TIGER

Pax asks lots of questions about me, but he doesn't tell me very much about him. Still, I enjoy talking with him. Sitting with him on the big bed, I feel like I'm hanging out with a friend. The longer Pax and I talk, the more I want to go on his mission. *Our* mission. I am about to tell him that when he suddenly jumps to his feet.

"It's late," he says. "I have to get back."

My stomach twists. "I wish you didn't have to leave."

"We can meet here again tomorrow," he says.

"Even if I'm not ready to go on the mission?" I ask.

"Yes," he says with a self-conscious smile.

"I'll see you tomorrow then," I say.

Pax looks into my eyes. "It's really important that you don't tell anyone about me."

"I won't," I promise him.

Pax smiles the warmest smile I've ever seen, and then he says, "I need my goggles back."

"Right." I slip off the goggles, and the room gets dark again.

"See you tomorrow, Tiger," Pax says softly as he takes the goggles from me.

I smile, just in case he's still looking at me. "See you tomorrow, Pax."

A few seconds later, I hear the hatch above me open and

then close. And then I sit down on the edge of the big thick bed, wishing Pax was still here.

FRIDAY, MAY FOURTH
0915

UNPLEASANT

Tiger steps out of The Room, and Liam and I meet her just outside the doorway. I expect him to give her a hug, but neither of them makes any attempt to initiate physical contact. Then I remember that Liam and his sister don't hug.

"I'm going in," I say to Liam.

A little while ago, everyone drew cards to determine the order that we will enter The Room today. I got "lucky" again and picked the highest card. Like yesterday, Liam asked if I wanted to switch places with him but I refused.

As I step into The Room, the stars blink away and the darkness takes me. I go through the unpleasant process of getting into my shield suit and, when it is done, I stand and wait for Kev. But will Kev come today or will it be someone else? Maybe no one will come at all.

Suddenly, the hatch in the ceiling opens, and Kev's face pops into view.

"Come on," he says, waving me toward him.

I take a deep breath. "Shield up," I say, and my face shield slides into place.

I climb up into the airlock, and Kev shuts the hatch behind me.

As soon as the smoke clears, Kev presses something into my right hand. *A gun.*

I don't like guns. Guns have the power to control someone

instantly. Some of them even have the power to kill. I don't want to hold that kind of power.

Very carefully, I pass the gun back to Kev. "I don't want this," I say.

"I didn't ask if you wanted it." He slides the gun into a pocket in my shield suit near my hip. "Just don't shoot me in the back, all right?"

"I'm not going to shoot you," I say. "I'm not going to shoot *anyone*."

Kev shakes his head. "I won't blame you if you change your mind."

He opens the hatch above us, and I follow him into the dark courtyard.

"This way," he says.

For a while, we reverse our path from last time, but then Kev opens a door that leads to an empty corridor that we haven't been in before. The black walls, floor, and ceiling here are padded. I feel myself bouncing with each step, enjoying it a little, until we turn a corner and I see dozens of motionless humanoid robots with bullseyes painted on their chests and faces.

"Time for target practice," Kev says to me.

"This isn't necessary," I argue.

"Have you ever fired a gun?" he asks me.

"No," I say.

"Then this is most definitely necessary," he says. "Ready. Aim. Attack!"

I don't think anything could have prepared me for what happens next. The air fills with gut-wrenching, heartbreaking screams. Screams of men, women, and children. The robots start moving stiffly, unnaturally toward me. I run, but there's nowhere to hide. One of them comes at me fast from the side and knocks me down, but it isn't satisfied with that. It covers my body with its body and presses me into the ground, squeezing the air from my lungs. I push and kick and try to get it off of me, but it is just too strong. Panic starts to overtake me, as I struggle to take an impossible breath. Kev grabs his gun and aims it toward me. An instant later, my attacker falls to the floor, dead. As I desperately try to catch my breath, Kev shoots down the closest of the approaching robots, each with a single shot.

"You still think this is unnecessary?" he asks me.

"This isn't real," I argue.

"If this *were* real, you'd be dead," Kev says, still shooting. "Do you want to die?"

"No," I say, remembering how much I dislike Kev.

He pulls the gun from my shield suit and puts it into my limp hands. "Then let me teach you how to stay alive."

FRIDAY, MAY FOURTH
1024

GOAT

When Unpleasant comes out of the starry room, her shoulders are tense. She doesn't relax them until she steps away from the stars and, even then, they don't relax all the way.

It's my turn to go in now, so I say goodbye to Paris, and I walk to the stars.

It doesn't take long to get dressed in my shield suit. When I climb off the cushion and look toward Nym's door, she's already there waiting for me. I start walking toward her.

"Put your shield up," she reminds me.

"Shield up," I say.

My face shield snaps closed.

As the Decon cleans us off, Nym asks, "How are you at climbing?"

There is very little about me that I'm proud of, but ... "I'm fairly good at climbing."

"Perfect," she says, sounding very pleased.

Less than a second later, the door to The Plant opens.

"This way," Nym whispers.

We walk fast down a few black hallways, and we stop underneath a hatch in the ceiling. There's a metal ladder on the wall next to it.

Nym points up. "We need to go through that hatch."

I start climbing the ladder and, when I reach the top, I push the heavy hatch open. Above the hatch it's dark, but I can see that the ladder continues up and up inside a very long tube.

"Hurry, Goat!" Nym says.

I learned yesterday that, when Nym tells me to do something like that, it's for good reason. And so I climb up as fast as I can, with Nym right behind me.

We climb higher and higher and higher, until the tube ends.

"We ran out of tube," I say to Nym.

She points to a big panel on the wall.

"There's a door here," she tells me. "Say, 'Open door.'"

"Open door," I try.

Nothing happens.

"Say it like you mean it," she says. "In a low, deep voice."

I try to figure out how to make my voice lower and deeper. "Open door," I say.

Nothing happens.

I try lower. "Open door."

Nothing.

I try deeper. "Open door."

The fourth try works! The door clicks.

Nym pushes the door open just a little, peers out, and then pushes the door open all the way.

"Come on," she tells me.

Once I'm through the door, I am outside, in a place about the same size as my family's living room back home. In the black sky above us, there are more stars than I've ever seen in my life. But how can it be night? When I went into the starry room a little while ago, we had eaten breakfast, but we hadn't yet had lunch.

"I like to come up to the roof because of the air," Nym says.

"Is it *uncontaminated* out here?" I ask.

"No, it's just as contaminated as inside The Plant." She

closes her eyes. "But, inside, you can't *feel* the air. I like the way it feels." Nym's face breaks into a smile as she feels the air.

I close my eyes like Nym, and I pay attention to the wind whipping against my shield suit. I never really thought about the *feeling of air* but, now that I do, I realize that it's one of the things that makes being outside different than being inside. It has been days since I've been outside. I don't think I've ever gone that long before except when I had the flu and spent an entire week in a hospital pod.

Nym screams.

My eyelids spring open. And I see ... a Predator. He's just a step away from us.

The Predator grabs Nym, and he reaches for his gun.

"Run!" Nym says to me through gritted teeth.

I do run. But I don't run away. I run *toward* the Predator with everything I've got, aiming to hit him where I know it will hurt him. I guess he isn't expecting my attack, because the top of my head slams into him at full force. With a groan, he bends forward, dropping his gun and letting go of Nym.

She runs.

In an instant, she's gone.

She left me.

The Predator grabs me and holds on so tightly that I can't breathe. My feet dangle in midair. I kick hard into him, but that only makes him angrier. His grip on me gets even tighter, and he reaches toward the floor for his gun.

I can't let him get that gun. If he does, he will probably shoot me and take me away. Just like the Predator did to that girl I saw yesterday.

Will Nym be able to help me if I'm taken by the Predator? Will she know where to look for me? Will she dare to go searching? She abandoned me here. But I don't blame her. She was trying to save herself. A little kid like her is no match for a Predator. Neither is a little kid like me.

In a last frantic attempt to get free, I jam both my elbows into the Predator's gut as hard as I can. One of my elbows digs deep into his stomach and up under his ribs. He lets out a grunt and falls onto the ground. After that, he doesn't try to get back up. He doesn't do anything at all. He just lies there. Like he's dead.

"Let's go!"

I look up and see Nym. In one of her hands is a silver gun … exactly like the one that's lying on the floor next to the lifeless Predator. Nym slides her gun into a pocket at her waist, then she grabs the Predator's gun and tucks it into a pocket on her leg as if she's done it a million times before.

"We need to get out of here," she says.

I follow Nym into another tube. It's like the one we climbed through before, except this one runs sideways instead of up and down. We crawl through the tube for a long while before Nym stops and leans up against the tube wall.

"We can rest here," she tells me.

I sit down across from her. Her face looks stressed, and her body is trembling a little. I guess the fear is still working its way through her. The way it's working its way through me.

Nym takes the Predator's gun from the pocket on her leg and examines it. With shaky hands, she makes some adjustments to it, and then she puts it back in her pocket.

"I told you to run," she says without looking at me. "Why did you stay?"

I hope it's for the same reason that *she* didn't abandon *me*. "Because we're friends."

She looks at me and smiles, but her eyes shine with tears.

"There's something I want to tell you," I say.

"What is it?" she asks.

"Yesterday, when we were hiding from the Predators, I peeked," I admit.

Her eyebrows pinch together. "What did you see?"

"I saw one of them shoot a girl with his gun, and then he took her away."

Nym shakes her head. "You shouldn't have looked. What if they'd seen you?"

"Where did he take that girl?" I ask.

"I don't know," Nym says. "I hope never to know. When the Predators take someone away, that person never comes back."

"Do the Predators *kill* them?" I ask.

She looks away from me again. "I don't know," she says.

"Did you kill that Predator on the roof?" I ask.

"I stunned him," she says. "He should already be awake by now."

"So those guns are just stun guns," I say, feeling a little better.

"It depends on the settings," she says quietly. "The guns have the capacity to kill."

My heart speeds. "What about the one you took from the Predator on the roof?" I ask. "What were its settings?"

Nym looks into my eyes. "His gun was set to kill."

My heart almost stops.

The Predator was going to shoot Nym—and me—with a gun that kills.

"So you saved my life," I say.

"You saved mine first," she says.

I decide to ask Nym something I've been wondering about. "A few nights ago, bad people kidnapped me from my family.

That's how I ended up here. Did that happen to you too?"

"I can't answer that," she says.

"Why not?" I ask.

"I just … I can't," she says.

My shoulders sink with frustration.

And then Nym looks right into my eyes, and she says, "But I understand what you're going through."

Maybe she just gave me an answer to my question.

Nym pulls out the Predator's gun again, and she hands it to me. "From now on, this is yours." She must see the fear in my eyes, because she adds, "I adjusted and locked the settings, so it can't kill anybody."

If my mom could see me now, sitting here holding a gun that almost killed me, she would be sick. But it's probably safer for me to have a gun than not. The Plant is extremely dangerous. Much more dangerous than anyplace I've ever been to back home.

"Thanks," I say to Nym.

She nods. "Now I guess I should show you how to use it."

FRIDAY, MAY FOURTH
1759

UNPLEASANT

Because I desperately needed a distraction from my anxious thoughts, after dinner I offered to do our laundry. We decided that I should wash our pajamas, t-shirts, socks, and underwear first, then we'll change into our pajamas, and I'll wash our sweatsuits.

When the dryer beeps to indicate that it's finished with the pajama load, I pull out our warm clean clothes and pile them on top of the machine. I suppose I could grab my nightgown and underwear and let the other kids come and fish out their clothes from the pile but, for some reason, I start folding Goat's Star Wars pajamas.

And then I fold Lizard's grey-green threadbare shirt and black-and-white striped leggings, and Harley's brown shorts and navy-blue t-shirt with a washed-out yellow logo, and Liam's plain grey t-shirt and boxers, and Tiger's dark-blue boys' pajamas, and Rain's purple-polka-dotted sleep shorts and tank top, and Paris' light-blue nightgown with a nearly-worn-off image of the Eiffel Tower on it. I also fold eight white t-shirts and eight pairs of white socks. The rest is underwear. Some underwear I can pair with its owner, but some I can't, so I leave the underwear in two tiny piles: one for the girls and one for the boys.

Afterward, I stare at what I have set out across the top of the dryer, and I realize why I felt the need to carefully fold the other kids' pajamas. These pajamas are the only real belongings any of us have left.

I drop my sweatsuit into the washer and put on my underwear and Hello Kitty nightgown. My mom gave me this nightgown on my birthday last year. She said I deserved to wear something nicer than a worn-out old t-shirt to bed. I'm really not sure why she chose this nightgown for me. It doesn't look like the kind of thing I would be caught dead in. I wasn't planning to wear it but, one night, I put it on because that t-shirt I always wore was in the laundry. Then I looked at myself in the mirror and thought, *I look cute.* Usually, when I look in the mirror, all I think is how ugly I am. But the Hello Kitty nightgown made me feel cute, even a little pretty. I wore this nightgown almost every night after that.

Tears have formed in my eyes again. *Stupid tears.* I've cried more in the past few days than I have in the past few years combined. I guess most people would say that, given my current circumstances, tears are warranted. But I wish I could control them.

I wipe my tears away, go to the toilet room, and vomit out what is left of my dinner. Then I rinse my mouth and face, and I go back to the common room. Goat and Paris are drawing with markers and colored pencils. Rain is staring at the cloudy blue sky in one of the "windows." Lizard is reading a book. Tiger and Liam are playing War. Harley isn't here, because he's in The Room.

"The first round of laundry is done," I tell the group.

One at a time, the kids disappear into the laundry room and emerge wearing their pajamas. Soon, everyone is dressed the way they were the first time I met them. But they look different than the first time I saw them.

Goat and Paris look older, though they still look very little.

Lizard looks more enigmatic.

Rain looks stronger.

Tiger looks more vulnerable.

Liam looks … more human.

Suddenly, the door to The Room opens. Harley comes out, appearing much less traumatized than yesterday, and Rain hurries inside to take her turn.

"Harley, your pajamas are ready," I say.

"Thanks," he murmurs in my direction.

"Once your sweatsuit is in the washer, I'll start the second load," I say.

"I can start it," Harley offers.

"I'll do it," I say. It doesn't make sense for me to go back to the laundry room just to start the washing machine, but I want an excuse to leave the common room, because I feel like I might need to vomit again.

When Harley returns from the laundry room, I head back in there. All of the clean clothes are gone, except for the white t-shirts and a few pairs of socks. I put them into a single neat pile. And then I stare at the plastic tub of laundry soap pods. There are enough to last over a month if we wash our clothes every other day. I toss a pod into the washer and set it to wash. As I listen to the water hiss into the machine, my tears begin to flow once more.

Why did they leave so many laundry soap pods? Will we be here long enough to use all of them?

Will we run out of food? Or water?

Will we ever see our families again?

Will we stay here until we die?

Unfortunately, the answer to each of those questions is unknown.

TUESDAY, MAY EIGHTH
0903

TIGER

It has been about a week since we've been kidnapped, as best we can tell. A few days ago, Paris made a calendar for the month of May, so we can mark off the days. She did a really nice job with it using her markers and Goat's colored pencils. She even personalized the calendar for us, adding little drawings along the edges: a cloudy sky with a bolt of yellow lightning for Rain, a motorcycle for Harley, an ocean with a girl swimming in it for Unpleasant, a goat for Goat, a man in a military uniform for Liam, a lizard for Lizard, and a tiger for me. It makes sense that Paris drew a tiger for me. Only Rain knows that I chose the name Tiger because of my dog.

Ever since breakfast, Paris has been staring at her calendar, which is sitting on the table beside her chair. She didn't even look up when Liam went into the star room.

All of a sudden, Paris says, "Might as well cross off today right now."

She takes her black marker and crosses today off with a big X. Normally, we don't cross off a day until after dinner, but it's Paris' calendar, so she can do what she wants.

But then she says, "Might as well cross it *all* off."

Paris begins to scribble over the whole entire month with her marker, even the days that haven't happened yet. She pushes so hard on the marker that the tip gets all misshapen. Her calendar gets darker and darker as the black ink covers over all the other colors.

I want her to stop ruining her calendar. "Paris, stop it!" I say.

She doesn't seem to hear me.

"Stop, Paris," Lizard tries.

Paris' marker leaves the calendar and moves onto the table. She's scribbling and scribbling. Everywhere. All over the table. Then the chair.

Without saying anything, Unpleasant calmly walks over and removes the marker from Paris' fist. She gives the marker to Goat, and then she puts both of her arms around Paris, the way Liam used to do with me when I was having a tantrum and our mom couldn't figure out how to make me stop. Whenever Liam did that to me, it just made me tantrum harder. But Paris only fights for a second or two, then she buries her face in Unpleasant's sweatshirt.

"My dad said, if I ever got lost, he would move heaven and earth until he found me," Paris cries.

"I'm sure he's trying to find you," Unpleasant says. "It's just ... we're very hard to find."

"Don't worry, Paris," Rain says. "We'll get out of here."

"Yeah," Lizard says. "We'll be out of here before you know it."

I'm not sure why Rain and Lizard sound so sure of that. Maybe they're not sure, but they're trying to comfort Paris. I used to think that Pax would help us get out. I'd thought maybe that was the "mission" he was referring to. But I don't think so anymore.

I try to remind myself that my family is looking for us. I bet they have the whole world searching for us right at this very moment. The police. The military. Everyone.

I just hope we're not impossible to find.

TUESDAY, MAY EIGHTH
0921

GOAT

Paris is finally starting to seem almost back to normal when Liam comes out of the starry room. I drew the second highest card this morning, so it's my turn to go in. But, just a little while ago, Paris was very upset. Maybe I shouldn't leave her.

"It's your turn," Paris says to me, looking at the starry room.

"I don't have to go right now," I say. "I bet other people would be happy to switch turns with me, if you want me to stay for a while."

Paris looks down at the marker-streaked table. "It's okay."

"Are you sure?" I ask.

She nods. "I'm okay, Goat."

I don't think Paris will *really* be okay until she gets to go home.

At first, like Paris, I was sure that our parents would find us. But they haven't found us yet. If the kidnappers have hidden us where our parents can't find us, then our only chance of getting home is in our hands. Nym said that she will help me, once she trusts me. I'm sure she'll trust me soon. Then I can get us all rescued.

I stand and walk straight into the starry room. Nym shows up as soon as I'm dressed in my shield suit. She hands me "my" gun and I slide it into a pocket at my waist, the way Nym usually wears hers.

As Nym and I stand in the Decon room, I ask her very

softly, "Remember how you said you're going to help me … once you trust me?"

Just before the smoke blocks my view of her face, her smile disappears.

"Yes," she says through the smoke.

I wait until the smoke clears away, and then I ask, "Do you trust me yet?"

Nym looks into my eyes. "Yes, Goat, I trust you."

"When are you going to help me then?" I ask, trying not to sound impatient.

"Today," she says.

So this is it. *Today is the day that Nym is going to help me get home.*

My heart races with hope … and fear.

Once we're in The Plant, we do a little bit of walking, and a lot of crawling through tubes, but no talking at all. Nym is more serious than usual, but that makes sense. Today is possibly our most dangerous day yet.

We pop out of a hatch into an empty room that we've never been in before. It is as tall as the gigantic room but much skinnier. Its six walls are covered in thousands of tiles, all the way up to the far-away ceiling. On each wall is a picture created entirely from the tiles: a coral reef, an erupting volcano, colorful birds, an ocean, a monkey cuddling its baby, and a green snake wrapped around a thick branch of a leafy tree. Each wall has its own tiled door than blends seamlessly with the wall around it.

A spiral staircase in the center of the room climbs through a massive chandelier made of stones that are as blue as the sky. I'd love to climb up inside that chandelier, but I doubt that rickety little staircase will help us get home. It seems to end at the dark glass ceiling.

Nym opens one of the doors very slowly and carefully—as if she thinks it could break—but she doesn't seem to find what she's looking for in the darkness beyond it.

She tries another door.

"Can I help you?" I ask her.

"Unfortunately not," she says, and then she cautiously opens yet another door.

I'm starting to worry that Nym doesn't know exactly how to help me get home. Maybe she's never actually done this before. I want to ask her about her plan, but I need to let Nym concentrate on what she's doing.

While Nym continues her search, I quietly walk over to the coral reef wall and run my fingers over the bumpy tiles. I can't believe how many tiles are set into the walls of this room. It took my dad three hours to tile the floor of our tiny bathroom just with plain grey tiles. It must have taken months to tile a room like this. Maybe years.

"Goat, run!" Nym says in a low voice.

I spin around and see that Nym and I are no longer alone.

Standing in an open doorway is ... a Predator.

He reaches for his gun. Nym reaches for her gun. I reach for mine.

The Predator aims at Nym. I aim at the Predator. Nym aims ... just behind me.

Something falls behind my back. I turn around and see a Predator lying lifeless on the floor. I turn back to fire at the other Predator ... But he's gone. And so is Nym.

Panicked, I race through the Predator's doorway and into the darkness. My shield suit mask switches to night vision, but there's nothing to see except the black walls of a tunnel. I run faster than I've ever run in my whole life, holding my gun ready. My heart pounds from both hard work and fear.

I nearly collide with the end of the tunnel. A wall. But this can't be the end. The Predator and Nym had to go somewhere. There must be a door. I search for a button or lever or something to open it, but there is nothing. And so I try using my voice.

I make my voice low and deep, the way Nym taught me. "Open door."

Nothing happens.

I try lower. "Open door."

Nothing.

I try deeper. "Open door."

"Go back, Goat," I hear.

It's Nym's voice.

But she's not here. I guess I'm hearing in my head what I think she would say ... what I *know* she would say. Nym would want me to turn back. I'm certain of that. In fact, I don't think she would have wanted me to come this far. She never wanted me to put myself in danger for her. But, all this time, she has been putting herself in danger for me. Including today. She shot the Predator who was behind my back, rather than shooting the one right beside her.

And so I don't leave. I sit on the floor, and I wait. Eventually, the door will open. Then I can go deeper into the tunnel. As deep as it is possible to go.

Strangely, I feel heat coming from the wall at the end of the tunnel. I walk over to touch it but, when my fingers get close, I pull them back. The wall is hot now, like the inside of an oven.

Suddenly, the entire wall slides open, and I gasp in fear. Behind it is nothing but fire. I hear a horrible metal sound, and then flames shoot out toward me, as if the tunnel has become the scorching mouth of a fire-breathing dragon. I turn away and run for my life, but the flames chase me. My shield suit tries to cool me down, but it is no match for the fire. My head feels dizzy and my eyes go blurry.

In the distance, I see the fuzzy outline of the doorway to the tile room. I keep running. Even though I feel like I can't run anymore. Even though the Predator who Nym stunned might be up ahead, and he might be awake now, looking for me. Even though I have no plan about what to do next.

When I burst through the doorway, there are no Predators. I yank open a hatch, dive into the tube on the other side, and pull the hatch closed. And then, I stop.

How am I going to get to Nym now?

"It's too late," I hear her whisper in my head.

Deep down, I know that's true. Nym told me just a few days ago, "When the Predators take someone away, that person never comes back." She didn't say, "No one comes back *unless they are rescued.*"

"Go home, Goat," I hear Nym say.

I can't go *home*. Not anymore. Without Nym, I have no idea how to get there.

And Nym is gone forever.

The hatch that I just came through is getting hot. The fire must be in the tile room now. I move away from it, away from Nym. And I don't stop. I keep moving through the tube. Heading back the way I came. I know that is what Nym would want me to do. But that doesn't make it any easier.

I don't let myself cry. I keep my eyes and ears alert, and I keep my gun ready, and I make my way back to the only home I have now.

Alone.

TUESDAY, MAY EIGHTH
1024

UNPLEASANT

I'm just settling into a game of War with Liam when Goat emerges from The Room. His face is soaked with tears and his expression is more distraught than I've ever seen it. His reddened eyes search for Paris but, once he sees her, he doesn't go to her. Instead, he walks to his hatch and descends into his bedroom.

Tiger heads hesitantly toward The Room. She drew the third highest card today, so it's her turn. She throws Liam an uncertain glance. He returns it with a reassuring nod. I'm not sure how Liam can feel confident enough to reassure his little sister after seeing Goat come out of The Room appearing the way he did. But I suppose it's better to face The Room with confidence rather than fear.

Paris walks over to Liam and me. "I'm going to go talk to Goat," she says.

"Let me go," I say.

It's probably best if I talk to Goat first.

Whatever happened in The Room traumatized him.

I don't want Goat's trauma to traumatize Paris too.

TUESDAY, MAY EIGHTH
1027

TIGER

I stand in the darkness, waiting for Pax. We have met up four times now. Each time Pax and I get together, we do the same thing: we talk. Sometimes we sit on the soft black bed. Sometimes we lie down on the bed, side by side, staring up at the ceiling.

I've grown comfortable with Pax. He talks calmly and softly. He talks even more calmly and even more softly when I start to get anxious. Pax respects my personal space. He never gets so physically close to me that I feel uncomfortable. He asks a lot of questions, but he doesn't get frustrated when I'm not sure how to answer them. He just tells me to do my best.

Every time I've come in here to meet Pax, I've fully intended to let him take me into The Plant. Every time, I've chickened out. Maybe today will be different.

"Hey, Tiger," Pax says, handing me the night-vision goggles.

"Hey, Pax," I say, putting them on.

We walk together to the bed and lie down.

"How've you been?" Pax asks me.

"I'm hanging in there," I say. "How are you doing?"

"Same old same old."

Pax uses that phrase a lot.

"I've been working on our mission," he adds.

Pax hasn't told me anything about the mission. And he

hasn't mentioned before that he has been actively working on it. I didn't realize he could work on our mission without me.

"How's it going?" I ask.

He takes a big breath. "Good, I think."

"I'm ready," I blurt out.

Pax rolls onto his side, so he can see my face. "Ready for what?"

"I'm ready to go with you on our mission," I say.

"Great … that's great," Pax says, and he jumps to his feet. "Let's get your shield suit on. You just need to lie down on the bed, and I'll trigger it to put one on you." Pax pulls a thin black box from one of his pockets and, a moment later, a small locker appears nearby. "Take off your clothes, and put them in the locker," Pax continues. "You have to take off the goggles too. The applicator won't work if you're wearing anything at all."

I don't want to take off my clothes, especially not with Pax here. But I think it would be even harder to take them off if he wasn't here. I feel safe with Pax. Not completely safe, but safe enough to do as he asks.

Pax turns his back toward me, and I remove my clothes and put them in the locker. I set Pax's goggles atop my clothes. And then, in the pitch-black dark, I make my way back to the bed and lie down.

"I'm on the bed now," I tell Pax.

All of a sudden, red light shines on the bed from above. I feel like I'm an actress onstage with a spotlight burning down on me. A *naked* actress.

Without warning, the bed grips onto me. Panic surges into me.

"Take slow deep breaths," Pax says calmly. "It'll be over soon."

I close my eyes and take slow breaths. Trying not to think. Trying not to feel.

A horrible pressure presses into my whole entire body all at once.

And then, the pressure is gone.

Someone takes hold of my hand. The touch is so gentle that it makes all of my anxiety melt away, as if the hand is a magic wand, casting a powerful spell over me. I look down at my body and see that I'm now wearing a black suit, like the one Pax wears. I turn and see Pax standing beside me, his gloved hand holding mine.

"Still ready?" he asks.

I smile. "Still ready."

He nods. "Let's get going then."

TUESDAY, MAY EIGHTH
1040

UNPLEASANT

Goat is lying on his bed, sobbing. It's hard to just stand by and do nothing, but it's best not to push someone when they're like this.

After a while, Goat's sobs finally lessen, and his breathing turns slow and deep. This is the stage when the body has released so much pain that it falls into a state of numbness. The pain isn't gone, but the person doesn't feel it so much. For the time being.

Goat turns his head, so that he's facing toward me and, finally, he speaks, "I'm never going back in the starry room."

I am about to reassure him that I will make sure that his wishes are respected. But then he says something that stops me cold ...

"I guess that means I can tell you everything."

Over the next several minutes, Goat tells me awful things about his time in a place he calls "The Plant," which sounds like it's the same place that Kev takes me. Goat's escort, a little girl named Nym, was abducted—and probably killed—by evil men called Predators, who Goat thinks are the same men who kidnapped us from our homes and brought us here.

Kev and I never encountered any Predators. At least not up close. But Kev is probably more skilled than Nym at avoiding them. After all, Kev is close to my age, and Nym is ... *was* ... only about nine years old. Upset grips me again. Even though I never met Nym, through Goat's words I feel as if I knew her. It sounds like she was a brave, fierce, caring, protective child. The kind of person who we need in this world. Even though I never knew her, the loss of Nym breaks my heart.

When I look at Goat, I see how much this loss has changed him. The fragile strands of innocence that still clung to him when we first met just one week ago are now completely gone. In their place is a web of sorrow that no child should ever know—but I know far too many kids *do* know it, even back home where it's supposed to be safe.

Now, Goat knows for sure that he isn't safe.

And, even though I guess I knew it all along, now I know it for sure too.

TIGER

Pax and I hurry along dark hallways, making turn after turn, as if we are inside a maze. Finally, he opens a hatch on the floor and crawls into a pipe barely big enough to fit inside.

Nervously, I follow him down the ladder that's on the inner wall of the pipe. The ladder takes us down. Deeper down and deeper still. Just before I am certain that it will never end, it makes a sharp turn and opens up into a little room. Actually, compared with the pipe, this is a *great big* room. It's nearly the size of my bedroom back home.

Pax invites me to sit on a red velvet couch across from the crackling fireplace.

"Welcome to my favorite place in the world," he says, stretching out on a plush brown chair.

He looks more relaxed than I've ever seen him. It makes me happy to see him like this.

"Do you like it?" he asks.

"It feels like …" Sadness stops me from speaking.

"What does it feel like?" he asks me softly.

I shake my head. I was going to say that it feels like home. But I don't want to think too much about home right now. If I do, I'm going to cry. And I don't want to cry in front of Pax, even though I think he'd understand if I did.

Pax jumps up and walks over to a corner of the room. He lifts the edge of the thick crimson rug and opens a small hatch on the floor beneath it. Then he withdraws … a gun. Its gleaming metal reflects the flames of the fire. Pax holds the gun out, offering it to me.

"Are you willing to use this?" he asks.

After what happened to Andrew, I don't even want to *see* a gun. I definitely don't want to *use* one. "Why would I need to use that?" I ask.

"To defend yourself," Pax says. "Our mission is dangerous. Just today, we lost someone."

My body stiffens. "I wish you'd told me that before I agreed to come with you."

"If you want, I'll take you back right now," he offers. "Just say the word."

"No." For some insane reason, I don't want him to take me back. "I want to stay."

"Are you willing to use this?" Pax asks again, offering the gun.

"I don't think you really know for sure what you'll do until it comes down to the moment when you have to make that decision for real." That's the best answer I can give. "But I've never used a gun before," I add.

He gives me a nod of approval. "I can remedy that."

Pax takes me to a place with spongy walls, where he teaches me how to use the gun to shoot training robots. In the beginning, the robots are immobile, then Pax tells them to move. At first, I have to force myself to shoot them, but it gets easier the more times I do it. Pax seems pleased with my progress, which makes me feel a little good and a little sick to my stomach. I'm relieved when he finally goes to the box on the wall and shuts everything down.

"Have you ever had to use a gun for real?" I ask him, as we head toward the exit.

He looks at me. "Do you want the honest answer or the answer you want to hear?"

"The honest answer *is* the one I want to—"

I stop speaking, because I hear a door slide open behind us. I spin around and see a hulking man standing in a large doorway, aiming a gun in our direction. Even though he is wearing a shield suit that matches ours, there is no doubt in my mind that this man is dangerous.

Without hesitation, Pax aims his gun at the man but, before he can fire it, the man fires his own gun, and Pax falls to the ground. Unconscious … Or dead.

I hold my gun with its barrel pointing down at the floor. I feel paralyzed, unable to raise it.

The man turns his gun on me.

"Drop your weapon!" he orders.

Pax takes a gasping breath. *He needs help.*

"DROP YOUR WEAPON NOW!" the man barks at me.

I might be able to help Pax. But only if this man is gone.

"This is your last chance," the man growls.

The only way to help Pax is to make this man go away.

I lift my gun and fire a single shot. Right at the center of the man's chest. Exactly like Pax showed me how to do on the targets.

The man goes down.

Suddenly, Pax leaps to his feet.

"You're okay!" I exclaim, feeling relieved, but also confused. Weirdly, Pax seems to be, not just okay, but perfectly fine.

"I didn't *actually* get shot." He cocks his head at the downed man. "That's one of the advanced training robots. Pretty realistic, isn't it?"

Anger builds inside me. "You were just *pretending*?" I ask.

Pax nods, looking a little smug.

"You shouldn't have done that," I say, moving away from him.

His face clouds with unease. "I needed to know what you would do if you had to make that decision *for real*."

"Now you know," I say, refusing to meet his gaze.

"I had to be sure you would defend yourself if I couldn't defend you," he says weakly.

"I wasn't defending *myself*," I say.

"What were you doing then?" he asks, appearing baffled.

"I was trying to protect *you*."

Pax looks truly distressed. "I'm sorry, Tiger."

I hold my gun out to Pax. Hesitantly, he accepts it.

"I want to go back to my room now," I say.

Pax nods. "As you wish."

That's the last thing he says until we're back inside the star room. Once we're there, he tells me that the bed will remove my shield suit automatically when I lie down. Finally, he climbs up the ladder and disappears into the light. The hatch opens, and then closes. Then I lie down on the bed, and it removes my shield suit.

Once my suit is off, my tears come hard and fast. They come even harder when I go to the locker and see that Pax forgot to take his night-vision goggles. I leave them there. Maybe Pax will come retrieve them once I'm gone.

I'm not angry with Pax anymore. Now that I've had a chance to think about it, I know that he was only trying to make sure I would be safe. Maybe he should have gone about it differently, but his intention was to help me, not to hurt me.

I know Pax cares about me. The way I care about him.

I wish I could tell him that I will be coming back here tomorrow.

I hope, with everything in my heart, that he comes back here tomorrow too.

TUESDAY, MAY EIGHTH
1142

UNPLEASANT

Tiger's eyes are wet when she comes out of The Room, but she doesn't appear traumatized. The door closes behind her, but I have no doubt that it will open again after lunch.

Not long after The Room closes, we are fed a meal of chicken and sliced carrots in a spiced curry sauce, with strawberry cobbler for desert. As always, the food is delicious, but it doesn't even begin to fill the hollow feeling in my stomach.

After lunch, The Room opens again. I walk toward the stars with a sense of urgency. I have to find a way to escape, and I have to do it as soon as possible. Every time someone enters The Plant, they are risking their life. Goat could have died today. Someone else still could.

My shield suit has just been applied when Kev meets me.

"Come on," he says, waving me toward him. "We're in a hurry today."

I don't bother to ask why. I know Kev won't answer.

After we go through the airlock, we head into the black hallways. We walk for a while before Kev opens a hatch on the floor that leads to a tunnel. I hate the claustrophobic tunnels here, although lately I've been handling them much better than I used to.

I take a deep breath and follow Kev down the ladder. This is the first time we've taken a tunnel downward without going upward first. This tunnel feels different from the others we've crawled or climbed through. It's cooler in here, and I smell a vague, rotten odor. I wonder if something died in here.

Suddenly, I hear a splash below me. I look down and see that Kev is now standing at the bottom of the tunnel in about a foot of what appears to be water. But this is no ordinary water. When his feet move, the water glows in his wake.

"Is that bioluminescence?" I ask Kev.

He smiles up at me. "That's right."

In school, we learned that certain microscopic organisms that live in bodies of water emit light when they are disturbed. These organisms were all but extinct prior to World War Three, but the substantial reduction in human impact on their habitat—due to the massive decline in the human population as a result of the war—caused them to thrive. I never dreamed I would see bioluminescence in person, because most of the places where bioluminescent organisms thrive aren't safe to visit. Like this place.

Kev pulls a two-person kayak out from a horizontal tunnel that intersects with ours.

"You have any experience with these things?" Kev asks me.

"A little," I say. "But that was years ago, and my dad did most of the work."

"Hopefully you're stronger now," Kev says. "I'm going to need your help once we get out into open water."

Open water? Is Kev going to take me out of The Plant?

I don't dare ask any questions. If Kev is planning to help me escape, I can't risk saying or doing anything to dissuade him, so instead I say, "Just tell me what you want me to do."

"For now," he says, "just hop in."

TUESDAY, MAY EIGHTH
1251

GOAT

A little while after Unpleasant leaves my bedroom, Paris comes in and sits down next to me on my bed. I tell her what I told Unpleasant. I don't want to scare Paris, but I need her to understand how dangerous The Plant really is.

"Please don't go in there ever again," I say to Paris when I'm done.

"What if going in there could help us?" she asks very quietly.

"It hasn't so far," I argue.

"There's a chance that it might," Paris says. "I think everyone believes that. Otherwise, why would they go back in there every day?"

"What if they're all wrong?" I ask.

"We *never* give up hope," Paris says firmly.

I said that same thing to her a few days ago, when Liam was locked inside the starry room and we didn't know if he would ever come out. My mom used to say, "When we give up hope, we give up living. And so we never give up hope, even when everything seems hopeless."

I don't want Paris to go back to The Plant, but if I can't stop her, I can at least help protect her.

"I hid a gun in the Decon room that's above the hatch," I say in barely a whisper. "It's wedged between the wall and the floor. There should be a pocket on the waist of your shield suit where you can hide it, in case you need it. Promise you'll take it with you if you go back into The Plant."

Paris nods. "I promise."

"When you come back from The Plant, hide the gun in the Decon room again." I take an uncomfortable breath. "Because I'm going to need it too."

If Paris isn't done fighting, then I'm not done either.

TUESDAY, MAY EIGHTH
1302

UNPLEASANT

Kev and I paddle quietly through dark winding tunnels. Every stroke of our paddles in the water brings a fleeting burst of pinprick dots of light—like tiny shooting stars. It is absolutely mesmerizing. So much so that I don't notice that the tunnel has grown narrower until Kev says, "Lean forward, as flat as you can get. I'll get us through this part."

Up ahead, there's only about a foot of clearance between the kayak and the tunnel walls. The claustrophobia that I thought I'd mostly conquered comes rising up to the surface, but I force it back down.

I curl my head and chest toward the kayak, trying to put my trust in Kev. So far, he hasn't led me into harm's way. I really do believe he's trying to help me. And, based on what happened to Nym, it's clear that he's putting his own life in danger in order to do so.

"All right," Kev finally says. "You can sit up now."

I sit up and my jaw falls slack in awe. We are now in wide open water, below an expansive sky filled with stars all the way to the horizon. Behind us, at the base of a tremendous rocky cliff, is a barely-visible sliver of open space from which we emerged.

The Plant must be perched on top of this cliff, but we are too close to the cliff to see it. A part of me is eager to see what The Plant looks like from the outside, but I suppose it's better that we can't. If we can't see The Plant then, hopefully, the

Predators can't see us.

"Stay close to the island, but be careful not to hit any rocks," Kev says. "We can't afford to damage the kayak. It's the only one we've got."

It's nearly impossible not to ask questions now. *Where are we heading? What will happen when we get there? Is someone waiting for us?* But, as much as I want to ask these questions and more, I stay quiet. It is pointless to ask Kev any questions. He won't answer them.

"There's a strong current up ahead," Kev says. "When we reach it, you need to do what I tell you. Even if it goes against your instincts. Even if it doesn't make sense."

I swallow and grip my paddle even more tightly. Almost immediately, I feel the current Kev told me about. It takes hold of our kayak with a force I hadn't anticipated, dragging us out into the open ocean. I try to fight it.

"Don't attempt to head back to shore," Kev says. "Keep us parallel to the edge of the island."

Everything inside me tells me to paddle back toward the island. We're getting too far away from it. What if the Predators spot us?

"Don't paddle toward the shore!" Kev shouts at me. "Paddle straight ahead!"

I force myself to follow Kev's commands and paddle straight, but the powerful current continues to drag us away from the island. We are so far away now that I can see a hint of red light glowing at the top of the cliff.

"Stop paddling!" Kev says, his voice serious.

I stop, even though my brain urges me to continue ... because it senses danger.

"The current is taking us out into the ocean," I say, worried.

"Let it," Kev responds quietly.

As we are carried away from the island, a monstrous structure perched on the tremendous cliff comes into view. With wide eyes, I gaze for the first time at the exterior of The Plant. It is lit only by dark-red floodlights and the glow of the night sky. From the outside, The Plant is a glimmering silver fortress protected by dozens of curved walls that come together at angles sharp enough to cut.

When I tear my gaze away and look back at the open ocean, I think I see other islands ahead of us in the distance. I wonder at first if my eyes are playing tricks on me but, the closer we get to them, the more certain I am that they are actually there. Some of the islands have buildings on them that look about the same size as The Plant, but far less menacing in appearance.

Kev points to the nearest island. "There's our destination," he says.

The relief that I feel at his words is overwhelming. *We're almost there.*

We're heading to an island that is much smaller than the one we came from. I don't see any buildings on it, only shrubs and trees. The shore is sand rather than rock, which makes it a safe place to land our kayak. Once we're close, Kev jumps into the warm water, and he helps me do the same. We drag our kayak up the beach and secure it out of sight behind some shrubs. Then Kev and I sit on the soft sand to rest.

"I want to show you something," Kev says, sounding energized.

"Okay," I say.

"Say, 'I want to feel you,'" he says.

"I want to *feel* you?" I ask.

He holds out his hand. "Now touch me."

Lightly, I touch Kev's fingers, and I pull my hand away in shock. It felt as if we were touching *skin-to-skin*, even though our hands are completely covered by our shield suits.

"It works on yourself too," he says.

I touch my opposite hand and, sure enough, it feels as if I am touching my hands together without anything between them. I run my fingers up my arm, taking in the astonishing sensation. It feels as if I'm not wearing anything at all.

Kev puts what feels like his bare hand on what feels like my bare shoulder. I freeze at the intimate touch. Suddenly, I feel intensely vulnerable.

I pull away.

"You don't want me to touch you?" Kev asks.

"No, I don't want you to touch me," I say. "I don't want *anyone* to touch me."

I see a splash of hurt in Kev's eyes. "I must have misread your signals," he says.

Did Kev think I *wanted* him to touch me like that? Is that why he brought me here?

A sudden wave of dizzying sickness crashes over me as my entire perspective shifts.

"I thought you were bringing me here to escape from the kidnappers," I say. "I thought you were going to help me go home to my mom and dad."

Kev stares out at the water, looking pained, but he doesn't say anything.

"I thought you were going to help me," I plead.

He looks deep into my eyes. "I tried," he says.

Kev can't help me. Or he won't.

I close my eyes for a moment and then open them, trying to appear even more vulnerable than I feel.

"I need a minute alone," I say softly.

Kev gives me a nod of understanding.

As I watch him walk away, I anxiously construct a plan.

Some of the other islands are not too far away. Maybe there are people there who can contact my family and get us rescued. I have no way of knowing unless I go there and see for myself, and this could be my only chance. I am certain that Kev isn't going to bring me out of The Plant again.

As Kev moves out of sight behind some trees, I gather my courage and make my move. I sprint back to the kayak and heave it up onto my shoulder. Then I race to the water, set the kayak in, and climb aboard. I paddle hard away from the shore, my adrenaline helping me travel faster than I'd ever be able to go under normal circumstances.

When I glance back, I see Kev running toward me. I'm sure his adrenaline is flowing too, and he will do everything in his power to prevent me from leaving him. I focus most of my attention on paddling and only a little on keeping tabs on my pursuer. Unfortunately, it turns out that Kev is an extremely strong swimmer, and he is rapidly getting too close for comfort. I throw all of my energy into paddling, and I don't dare to look back.

Suddenly, the kayak tilts. I plunge into the water with a feeling of suffocating dread. Kev pulls me underwater. I kick him, trying to force him to let go of me, but he holds on so tight that he squeezes the air from my lungs. Even though my shield suit still seems to be providing me with plenty of fresh air, I can't seem to get enough oxygen.

I take the deepest breath I can manage and slam my helmet into Kev's. Finally, he loses his grip on me, and I am set free. When I surface, I spot the abandoned kayak about ten feet away. I propel myself toward it, leaving Kev in my wake. Once I am less than an arm's length away, I reach for it. But, just before my fingers make contact, an agonizing pain hits the back of my head.

And the world goes black.

TUESDAY, MAY EIGHTH
1403

TIGER

We don't have any clocks here, but I don't need a clock to know that Unpleasant has been in the star room for longer than anyone has been in there before. When I see the concerned look on Liam's face, I know that he knows it too.

Unpleasant has been gone too long.

Maybe she isn't coming back.

TUESDAY, MAY EIGHTH
1424

UNPLEASANT

I wake up feeling more exhausted than I ever have in my entire life. The way I felt at the end of my first visit to The Room was nothing compared to this. The back of my head throbs uncontrollably, making it hard to gather my thoughts.

My bleary eyes scan my surroundings. Although it is dark, the night vision of my shield suit allows me to see that I have been brought back to The Room. I'm lying on the black bed, bathed in red light. Kev emerges from the darkest shadow and strides toward me. No doubt he is furious with me for what I did. Who knows how he will retaliate? I reach for my gun, just in case, but then I remember, Kev didn't give it to me today.

Kev gently places his hand on my forearm. Unlike when we were on the beach, I feel our shield suits between us. We are no longer able to feel each other skin-to-skin. Even so, I pull away from his touch.

"I have no desire to harm you," he says softly.

I don't believe that anymore.

"My head hurts pretty bad. Maybe I should be checked out by a medical pod to make sure there's no internal damage," I say to see how he'll respond.

"You were shot with a stunner," he says. "Now that you're awake, there's nothing to be concerned about. There should be no significant aftereffects. The discomfort will resolve shortly."

"Who shot me?" I ask, not expecting an answer.

"I did," he says.

Apparently, Kev is answering questions now.

"What did you do to me after you stunned me?" I ask, looking him straight in the eyes.

He could have done *anything* to me.

"I brought you home." His eyes don't show even the slightest hint of deception.

I shake my head. "My home isn't here."

"It is now," he says, and then he abruptly walks away.

I hear the airlock door open and then shut.

Kev is gone.

Unsteadily, I pull myself to my feet, trying to salvage enough of my broken strength to speak to the woman in The Room. I need to know if she is going to make good on her promise.

"I need to talk to you!" I call out toward the dark walls of The Room.

No one responds.

"Answer me!" I shout.

"Is something wrong?"

The sound of the woman's calm voice kindles the fire of my anger.

"Is your name Nevah?" I ask.

"It is," she says.

"Did you send Kev to help me?" I ask.

"I did," she says.

"Well, that didn't work out," I say. "You need to send someone else."

"That won't be necessary," she says.

"Why not?" I ask.

There is a moment of silence, and then she says, "Our

mission is complete."

My heart pounds. "I thought our 'mission' was to help me go home," I say.

Nevah doesn't respond.

My strength is fading and, along with it, my sense of hope.

"Did you ever have any intention of helping any of us escape from here?" I ask.

"No," Nevah says. And, with that, my last shred of hope tears in two.

Whatever strength I mustered is now gone. My head is throbbing so hard that I can barely stand. I shuffle over to the bed and lie down.

"Our deal is off," I say weakly.

As the bed takes hold of me, I brace for the wrath of Nevah or the kidnappers or whoever is actually in charge of things here. I am done being afraid of them.

I am done being afraid.

The second bed descends and locks me between the two beds. Then the second bed rises away, leaving me undressed. I turn and see my clothes sitting in the locker, just as I left them. I stare at them, waiting for something bad to happen. But nothing does.

And so I pull on my clothes and stagger over to the door.

Wondering if it will open.

TUESDAY, MAY EIGHTH
1432

TIGER

Unpleasant is standing just inside the doorway of the star room. She takes a few unsteady steps into the common room, and then she does something she looks too exhausted to do ... She speaks.

"I'm assuming that all of you have spoken with the woman inside The Room. Her name is Nevah. You told her your deepest secrets and desires, because she tortured them from your lips. Then she promised you something that you want so desperately that you're willing to do anything to get it, even make a deal with the devil. But when you deal with Nevah, you won't win. Putting your trust in her puts you in grave danger. That mistake could cost you your life. It almost cost me mine."

Unpleasant seems as if she has something more to say but, after a moment, without saying anything further, she walks over to a chair and sits down facing a "window."

Harley quietly stands and walks into the star room. To take his turn. I am not surprised by his actions. Despite what Unpleasant just said, if it was my turn to go into the star room now, I would go.

I don't trust the woman in the star room. I never did, and I never will. But I trust Pax.

Pax wants to help me.

I know he does.

In a way, he already has.

TUESDAY, MAY EIGHTH
2135

UNPLEASANT

Today, every one of the kids who was supposed to go into The Room after me went ahead and took their turn. None of them were dissuaded by my words. Fortunately, every one of them returned apparently unharmed. Maybe I should have told them more. Maybe I will say more tomorrow. First, I need to tell Liam exactly what happened to me.

Once we are alone in my bedroom for the night, I tell Liam *everything*, even what Kev was hoping to do with me on the beach, though I worry that maybe I should have withheld that final detail. When I am through, I finally look into Liam's eyes. The way he is looking at me is utterly nonjudgmental. Understanding. Accepting.

"I'm sorry I made you listen to all of that," I apologize.

"Don't be sorry," he says. "I told you that you can tell me anything."

Tears spring into my eyes. "You're the first person in my entire life who has ever made me feel like that might actually be true."

Liam gives a conflicted smile. "I feel that way about you too."

A few hours ago, when Kev and I were on the beach, I told him that I didn't want *anyone* to touch me but, the moment I said it, I realized that it wasn't the truth. There *is* one person in the world who I wish would touch me …

Without speaking, I lean toward Liam, so close that I can feel his breath. He closes his eyes and moves nearer. His lips are about to touch my lips ...

My heart races with panic. I pull back.

"What's wrong?" he asks so gently that it makes tears start down my cheeks.

"We were going to kiss," I say.

"And you don't want to," he says.

"I *do* want to kiss you." My heart pounds even harder when I say that. "It's just that ... If this doesn't work out ... we're kind of stuck here. It could be very ..."

"Unpleasant."

"Yeah," I say.

"What makes you think this isn't going to work out?" he asks.

"Nothing in my life ever does."

Liam shakes his head, but not in a mean way. "You can't stop living your life because you're afraid that something is going to go wrong."

"I know, but ..." I start.

"You like swimming, right?" Liam asks.

"I love swimming," I say.

Liam goes on, "What if you had been too afraid to learn how to swim, and all you did your whole life was stare at the water, believing that if you got in it, you were going to drown?" His hand touches mine. I stare at our hands. Touching. Liam continues, "It's hard to swim until you *believe* you can do it."

For a moment, I *believe* that Liam and I could kiss each other without our friendship shattering into bits. Just before that feeling fades away, I close my eyes and I lean toward him. This time, I let my lips press against his. His arms take hold of me. Instead of feeling as if he's pulling me underwater—where there isn't any air to breathe—I feel as if he's lifting me up to the surface—where there's enough air to go on breathing forever.

Maybe it *is* possible that this kind of relationship with Liam will work out. Maybe we will grow together instead of apart. Maybe kissing him will always feel the way it does right now … like magic.

Suddenly, the lights in my room go a menacing red. The beautiful quiet is broken by a horrible alarm. Loud and unrelenting.

Liam pulls his mattress off the floor. Cautiously, he lifts open the hatch, and we peer down into the common room.

Standing there all alone, bathed in red light, is Rain. Around her are a jumble of wires that have been pulled from the walls, as well as seven movie screen "windows" lying broken on the floor.

Liam and I climb quickly down the ladder.

"I'm sorry. I'm sorry," Rain keeps saying over and over.

"What did you do?" Liam asks her.

"I was trying to help," she says.

As the other kids appear at their hatches, Liam's focus pulls away from Rain. I follow his gaze toward The Room. Its door is closed, but there is now an open panel beside it. On the panel is a lever and what looks like a steering wheel. Above the lever I see: "Door 029."

My eyes widen as I notice a second open panel on the same wall, just a few feet away. This one is labeled "Door 030." If there is a door near that second panel, we've never seen it open.

Liam walks directly to the second panel. "What's this?" he asks Rain.

"I don't know," she says. "That opened when the lights turned red."

Liam shifts the lever, and then he rotates the wheel. As he does that, a door slowly cranks open, revealing a narrow red-lit corridor beyond it. Warily, Liam starts into the corridor. The rest of us follow.

Liam turns to us and holds up his hand. "Wait here."

"We need to stick together," Paris says. "You said so yourself on our first day here."

"I was wrong," Liam says, and then I notice that he's trembling.

I look into his eyes. "No, you weren't," I say. "You were absolutely right."

Liam returns my gaze and exhales. "All right. Everyone stay close."

The eight of us walk down the skinny corridor. After about twenty feet, there's a ladder heading up. We climb it, Liam leading the way.

At the top of the ladder is a room almost as big as the common room but, unlike the common room, it looks vibrantly alive. Screens fill nearly every available space on every wall, but the data they display makes no sense.

"It looks like the cockpit of a spaceship," Goat says, his jaw agape.

Harley sits down in one of the six empty chairs here, and he examines the information on the screens. "It's a submarine," he says. He sounds absolutely certain of that.

"How do you know?" I ask him.

"Virtual reality sub games used to be my life," Harley says, focusing on another screen with rapt interest. "For years I spent practically every weekend playing them."

"Why isn't there anyone driving the submarine?" Goat

asks.

"Maybe it's remote-controlled," Lizard suggests.

"Or on autopilot," Harley says.

"But where are the bad men?" Paris asks.

"If they were on board, they would have come for us by now," Rain says.

"She's right," I say. "There's no one here but us."

"Maybe I can figure out how to pilot this thing," Harley says, reaching toward a screen.

"Don't *anyone* touch *anything*," Liam warns. "The submarine is probably in some kind of emergency mode. Something important might have been damaged."

"If something got damaged, then what happens?" Rain asks.

"Generally, if a sub is significantly compromised, it will automatically surface," Harley says, his eyes fixed on the screens.

"Where will it surface?" Lizard asks.

Harley shrugs. "Wherever we are."

"But where are we?" Tiger murmurs.

Harley walks over to a table in the middle of the room. There's a large screen on the tabletop, but the screen is dark. "There should be a map here showing our location, but the screen isn't displaying anything." He heads back over to the lit screens on the walls.

"What happens if we surface in the middle of nowhere?" Lizard asks.

Her question hangs in the air. There is no reassuring way to answer it.

Finally Paris says, "The men will come for us."

"When they do, they'll be angry," Lizard says.

"What if they're so angry that they don't come?" Tiger

asks.

"Hopefully, they'll come," Paris says, sounding uncertain.

I don't know what to hope for.

TUESDAY, MAY EIGHTH
2223

TIGER

While Unpleasant, Liam, Rain, and Harley try to figure out the monitors in the control room, Paris, Goat, Lizard, and I explore the rest of the submarine. The sub is mostly filled with machinery, along with hundreds of pipes that weave along the ceilings like silver snakes.

We are about to go back to the control room when Paris says, "We haven't checked the starry room yet."

"I guess we should have a look in there too," Lizard agrees.

And so the four of us go to the common room, and Lizard pulls the lever next to the star room and cranks open the door. The room on the other side of the door doesn't look like it could possibly be the same place I was in just hours ago. It looks like a plain ordinary room, and not a very big one. Not nearly as big as I remember.

"This can't be the right room," I say.

"It has to be," Lizard says. "It's the only one here."

Paris points toward one of the walls. "But there was a door, way over there, past this wall. And there was a hatch on the ceiling. The door and the hatch are how you get into The Plant."

"The Plant doesn't exist," Lizard says. "Think about it. When you came into this room, all you saw and all you felt was darkness and lights, until you put on your 'shield suit.'" She looks as if her own words hurt her to say them. "It was all just some kind of super-high-tech virtual reality game."

But I saw Pax before I put on the suit.

Actually ... I didn't see him until I put on *his goggles.*

I felt Pax touch me.

But only after I put on the suit. He never actually touched me before then.

"It felt so real," I murmur.

"It felt real to me too," Lizard says.

"Now nothing feels real," Paris says.

Goat turns toward the doorway, as if he suddenly isn't comfortable in this space anymore. "We should probably go back to the control room," he says.

"Right," Lizard agrees.

"I'll meet you there," I say, and then I add, "I need to use the bathroom."

"We'll wait for you," Lizard says.

"That's okay," I say. It's bad enough that I just announced my bodily needs to Lizard, Goat, and Paris. I definitely don't want them waiting for me while I relieve myself.

Lizard shrugs. "All right. We'll meet you up there."

She leads Goat and Paris toward the control room, and I go off to the toilets.

But, after I'm through, I don't join the others.

TUESDAY, MAY EIGHTH
2240

UNPLEASANT

By the time Lizard, Goat, and Paris return to the control room, we still have very little information to report. It appears that the course of the submarine is locked in and encrypted. We can't view it or change it without permission. So, basically, we're still at the mercy of our captors.

Strangely, the kidnappers don't seem to be inflicting any punishment on us for venturing into the forbidden parts of the submarine. True, there is a horrible alarm blaring throughout the sub, and all of the overhead lights now glow red rather than white, but those are probably automated responses of the sub to damage. No disembodied voices have scolded us or even spoken to us since we ventured out of our permitted living space. There has been no painful "rain," deafening banging, or icy air conditioning. Although it is a relief not to suffer additional abuse from our kidnappers, I can't help feeling on edge. I expected that they would have taken some action against us by now. I wonder why they haven't.

"So what happens now?" Lizard asks.

"As long as we're still seaworthy, we'll probably continue on our current course to wherever it was we were originally heading," Harley says. "It's also possible that the kidnappers can alter our course remotely to bring us to a different location."

"Could they come here to us?" Rain asks.

"They could," Harley says. "They can either cause the sub to surface and meet us there, or they can dive down here and enter the sub while it's underway, probably via the escape chamber."

Paris brightens. "There's an escape chamber?"

Harley brings up a three-dimensional holographic model of the submarine. "It's over here on the port side," he says, zooming in on the model.

"We saw that on our tour just now," Paris says. "But we couldn't figure out what it was."

"If there's an escape chamber, why don't we use it to escape?" Rain asks.

"For one thing, we're currently six hundred twenty-three feet below the surface, so unless you found some scuba gear on your tour *and* you're experienced at surfacing from that kind of depth, you'd be committing suicide. And, even if you did have scuba gear, and you knew how to use it, you'd probably end up surfacing in the middle of the ocean, where no one would ever find you."

"Can we disable the escape chamber, so the kidnappers can't use it?" Lizard asks.

"I think so," Harley says. "An escape chamber is an underwater airlock. It has an interior door and an exterior one. The exterior door won't open unless the interior door is closed and locked. So as long as we keep the interior door open, the kidnappers can't use the chamber to board the submarine."

"How are we going to keep the door open?" Goat asks.

"Put my mattress there," Liam says. "I won't need it any time soon."

Unfortunately, that is probably true. It looks like none of us will be getting any sleep tonight.

"We should also secure all of the exterior hatches as best

we can," Harley says. "It won't stop the kidnappers from getting to us, but it might give us some warning if they try."

"We should gather up things we can use as weapons," Lizard suggests.

I rise to my feet. "Let's get started."

WEDNESDAY, MAY NINTH
2311

TIGER

I sit on the floor of the star room, missing both its stars and its darkness. But most of all, I miss Pax. I feel like maybe he's waiting for me in The Plant, just on the other side of these walls. But he can't be. Because there is no Plant.

Now that I look more closely, I spot the wall panels that conceal the physical objects I encountered here. I can see where the black bed and the white table must be hiding. And where the clothes locker must be hidden. I know there is other stuff inside these walls too, for example, whatever "handed me" Pax's goggles. And whatever undressed me and put me on the white table the very first time I came into this room … after I passed out. Everything I felt here was either hidden in these walls or simulated by my "shield suit."

I was never touched in this room, at least not by anything human.

And even though I know now that every single thing that happened to me in this room was a lie, I can't make myself leave it. This is where I met Pax. And where I last saw him. This is where I was hoping to see him again.

But I won't ever see him again.

Pax isn't gone. Someone can't be gone if they were never here.

He isn't dead. Someone can't die if they were never alive.

Pax just never *was*. He was never real.

But to me Pax *was* real. He was my *real* friend. On the first day we met, Pax said he would help me, and he did. Pax helped me to be brave. Brave enough to bond with him. Brave enough to do things that scared me. Brave enough to defend my buddy, even if it put my own safety at risk. Pax helped me to be brave like Liam … and like Andrew.

I guess now I need to be brave enough to say goodbye to Pax.

Behind me, I hear the star room's door start to crank open and the abrupt "unmuting" of the horrid emergency alarm. I turn and see Rain peeking in through the partly-open doorway.

"Sorry to bother you," she says when she sees me. "I was just trying to find some peace and quiet."

"I guess it's time to let someone else have a turn in here," I say.

I start to get up, but Rain shakes her head. "No, you should stay."

She steps out of the doorway and cranks the door closed, bringing back the quiet once more.

And so I stay.

WEDNESDAY, MAY NINTH
2346

GOAT

Liam finally figured out how to turn off the emergency alarm, which is good because I think it was starting to drive everyone crazy.

"Now that it's quiet, maybe I can think straight," Harley says.

"I still hear something," Paris says.

"The alarm is probably just echoing around in your brain," Lizard says.

"No," Unpleasant says. "I hear it too."

Everyone is silent for a minute, listening. And then I hear the sound that Paris and Unpleasant were talking about. It's very soft. A little bit like an alarm, but not exactly.

"Something's beeping," Unpleasant says. "But it's not coming from in here."

Liam stands up. "I'll check it out."

Paris and I go with him to follow the sound. We climb the ladder out of the control room and walk down the hallway, heading toward the beeping. And then, on the hallway floor next to the escape chamber, I see something that's not right.

A little while ago, I helped put Liam's mattress between the escape chamber's inside door and the door jamb, to block the door from closing, so the bad guys wouldn't be able to use the escape hatch to get into the submarine. But now, Liam's mattress is lying flat on the hallway floor, instead of where we left it. And the escape chamber door is closed.

Somebody reversed what we did.

Liam looks through the escape chamber window, mutters a curse word, and leaps over to the computer screen next to the door.

"Who wasn't with us in the control room just now?" he asks Paris and me.

"Rain ... and Tiger," Paris says.

Liam slams his fist against the wall near the computer screen. "How the hell do you get this thing to abort?" he mutters.

Paris and I look through the escape chamber window. The chamber is almost completely filled up with water. And there's somebody *in* the water. They're wearing blue sweatpants and a blue sweatshirt, like the ones we are wearing.

Whoever it is isn't swimming or floating. They look dead.

And then I see the person's face.

"It's Rain," I say.

A second later, the water stops rising, and then it starts to fall. Liam comes back over to the window. He takes another look through it, then he turns to Paris.

"Get Harley and Unpleasant, and bring them here right away," he says.

Paris runs off toward the control room.

"Keep an eye on Rain," Liam tells me. "I need to find Tiger."

After he races away, I stare through the escape chamber window—helplessly watching Rain's lifeless body drift around in the sinking water. Not even a minute later, Unpleasant and Harley come running down the hallway with Paris. Unpleasant takes a quick look through the chamber window and then tries madly to pull the lever to unlock the door.

"Why won't the stupid door open?" she shouts.

"It won't unlock until the pressure is equalized with the inside of the submarine," Harley says, looking at the computer screen. "We're almost there."

It feels like forever before the light above the door turns from red to green. Then Harley releases the door and cranks it open, and Unpleasant runs to Rain.

Rain is lying like an abandoned rag doll on the floor. Her lips are blue, and her open eyes don't blink. She doesn't respond at all to Unpleasant's shouts.

Without saying anything, because my voice is too shaky to speak, I walk into the escape chamber and kneel down next to Rain in the ice-cold puddle of water on the floor. I put both of my hands in the center of Rain's ribcage, and I push down, hard and fast, a bunch of times in a row. Then I pinch Rain's nose shut and breathe into her lungs, watching her chest rise and fall.

I learned to do CPR when I was watching our pig, Gertie, have her piglets. When piglets are born, they start wiggling around right away. But there was one piglet that didn't wiggle at all. He looked dead, but my mom told me that, sometimes, even if a baby doesn't seem to be alive when they are born, they still have a little bit of life left inside them. If you massage their heart and help them breathe for a little while, sometimes they'll start breathing on their own. My mom said CPR doesn't always work. But it worked on the little piglet. We named him Miracle.

After that bully left Mary and me with her lifeless kids, I tried CPR on them. I hoped that maybe there was still a little bit of life left in them, just like there was in Miracle. I kept trying and trying for four hours—until my mom got home from work—but I couldn't get the babies to start breathing again.

My mom said CPR won't work if somebody's life is already gone. But she said it was good that I tried. She said it's never wrong to try.

And so, even though Rain doesn't seem to have any life left in her ... I try.

WEDNESDAY, MAY NINTH
2358

TIGER

The door to the star room cranks open again. I turn around expecting Rain, but it's Liam. His eyes are crazed. I've never seen him look like this before. It scares me.

"What are you doing in here?" he asks me. His voice falters as he speaks.

I don't want to explain about how much I miss Pax. So I use what Rain said to me instead, "I was just looking for some peace and quiet."

"When was the last time you saw Rain?" he asks me.

"A little while ago," I answer. "She came in here and said she was looking for peace and quiet too."

Liam lets out a curse under his breath, and then he says, "Come with me."

WEDNESDAY, MAY NINTH
0002

UNPLEASANT

Liam appears at the escape chamber door with his little sister in tow. Tiger's face contorts in shock when she sees the scene. Goat, Paris, Harley, and I are sitting cross-legged on the wet floor around Rain's body. Our own bodies are as still as death.

"Rain's dead?" Tiger squeaks out.

"Not anymore," I say. "Goat got her breathing again."

I can almost feel the relief that appears on Liam's face.

Tiger steps into the escape chamber. "Rain—" she starts.

"She hasn't woken up yet," Paris tells Tiger.

Liam's face once again looks concerned. I'm concerned too. It's possible that Rain will never wake up. That's what happened to my aunt after she had her heart attack. The doctor said that her brain was deprived of oxygen when her heart stopped. Even though they got her heart beating again, her brain was too badly damaged to recover.

"Let's get these wet clothes off her," I say. "We can dress her in her pajamas and set up a bed for her in the common room."

"I'll bring up her mattress," Harley says, heading away.

Liam scoops Rain off the floor and carries her toward the common room.

"Goat, Paris, you should go change out of your wet clothes too," I say.

The two of them nod and head off.

Tiger remains standing just inside the chamber doorway. "What can I do?" she asks me.

"I'm going to need help getting Rain into her pajamas," I say.

"I can help you with that," she says.

"Thanks," I say.

I know Tiger isn't a fan of hugs, but she really looks like she could use one right now. I walk over to her and, very gently, put my arm around her. Surprisingly, she throws both her arms around me and hugs me tight.

Maybe Tiger never liked hugs back home. I know I didn't. But our circumstances here are pretty dire, and tonight they got even worse.

I guess we could all use a little comforting right now.

WEDNESDAY, MAY NINTH
0031

GOAT

Everyone except for Liam, Unpleasant, and Harley is in the common room—the way we usually are on a normal day here. But nothing is normal now.

Rain is lying on her mattress on the common room floor. Her skin isn't bluish-purple anymore, and she's wearing her pajamas, so she kind of looks like she's asleep, but Unpleasant said that Rain is very ill, and we don't know yet if she's going to get better. Paris and I sit next to Rain, watching over her. Lizard and Tiger watch from a bit further away.

"Is it true that Goat saved Rain's life?" Lizard whispers.

"Yeah," Tiger answers. "It's good that he knew CPR."

"I don't know if that's such a good thing," Lizard says. "Rain was nothing but trouble."

My chest squeezes tight. *Does Lizard think I shouldn't have tried to help Rain?*

"Rain made some mistakes," Tiger says firmly.

"She pushed me into The Room *on purpose*," Lizard says. "And she took it upon herself to mess with the submarine's wires, all on her own, without considering the risks. She *broke* the submarine."

"The submarine isn't broken," Tiger says. "It's still running."

"All of the lights are red," Lizard says. "Something isn't right. If the submarine fails, we could all die."

"If we die, it's the kidnappers' fault, not Rain's," Tiger argues.

"Why are you sticking up for her, Tiger?" Lizard asks.

"I don't want *any* of us to die," Tiger says.

"It doesn't really matter," Lizard says.

Paris whips around. "How can you say that?"

"The chances of us getting back home are probably zero," Lizard says. "If we're not going to make it back to our families, what's the point?"

I finally stand up and face the others. "The point is we're alive."

"Goat's right," Tiger says. "And we don't know what's going to happen next."

Lizard stares down at the floor. "What if things get worse?"

"Then we'll deal with it," Paris says. "All eight of us."

"It's only seven of us," Tiger says. "Unless Rain wakes up."

Lizard's eyes go narrow. "*Even* if Rain wakes up, it's only seven of us," she says, and then she stomps away toward the bathrooms.

WEDNESDAY, MAY NINTH
0036

UNPLEASANT

Liam and I are sitting side by side in the control room. I'm wearing his sweatpants, because mine got wet when I was with Rain in the escape chamber. Liam insisted that I wear his until mine dry out because he thought I looked cold. He was right, I was cold.

"I kind of suspected that The Room was virtual reality," Harley abruptly says, breaking the silence. "On the second day in there, I tried testing it. I did everything I could think of—short of throwing myself off the top floor of The Plant—to see if I'd actually die. Probably because I was distracted by all my experimenting, a bunch of Predators snuck up and grabbed me. Ryn tried to help me, but they grabbed him too. They took us to their lair and started torturing us. It was so bad that I was convinced that I was going to find out the hard way that my VR theory was wrong. But then an alarm sounded, and the Predators ran off and left us there. Ryn's shield suit had been ripped open and his guts were … well … it was brutally obvious that he was dead. I carried his body all the way back to The Room. I didn't want to leave him where the Predators could find him, in case he was real …"

I remember how, our third day here on the sub, Harley sat on the floor of The Room after his time in there, appearing paralyzed with shock. Now I understand why.

"Did Ryn die in your simulation too?" Harley asks us.

"I had a different escort," I say. "He didn't die though."

Harley and I look at Liam, waiting for his answer.

"I was on my own in there," Liam murmurs as if he is speaking only to himself, and then he stands. "I'm going to go check on the other kids."

"They should be fine," I say. "I left them all together in the common room, and I asked Tiger to come get us if anything changes."

"They're not *fine*," Liam says. "Rain nearly died tonight … She still might die." He shakes his head. "I *can't* lose any of these kids—"

Suddenly, the sub jerks in a horrible way. I nearly fall out of my seat as the sub angles sharply upward. Liam rights me just in time.

"What the *hell* was that?" Liam shouts out.

"Everything changed all of a sudden on the monitors," Harley says. "I'm not sure why, but we're surfacing."

With that realization, ice-cold panic surges into my veins.

GOAT

Rain is the only one of us who doesn't scream. The rest of us scream and grab onto chairs or tables and hold on for our lives. I brace Rain against the wall using my feet, so she doesn't slide away.

"What's happening?" Paris cries out.

"Maybe Harley figured out how to control the submarine," Tiger says.

"What if it's the kidnappers who are doing this?" Lizard asks, sounding upset.

"I need to go to Liam," Tiger says.

Lizard throws one of her arms around Tiger. "No, it's too dangerous," she says. "Stay here."

The sub hits something with a loud boom. Anyone who wasn't holding on, or being held, would have gone flying.

There's a strange thudding and pounding and more thudding and then …

It's quiet.

WEDNESDAY, MAY NINTH
0042

TIGER

Liam and Unpleasant come running into the common room.

"Is anyone hurt?" Liam asks us.

Everyone says that they're okay. Except for Rain, because she's still asleep.

"We've surfaced, right?" Lizard asks.

"Apparently," Liam says.

"So the men will be coming for us now?" Paris asks, clutching Goat's hand.

"With any luck, they're going to pick us up in a boat or helicopter and take us somewhere else," Liam says, trying to sound reassuring.

"We should go get our weapons," Paris says, and then she adds something Liam says a lot, "Just in case."

"Let's collect everything we need," Liam says, "and then we'll all wait together here in the common room. Agreed?"

Everyone says that they agree … except for Rain, of course.

"I'll tell Harley," Unpleasant says.

WEDNESDAY, MAY NINTH
0045

UNPLEASANT

Liam and I go together to get Harley, even though it doesn't really take two people to do that. We find Harley studying the screens in the control room.

"Look at this," he says to us as we enter.

Liam and I look where he points. On a cluster of eight screens are grainy images of the inside of a building, maybe a warehouse.

Harley goes on, "Those are live video feeds from the mast of the submarine. Our deck is no longer underwater. But, according to our depth indicators, we're still two hundred thirty-four feet *below* the surface."

Liam's eyes widen. "So we've docked inside an underwater station."

My eyes scan the video images of the large empty chamber that the sub now occupies. Strangely, there are no signs of life at all.

"Shouldn't somebody be here to meet us?" I ask. "Where are the kidnappers?"

"I'm sure they're on their way," Liam says, without taking his eyes off the screens.

The feeling of dread grows inside me. "I'll gather the other kids."

WEDNESDAY, MAY NINTH
0048

TIGER

Unpleasant pokes her head into the common room. "Change of plans," she says. "We're going to wait in the control room."

"Why?" Lizard asks.

"We need to keep an eye on the monitors," Unpleasant explains.

Lizard, Goat, and Paris grab our weapons and head up to the control room. Unpleasant and I lift Rain on her mattress and bring her to the hallway below it. It would be too risky to carry Rain up the ladder, so we decide to leave her here, on the main floor. I volunteer to stay with her, and Unpleasant volunteers to keep me company.

From down here, Unpleasant and I listen as Harley explains that we've docked inside an underwater hangar of some sort. Weirdly, the kidnappers don't seem to be coming for us yet. It's as if they're giving us time to prepare for their arrival. But we've already prepared in the only ways we can think of—

Out of the corner of my eye, I sense some movement. I look down at Rain in time to see her eyes snap shut.

"Rain, you're awake," I say.

She grimaces and opens her eyes, squinting against the dim red light.

"I've been awake for a while," she says. "I just wasn't sure I wanted to be."

"How are you feeling?" Unpleasant asks her.

"Alive," Rain says. "Otherwise I feel okay."

"So you went in the escape chamber because you wanted to die?" I ask.

Unpleasant gives me a look that makes me think that I've asked a question that shouldn't have been asked. But why not ask it? I'm just trying to understand what Rain was thinking.

"Yes, I wanted to die," Rain says.

She answered my question, so I ask another one. "Why did you want to die?"

"Because I didn't want to be trapped in a place where everyone hates me," she says. "But when I was standing in that chamber, with the water rushing in, it gave me time to think. The pocket of air between the water and the escape hatch was getting smaller and smaller, and I knew that, when the escape hatch opened, I was going to drown. I would be dead. Gone. No more second chances. And I realized that I didn't really want to die.

"I dove down to the control panel to stop the water from coming in but, when I did that, some water got in my nose, and I panicked, and then I swallowed a whole lot of water, and I needed air, but I couldn't get it. And all I could think was, *It's over.* And it was. The whole world disappeared.

"I woke up on the common room floor and, at first, I thought I'd been really lucky that someone had rescued me. But then I heard Lizard talking about how if I had died it would have been a good thing, and I thought maybe it would be better for the rest of you if I wasn't here."

"She was just angry with you," I say.

"Everyone hates me," Rain argues.

"I don't hate you," I say.

"I don't hate you either and Liam doesn't," Unpleasant

says. "And Goat saved your life. Paris and Harley and I were right by his side when he did it. I don't think anyone here hates you. They might be angry about some of the things you did. Very angry, maybe."

Tears form in Rain's eyes. "So what do you think I should do?"

"You can apologize," Unpleasant says gently. "And then you can show that you want to be part of this team. That you won't take actions on your own that could put any of us in jeopardy. Not even yourself. You got a second chance, Rain. Don't screw it up."

Tears fall down Rain's cheeks, but she doesn't say a word.

UNPLEASANT

There was a time in my life when I wanted to die, but I never tried to make it happen. I guess that's because, unlike Rain, I tend to think things through to an almost obsessive degree before I do them. And every possible outcome of killing myself was bad.

I thought of all the people who would be upset if I died: My dad. My grandmother. My uncle. My cousin. Hesper Johnson, the only person at my school who didn't laugh when I was being humiliated. Mr. Rainville, the only teacher who didn't make me feel like I was a waste of their time. And my mom. I'm sure all of those people would have eventually gotten over my death and moved on with their lives, except for my mom. I don't think she could have gone on if I committed suicide. I didn't want to end her life, and so I never ended mine.

As soon as Rain says she's feeling up to it, Tiger and I help her climb the ladder. When we enter the control room, relief spills over Liam's face. The other kids turn and look at Rain, and they keep looking. Liam offers her his seat, since it's the closest to the ladder, but she waves him off and sits on the floor.

Finally, Rain speaks, "I want to apologize for the reckless things I've done. I put all of you at risk because of my actions. And that wasn't right. I know my apology probably doesn't mean very much to any of you, because you don't trust me, and I respect that. I know it's going to take time for me to earn your trust. But I hope I get that chance. I want to be part of this team … if you'll have me."

Rain takes a shaky breath and her lower lip quivers. She seems to be finished talking, but no one makes any response to what she said. I understand why they might hesitate, though. An apology is only words. They want to see if her actions back it up.

But Rain is hurting right now. She needs to know that someone cares about her. And so I walk over to her, and help her to her feet, and give her a hug. And then Paris comes and hugs her too. And Liam. And Goat. Tiger shakes her hand. Harley holds out a fist and lightly bumps it with Rain's. And Lizard gives her a nod, which means a lot coming from Lizard.

And then everyone goes back to watching the monitors.

And waiting.

WEDNESDAY, MAY NINTH
0543

GOAT

We've been all together in the control room for a long while now. There have been no more alarms or beeps or thuds or booms. Nothing has changed on the monitors. According to the submarine's cameras, the hangar that we are inside is still deserted.

"Why hasn't anyone come for us?" Paris asks softly.

"I don't know," Liam says.

"Maybe they're waiting for us to come out," Harley suggests.

"You might be right," Liam says.

He stands up from his chair. Everyone else stands up too.

"It looks like we're all in agreement," Lizard says.

"All right then!" Harley says. "Let's roll!"

WEDNESDAY, MAY NINTH
0548

UNPLEASANT

We probably resemble a group of preschoolers heading off on a make-believe adventure—with our makeshift weapons and ragtag uniforms: a mix of pajamas, underwear, and sweatsuits. But this is no children's game.

I help Liam dismantle our crude efforts at securing the main hatch of the submarine, then he unlocks it and spins the wheel beneath it. There is a subtle sucking sound as the hatch opens. A bit of water drips onto my forehead. I wipe it away and climb the ladder, clutching my weapon—a heavy crowbar that we found in a tool locker.

I step out onto the top of the submarine and look down at the imposing black vessel beneath me. What I see doesn't seem real. But this must be real. I'm not wearing any kind of suit to fool me, and the surface under my bare feet feels cold and rough.

The submarine rests in a thin channel of water, and a delicate-looking walkway bridges the space between the sub and the floor of the hangar.

Strangely, even though we are now emerging from the submarine, no one has come to intercept us. The kidnappers *must* be watching us. *What are they waiting for?*

Once we have all exited the sub, Liam closes the hatch. He tests the walkway with his foot, and it seems sturdy enough, so he cautiously heads across. After he has reached the other side, we follow, crossing one at a time. Although the walkway quivers a bit as we traverse it, it manages to hold.

We move as a group across the smooth grey floor, heading toward the only doorway. Since none of us is wearing shoes, our footsteps are quiet, but this feels like the kind of space where sound would echo endlessly. My supposition is confirmed when Liam unlocks the heavy metal door and it creaks open. If the men somehow didn't already know that we are here, they know now. The deep echoes have no doubt alerted everyone in this place that we are making a move.

Liam peers through the slightly-open doorway, weapon in hand, looking like a swat officer in a movie, and then he pulls the door open all the way, revealing a second door just a few feet ahead of us. The second door refuses to open, though. The light above it is red.

"This looks like an airlock," Liam says. "We probably have to close the first door before the second one will open."

We all step inside the possible airlock and Liam pulls the first door closed. The tiny room fills with odorless white smoke, just like the airlocks at The Plant. I close my eyes and try not to breathe, hoping the smoke clears quickly. Despite my claustrophobia issues, the airlocks in The Plant never really bothered me. Maybe that's because Kev was my guide there, letting me know the supposed right path to take. Here, we have no reassurance that this is a relatively safe way to proceed. What if it's not? What if the second door doesn't open, and the first one locks, and we are trapped inside here for the rest of our lives?

Before I can consider any other horrible scenarios, the second door slides open, revealing a cylindrical dark chamber with no further doors.

"It's an elevator," Tiger says, pointing to the buttons on the wall.

There are only two choices: "G" and "ONE."

Liam pushes both buttons, but only the "ONE" illuminates.

About a minute later, the elevator seems to click into position, and the door reopens. I feel my eyes go wide and my jaw fall slack. Ahead of us is the most extraordinary place I've ever seen. It is vaguely reminiscent of a luxury hotel combined with an aquarium, but far more spectacular than either one. Its rounded walls feature large windows framed by glistening silver. Outside those windows is a bright blue-green ocean teeming with fish: schools of silver ones, and yellow and black ones, and brilliant blue ones. A crystal-clear spiral staircase blooms from the center of the room toward a glass ceiling that sparkles with sunlight shrouded by the ocean. The staircase sends out four branches, each curving upward, like the petals of a flower, to reach one of the four stories of this impressive structure.

"Where are the bad guys?" Paris asks.

Unbelievably, I'd nearly forgotten about the kidnappers. Maybe that's because it doesn't seem possible that anything bad could exist in a place this magnificent.

"They must be here somewhere," Liam says, bringing me back to reality.

He starts up the staircase, and the rest of us follow. Cautiously, we explore each of the four seemingly-unoccupied stories, peering through doorways to discover numerous spaces … A work-out room with state-of-the-art equipment. Two apartments, each with a living room, a spacious bathroom, and a bedroom with a king-size bed. An automated store with fully-stocked vending machines. Another two apartments. A mini hospital with eight treatment pods. An aquaponic greenhouse without any plants or fish. A room of pumps and

277

humming equipment that must be responsible for keeping this place alive. Four more apartments. A digital library and interactive virtual education room stocked with over two hundred million books and lessons. A kitchen with a pantry full of canned and boxed food items. A laundry room. A provisions room with everything from cleaning supplies to toilet paper to toothpaste. And a room of monitors, all of which display nothing on their screens when we turn them on. This entire place looks ready for occupants—complete with crisp linens on the beds and clean fluffy towels in the bathrooms—but there is no evidence that there have ever been occupants here.

Liam exhales once we have explored the final room. "I guess we've seen it all."

"I'm so tired," Paris says.

"Me too," Goat agrees.

"Let's go back to the sub, so you can get some sleep," Liam says.

"Why don't we sleep in here?" Paris asks.

"I think it's best if we stay in the sub for now," Liam says. "We don't know if this place is ours to occupy."

One by one the others agree. And so we all head back to the place that was once our prison.

And, in a way, still is.

WEDNESDAY, MAY NINTH
0702

GOAT

I was almost too tired to drag my mattress up to the common room, but Liam said we should all sleep here, instead of in our bedrooms, so we can be together. He's right, I guess. The bad guys could come at any minute. But until they do, we need to get some sleep.

As soon as I close my eyes, a quiet sound makes me open them. In the red light, I see Liam and Unpleasant creeping out of the common room. I wonder where they are going, but I'm too tired to ask. I'm too tired to do anything but sleep. And so I close my eyes again.

UNPLEASANT

I would like nothing more than to lie down and rest right now, but Liam asked me if I would accompany him on a walk, and I want to be there for him, the way he always seems to be for me.

I follow Liam back into the underwater compound and up to the top of the spiral staircase. Then we walk past each of the rooms, looking inside every one. It feels like we are repeating what we just did with the others, except that, this time, in each room, Liam calls out, "Hello! Is anyone here?" Not surprisingly, there is no response to Liam's calls.

We finally make it back down to the lowest level, after having reexplored the entire compound. I hope that Liam is satisfied. Maybe now we can rejoin the others on the sub and get some much needed rest.

But Liam doesn't head for the elevator. Instead, he tilts his face up toward the ceiling and calls out, "Where the hell are you?" His voice echoes loudly in the space. Rupturing the quiet.

"There's no one here but us, Liam," I say, unsure of why he hasn't already come to the same conclusion.

"There *has* to be," he says quietly.

"The kidnappers are probably planning to keep us here until they're ready for us," I say. "I think they're fairly certain that we can't escape from this place on our own."

"But he was supposed to be here," Liam says, almost to himself.

"*Who* was supposed to be here?" I ask.

Liam shakes his head, as if he's fighting to wake up from a nightmare that won't let him go, and then he whispers, "My dad."

Is Liam losing his mind? Or is the stress and lack of sleep starting to get the best of him? Or maybe his heart just doesn't accept the fact that our parents haven't come yet to rescue us.

"Your dad doesn't know where we are," I say gently.

Liam finally looks into my eyes. "My dad helped kidnap us."

My blood turns cold. "What?" I breathe.

"Your dad did too," he says.

I back away from him. "You're not making any sense."

"The night we were kidnapped, a global war was imminent, even worse than World War Three," Liam says. "Our dads had us put in that submarine because it was the only way they knew of to protect us. The sub was supposed to take us to a place where we would be safe. My dad *promised* he would be there."

My tired mind tries to grasp what Liam is saying. His story sounds like the mutterings of someone who has gone mad but, knowing what I know about my dad, there is a very small chance that everything Liam is saying is one-hundred-percent true.

"What does your dad do for a living?" I ask Liam.

I don't usually tell people what *my* dad does for a living. From the time I was little, he told me that it is best not to talk to strangers about his profession. The only people who knew anything about it were close friends and family. Navy SEALs like to keep their work private.

"My dad works for a research firm," Liam says. "But he's a former SEAL."

And so what Liam told me might be true.

But is it really possible that my own dad had me kidnapped?

"My father wouldn't have done all this without telling me," I say.

"There wasn't time," Liam says. "My dad is the only one out of all of our dads who isn't currently deployed. He told *me* the truth so there would be someone on the sub who knew what was going on."

"Why didn't you tell me this before now?" I ask.

"Back when we were trapped in that submarine, if I'd told you that our dads had us locked up in there because the world was about to be destroyed, you would have thought I was crazy."

To be honest, I don't think I would have believed Liam back then. And I'm not sure whether to believe him now. But I don't think he's crazy. I have an even more terrible concern.

It seems unlikely that World War Four just suddenly happened out of nowhere. There was no indication of any significant unrest in the world in the days before we were kidnapped.

Liam has been keeping secrets from us the entire time we were on the sub. What if what he is telling me now is a lie?

What if Liam is one of the bad guys?

And so I am left with two horrible possibilities ...

Either Liam is telling the truth, and the world is coming to an end.

Or he is lying, and my world is coming to an end.

Tears flood my eyes as my fears come crashing down around me. I bolt up the staircase, trying to flee them, even though there is no escape. The only thing that keeps me from falling apart is that I know exactly where I'm heading and what I'm going to do when I get there.

WEDNESDAY, MAY NINTH
0745

TIGER

DING. DING.

I feel like the bell woke me from the deepest sleep of my life.

It's meal time. Breakfast, I guess.

When I think about it, I *am* hungry, but I'm more tired than hungry. Even so, I should probably eat. I sit up on my mattress and see the others walking their sleepy selves to the boxes in the food dispenser.

And then I notice that two of us aren't here: Liam and Unpleasant.

But where are they?

Why aren't they with us?

WEDNESDAY, MAY NINTH
0748

UNPLEASANT

I move through the kitchen pantry, opening boxes, removing packages from inside them, gathering what I'm going to eat. I need to make my pain go away, even if it's only for a little while. I need to feel numb. And there is enough food here in this pantry to make that happen. The urge to eat rises inside me like a wave about to smother me. I ache for food. In my mouth, in my throat, in the pit of my stomach. It is the only thing in the world that I want now.

But a sudden thought stops me cold.

It might be the only thing capable of stopping me right now.

I don't want to hurt the other kids.

If what Liam told me is true, who knows how long we're going to be trapped here? The food in this pantry isn't going to feed eight people for very long. If we run out of food, we'll die of starvation. What's worse, we'll have to watch each other die of starvation. No matter what I do in this moment, that horrible scenario may eventually play out. But I can't … I won't … allow myself to hasten its arrival. I won't waste our precious food. I won't give in to my urge to binge. Not now, and maybe not ever again. That thought makes my throat burn with anxiety.

I lie down on the floor and stare up at the ceiling. I don't allow myself to move, except to breathe. I count each breath, in and out, the way the stupid therapist said to do when the world is spinning so fast that it's making me sick.

I will stay right here on this floor until my urge to binge passes.

It will pass, I promise myself. *It will pass.*

I hug my body, thinking about how it felt when Liam held me last night. The way his touch seemed to lift me up. But now, when I try to lift myself up—even just enough so there is sufficient air to breathe—it feels impossible.

Suddenly, through the blur of my tears, I see Liam. His concerned eyes look at me, and then at all of the packages of food strewn about me.

"What happened?" he asks.

It takes a few moments before I feel like I can speak.

"I wanted to make the pain go away," I finally say.

"How?" he asks.

"By eating so much that my stomach feels like it's going to explode," I say. "And then I was going to vomit it all out."

His forehead creases. "Have you done that before?"

"Too many times," I say. "I'm even more screwed up than you realized, aren't I?"

"Nobody is normal once you get to know them," he says, still looking concerned.

"I thought *you* were pretty normal," I say.

"Well, I'm not," he says, looking straight into my blurry eyes, and then he swallows hard, "I don't know how I would have made it this far without you."

"Why should I believe anything you say?" I ask him, pleading for an answer that makes sense.

"You don't trust me?" he asks.

"I'm trying, Liam," I say. "I am really trying. But it's hard to know what to believe."

"I understand." He reaches to his waist and slides his thumb under the top of his boxers. I freeze until he flips the waistband over and pulls out a tiny black plastic case—about the size of a dime—from a tear in the seam. Liam opens the case. Inside is a data storage chip. Liam continues, "My dad gave me this."

"What's on it?" I ask.

"He didn't say," he says.

Liam and I walk to the room with all those blank monitors. Liam sits down at a terminal off to the side and examines the input slots. There are spots to insert any type of input I can think of, even some that I don't recognize. Carefully, Liam inserts his chip into one of the slots. A moment later, three icons appear on one of the screens. He touches the first one, a plain yellow folder labeled simply: "1MAY."

The folder opens, and my breath catches in my chest. I stare at the image that now fills the screen. It shows six men sitting in a darkened room, wearing faded green cammies. I point to one of the men in disbelief.

"That's my dad," I whisper.

Liam doesn't have to point out his dad. In the lower right corner of the main image is a small square picture of a man who looks unmistakably like an older version of Liam.

A red arrow sits over the center of the larger image. Liam touches it, and the video begins to play. It's a recording of the conferencing system that my dad uses on those very rare occasions when he gets to talk to us during his deployments. When I was younger, my mom used to record our video calls, so I could rewatch them again later, because I never got enough of seeing my dad during our always-too-brief conversations.

The man sitting next to my dad speaks first. "Hey, kiddo," he says in a gravelly voice. "I didn't say it enough, but you know I love you. Whatever happens in your life, I want you to keep going ... *Never* give up ..." The man's jaw clenches tight, an expression that makes me wonder if he's trying not to cry, even though he looks too strong to ever cry.

The man nods at my dad, and my dad looks right at the camera. It almost feels like he can see me through the screen. I focus on every movement, every word. "Hi, Button," my dad says. "Sorry, I guess you're too old for a nickname like that." His forehead furrows painfully. "Anyway, when I was your age, I was ... a lot like you. In good ways and in bad ways. I used to spend a hell of a lot of time and energy pushing away the people who cared about me the most. I still do that sometimes. I wish I could have convinced you to stop pushing."

One at a time, each of the other men speaks, saying the kinds of things that might be privately uttered to loved ones by people on their death beds. They sound like they're saying their final goodbyes.

Liam's dad is the last to speak. "Little girl," he starts out, talking to Tiger, "You're one of the most courageous people I ever met. I know you won't believe that, but it's true. And, my son ... I just ... I'm sorry."

And then the video is over.

Liam stares at the image, frozen on his father's final word to him. I can't help but wonder what his dad was apologizing for.

Liam shakes away what he's seen and turns to me. "Your nickname was Button?" he asks.

"No," I say.

"Then why would your dad call you that?" he asks.

"Do you remember, about eight years ago, when those Delta Force guys were supposedly captured and held hostage, but it turned out it was all a hoax?" I ask.

Liam nods. "Yeah."

In videos that were released to the public, the Delta Force guys said and did horrible things. The videos looked so authentic that even the experts couldn't tell that they were manufactured. It terrified me to think that someday I might see a video like that of my dad, and I wouldn't know whether or not it was really him.

"Back then, I asked my dad how I would know if a video I saw of him was real," I say. "He thought about it and said that, if he was going to say anything to or about me, he'd use a code word. I asked him to use Button. Only my dad and I knew about that."

And so I know that what I just saw was real.

Liam closes the video and touches the second icon on the screen: an unlabeled small blue square. An instant later, a checkerboard of dark boxes fills the screen. One by one, the boxes populate with a single word: "Connecting." The word flashes every second or so.

"Connecting?" I ask. "To what?"

And then comes a disappointing change in one of the boxes. The word "Connecting" is replaced with "Live feed unavailable." But, a moment later, the darkness fades into an image of the west coast of the United States as seen from outer space. The timestamp is from May first of this year at 08:23:05 UTC. And then an image of Australia appears in a different box, with a timestamp a few minutes earlier.

They're satellite images from the night we were kidnapped.

Slowly, more images fill the dark squares. All have a timestamp from May first ... except for one. At the bottom of the newest square to populate is a word in red: "LIVE," along with a timestamp from May ninth and a clock that starts at

13:17:36 UTC and ticks ahead with each passing second. This image features the United Kingdom, but most of the land is shrouded in grey-white clouds. I touch the image, and it enlarges to fill the screen. When I zoom in for a closer look, I realize that what I'd thought were clouds are actually plumes of smoke. I can only see glimpses of what is beneath them, but what I see turns my stomach. There are horrifying *holes*. Places where homes and buildings abruptly end, leaving nothing but grey emptiness.

When I minimize the image, I see that the main grid is now fully-populated. Liam enlarges an image of the east coast of the United States labeled "LIVE." He zooms in on Washington, D.C., which is mostly obscured by plumes of smoke. He zooms in further ... and further ...

"The White House is gone," he breathes. "And so is the Pentagon." He zooms in on an area just to the east. An area of nothingness. "My house is gone too," he says, and his hand falls from the screen.

Maybe I shouldn't do it, but I zoom out and then zoom in on my hometown. When I see what's there, my throat squeezes tight. My entire town has vanished. There are no houses. No trees. It's as if I'm looking at the surface of the moon rather than the place where I once rode my bike, and went to school, and lived almost every day of my life.

I go back to the main screen and select the third—and final—icon. A ray of hope illuminates inside me as the MilComm insignia appears on the screen. MilComm is the secure messaging system that we use to contact my dad during his deployments. But, when the system finally opens, a single line of text repeats over and over, all the way down the screen: "Secure connection failed." I scroll down to the very bottom and read: "MilComm fatal system error. No route to host."

My tiny ray of hope flickers into darkness. I'm sure our dads were certain that we would be able to use this system to communicate with someone who could help us. My dad told me that the MilComm system is indestructible. He said the only way the system would go down was if the entire planet was essentially annihilated.

"What about our moms?" I ask Liam, my voice shaking. "Our dads couldn't have just left them there to die."

"My dad said our moms were going to be taken to an underground bunker. He said it wasn't as safe as a submarine, but he only had access to one sub and that sub would only accommodate eight people. The kidnappers and their families were supposed to end up in the underground bunker with our moms."

"The kidnappers?" I ask.

"They were buddies of our dads. Former military," Liam says.

There is no doubt in my mind now that Liam has told me the truth. Our dads arranged to have us kidnapped and put on that sub. It was the best way they could think of to protect us. They believed that our lives were in imminent danger. They believed that the world was about to come to an end.

And it did.

WEDNESDAY, MAY NINTH
1200

GOAT

DING. DING.

It's time to eat again. I crawl out of bed, take one of the little boxes of food from the dispenser, and eat without thinking about what I'm eating. I'm still mostly asleep and only a little bit awake. Liam and Unpleasant are back with us, after they missed breakfast. Liam's eyes are red and puffy, and so are Unpleasant's. It looks like they've both been crying.

After I finish my lunch and put the empty box in the dispenser, I lie back down on my mattress. Just as soon as I close my eyes, I hear someone clear their throat, so I open my eyes again. Liam and Unpleasant are standing up.

"I need everyone to come with me," Liam says. "There's something I need to show you."

Quietly, we follow him inside the hangar, and up in the elevator, and upstairs. He takes us to the room with the computers. And then he tells us a story that sounds like a horrible nightmare. It's about us. And the world. The worst part is, he says the story is true. Then he shows us proof.

When Liam is done, everyone is crying except for Unpleasant, Liam, and Harley.

"You knew about all this the whole time we were on the sub?" Harley asks Liam.

Liam nods. "Most of it."

"And you let us believe that we were being held hostage by

a bunch of lunatics?" Lizard asks.

"Our dads thought it was best if we were in the dark about things until we got here," Liam says.

"But *your* dad told *you*," Harley says. "We should have *all* been told."

"We shouldn't have been kidnapped like that," Lizard says.

"If your mom or dad had asked you to go willingly, would you have gone?" Liam asks.

"You did," Harley says.

Liam shakes his head. "Who says I went willingly?"

"Did our dads tell the kidnappers to shave off our hair?" Rain asks.

"I don't know," Liam says. "My dad didn't mention that."

"Why would our dads let the starry room be mean to us?" Paris asks.

Liam rubs his forehead as if it hurts. "Who knows if they meant for everything to happen the way it did. You never really know how things are going to go down until they do."

"Maybe our dads didn't know about the starry room," I say. "*They* didn't open it. The *submarine* did."

"*Somebody* was controlling the submarine," Lizard says.

"Actually, as far as I can tell, the sub was controlling itself," Harley says. "It appears that it was designed to autonomously transport people here and meet all of their basic needs along the way."

"So, once our dads had us dropped off in the sub, an artificial intelligence program was in charge of *everything*?" Lizard asks.

"Including babysitting us?" Tiger asks.

"I think so," Harley says.

"But why would a *submarine* be mean to us?" Paris asks.

Rain looks down at the floor. "Because I broke its

'window.'"

It *is* true that the starry room opened for the first time a little while after Rain kicked the "window" off the wall.

"Then why did it punish *all of us*," I ask.

"It wasn't trying to punish us," Tiger says softly. "It was trying to help us."

Unpleasant nods her head. "It was teaching us to face our fears. Not always directly, though. More like the way you work through things in your dreams."

"It was a little harsh with us, don't you think?" Lizard asks.

"The world is fairly harsh right now," Harley says.

"Do you think the AI is still babysitting us now?" Tiger asks.

"It must be," Unpleasant says. "It wouldn't bring us all the way here and then abandon us."

It makes me nervous to think that an AI is responsible for looking after me. I guess maybe *some* AIs are better babysitters than *some* human beings. But I'm not sure about this one.

"So what do we do now?" Rain asks.

Liam swallows hard. "I guess we settle into our new home."

WEDNESDAY, MAY NINTH
1337

UNPLEASANT

I don't think there's anything I can do right now to help the other kids cope with what has happened. They seem like they need some time to process what they've learned. So I collect everyone's dirty clothes and take them to our new laundry room. It's much bigger than the one on the submarine, and an entire wall provides a view of the ocean.

As I begin the wash, Liam enters with his rumpled sweatshirt balled up in his arms.

"Am I too late?" he asks.

"No," I say. "I just started the machine."

He lifts the lid on the washer and drops his laundry into the swirling water, then he leans against the dryer. "How are you holding up?" he asks me.

"I think I'm still in shock," I say. "But, at least for right now, I don't want to eat myself sick."

"Did you do that a lot back home?" he asks.

Exhaustion dulls my resistance to answer him honestly. "I used to do it a few times a week, but then one night I vomited up some blood, and I got scared. After that, I got it down to about three or four times a month. But even that is way too much. It's just that, when I'm feeling really bad, I can't *not* do it."

"You didn't do it today," he says.

"We can't afford to waste any food here," I say. "I'm okay

with hurting myself. But I don't want to hurt anyone else."

Liam looks down at the floor. "By hurting yourself, you *do* hurt other people."

"I know," I admit. "But I've been doing this for so long that it feels like I need to do it in order to survive."

"When did you start?" Liam asks.

"In sixth grade. I got a little chubby, and my two 'best friends' started saying hurtful things about me behind my back. When I asked them to stop, they beat me up in the gym locker room. They stomped on me so hard that they broke my arm. But that didn't stop them. Every time I went to school, I was bombarded with nasty comments or surreptitious punches or 'accidental' shoves. I felt like a ticking time bomb. Like I was racing closer and closer to the moment when I explode and disappear."

"We're all time bombs," Liam says. "Everyone in the world is dying from the day they're born. We're all going to disappear someday."

"Thanks for the pep talk," I say.

"Sorry," he says. "I suck when it comes to stuff like this."

"No, you don't," I say. "I don't know exactly how you do it, but you always seem to make me feel better. I don't think it's *what* you say. I think it's the way you look at me."

He cocks his head to the side and his brow furrows. "How do I look at you?"

"Like I matter," I say.

Instead of seeming pleased by what I said, Liam seems disquieted by it.

"What's wrong?" I ask him.

"There's something I need to do," he says.

WEDNESDAY, MAY NINTH
1356

TIGER

I could be happy here, pedaling this stationary bike toward a giant window with a view of the inside of the ocean. But I'm too sad to be happy.

I keep thinking about my last night in my house. Just before I went to bed, my mom and I read a chapter of *Harry Potter*, the same way we always did. She read the narration, and I read the dialogue using silly voices that made my mom laugh, just like always. My dad came into my room to say goodnight a few minutes later. He acted pretty normal, except that he lingered longer than usual. It wasn't long enough that I questioned it at the time but, now that I think about it, I'm sure he knew it could be the last time he ever wished me goodnight. He touched two fingers to his lips and then to my forehead, which is the way he always kissed me at bedtime, because I don't like regular kisses. That night, he held his fingers on my forehead for a much longer time than ever before. It was as if he didn't want to lift them—

A sudden reflection appears in the glass of the ocean window. I turn and see Liam standing just inside the doorway to the workout room.

"Can I join you?" he asks me.

I wipe the tears from my eyes. "Sure," I say.

Liam steps up onto the treadmill that's beside me and starts walking, but his walk quickly transforms into a jog.

"Do you remember when we were on the way home from Andrew's funeral, in the back seat of the car, and you said you didn't feel like you mattered anymore?" he asks me.

"Yes, I remember," I say.

"Did you really believe that you didn't matter?" he asks.

"I said that because I was angry at you," I say.

"At *me*?" Liam asks.

"During Andrew's funeral, you said that you wanted to be a Navy SEAL," I say. "Dad was a SEAL and he lost both his legs and nearly died. Andrew was a SEAL and he *did* die. I was afraid I was going to lose you too."

"Why didn't you say that back then?" he asks.

"What *I* wanted wasn't going to change anything," I say. "Just like it didn't change anything for Andrew. What *I* wanted didn't matter."

"But *you* mattered to Andrew," Liam says.

Tears fill my eyes again. "I know," I say.

"And you matter to *me*," he adds.

"I know that," I say.

"You do?" Liam asks.

"Sometimes I wasn't so sure when we were back home," I say. "But *now* I know I matter to you."

He exhales softly. "Good."

Without another word, Liam picks up his pace, and so do I. Both of us race toward the big window that looks out on the ocean. Me on my stationary bike, and Liam on his treadmill. Him running. Me pedaling. Traveling together, even though we're barely moving at all.

WEDNESDAY, MAY NINTH
1421

UNPLEASANT

While I wait for our clothes to finish drying, I sit and watch a school of orange fish dart back and forth in the calm blue ocean. It's good to see that the fish are alive and well here. It gives me hope that maybe the Earth hasn't been completely destroyed. Only time will tell though. The aftermath of war can be far worse than the initial insult.

A soft sound behind me makes me jump. I spin around and see Lizard standing in the doorway. Like me, she's wearing her pajamas, making her look a little vulnerable. I assume she's here to see about her sweatsuit.

"The laundry is in the dryer," I tell her as I glance at the timer. "It should be ready in about ten minutes."

"Okay, thanks." She awkwardly turns to go, but then she seems to change her mind. She turns back toward me, but stares at her feet. "I came by a while ago, and I heard you talking to Liam …"

My pulse quickens, and my cheeks burn uncomfortably. I didn't want anyone to hear what I said to Liam. I'm not even sure if I really wanted Liam to hear it.

"I shouldn't have stayed to listen," Lizard continues, "but when I heard what you were saying … it made me think that, maybe, you might understand."

"Understand what?" I ask her.

Her gaze finally meets mine. "Those bruises you saw on me

... They were from back home." She looks away, as if she's embarrassed by her admission. "I was my stepdad's personal punching bag," she adds. "I never told my mom or dad."

I think of all those horrible bruises on Lizard's body. It's hard to imagine a grown man doing that to a child, especially someone who he was supposed to care for.

She shrugs self-consciously. "Half the time I deserved it."

Her words make me shudder. "You *never* deserved that," I say.

"It doesn't matter now," Lizard says.

"It *does* matter," I say. "Because even after the bruises disappear, the scars inside you are still there."

Lizard's gaze softens. Maybe she finally believes that I do understand.

"Those scars don't go away, do they?" she asks.

"I hope they do for you," I say. "They haven't for me. Not yet anyway."

"Liam will help you," Lizard says.

"The only person who can really help me is me," I say. "But it does help to talk about it with someone who cares. If you ever want to talk about it, just let me know, all right?"

She smiles a little. It's a somber smile, but it's the most I've ever seen Lizard smile. "Can I ... wait for the laundry with you?" she asks. "Maybe we could talk."

"Sure," I say.

I nod at the seat beside me, and Lizard sits down.

And we talk.

WEDNESDAY, MAY NINTH
1745

GOAT

Our new "home" gave us dinner tonight. I guess that means it is going to take care of us, like the submarine did. That's good … I hope.

Liam and Unpleasant said we could each pick our very own apartment here, but Paris and I decided to choose one apartment for the both of us.

I crawl into the great big bed, and Paris climbs in after me. We lie down side by side and look up at the clean white ceiling, and my eyes fill with tears.

"Are you okay, Goat?" Paris whispers.

I tell her the truth, "I'm not okay."

"I'm not okay either," she says.

Paris takes a big breath, and then she grabs my hand and holds it tight.

"We can't let this break us," she says.

"We won't," I say.

"Promise?" Paris asks.

I wipe my eyes with my fist. "I promise."

WEDNESDAY, MAY NINTH
1835

UNPLEASANT

I just took the most luxurious shower I've ever taken. The water smelled like lavender, and the towel that I used to dry myself afterward was the softest I could ever imagine. Liam postulates that the high-tech submarine and this opulent underwater structure were meant for the executives at his dad's company in the event of a catastrophe. It sounds like, unfortunately for the executives, they weren't aware that a catastrophe was coming until it came.

I enter the bedroom of the apartment that Liam and I have selected as ours. We decided that we will share the same apartment, at least for now. We don't have much privacy, though. We've left our doors unlocked, telling the other kids that they can come by whenever they need us, even in the middle of the night. We want them to know that we're all in this together. No one here should ever feel alone.

I join Liam in the tremendous bed. Like the towels, the sheets are unimaginably soft. Even softer than my Hello Kitty nightgown, which is what I'm wearing now. Liam is wearing his grey t-shirt and boxers. Being in bed with him like this feels extremely intimate. Even more intimate than last night's kiss.

But, even after I settle in bed, Liam remains facing away from me.

"I'm sorry I didn't tell you the truth until today," he says.

"Maybe it would have been easier for you if you'd known what was really going on from the beginning."

"I don't think there was an *easy* way to do this," I say. "Actually, I think it would have been harder for me if I'd known that my dad had me sent away before I saw with my own eyes why he did it."

"Do you think there's any chance our dads are still alive?" Liam asks me.

I shake my head. "If they were alive, we would know it."

Liam is quiet for a while before he says, "Back when we were on the sub, I wasn't convinced that what my dad told me was the truth. I thought it was possible that everything we were going through was some kind of elaborate test. Especially what happened in The Plant."

"What happened to you in The Plant?" I ask, hoping he'll finally answer.

He inhales deeply. "Every time I went in there, no matter what I did, I was ambushed by Predators. They clamped weights to my arms and legs and tossed me into a network of dark tunnels filled with electrified water that made my flesh burn. There were dead bodies in the water ... so many bodies that it was impossible to avoid bumping into them. It was like a horrific maze. The only escape was through hatches on the ceiling. Most of them led nowhere, and I had to climb back down into the painful water to find another one. Eventually, though, I always found a hatch that led to an escape."

"But you knew all that wasn't real," I say.

"I figured it had to be some kind of virtual reality simulation, even though I'd never seen VR *that* convincing," he says. "I was sure there was no actual danger. But that didn't make the pain less real. The thing is, as bad as it was, when I left, I always wanted to go back."

"Why?" I ask. The only reason I went back into The Room day after day was because I was hoping to find a way to escape from our captors.

"I felt like I was overcoming my weaknesses," he says. "After a while, I actually started to believe that I might someday become a person my dad would be proud of."

"You don't think your dad was proud of you?" I ask.

"I wasn't the kind of son he wanted," he says. "My brother, Andrew, was. He was a SEAL, like my dad. When Andrew died, I said I wanted to become a SEAL, to finish what Andrew started. After that, my dad got me scuba certified and, to celebrate, he took me on a cave dive in Mexico. He was so excited about it, because it was his favorite dive in the world. We were deep inside the cave, and I was moving through this really narrow underwater passageway, and my light went out, and suddenly it was pitch black. I panicked. Not just a little panic, but a full-on freak out. I took my regulator out of my mouth. How the hell did I expect to breathe without an air hose? After that, I was sure I could never be a SEAL. We both were. When we finally made it back to dry land, my dad told me that he was disappointed in me. It was the worst thing he'd ever said to me. I think maybe that's what he was apologizing for in that video."

My mind jumps back to what Liam's dad said to him in the goodbye video: *I'm sorry.* He offered no explanation, but the way he looked into the camera, with his eyes filled with pain, I could tell that his words came straight from his heart.

Liam's dad could have been apologizing for *anything.* But maybe he was apologizing for *everything.* For all those cutting things that we say and do to people we love out of anger or frustration. The things that we later regret but never revisit because we're afraid to stir up bad feelings. There are so many apologies that I wish I'd made. So much I wish I could say to the people I loved …

"I'm sure your dad was proud of you," I say to Liam. "You're courageous and smart and … kind. And kindness is the most important thing of all. I think that's why I haven't been afraid to let you see the real me. Not the me who I created to show to the world. The raw and imperfect me. The one I'm still too scared to let anyone else see."

Liam turns toward me and looks into my eyes so deeply that I feel like he can see all the way to my soul. "I feel *exactly* the same way," he whispers.

I close my eyes and feel our lips meet. We kiss so intensely that I can barely think. So fiercely that I can barely breathe. It's different than last night's kiss. Now, when I kiss Liam, there are no uncertainties in my mind … no fears.

When our kiss ends, I gaze at Liam, struggling to catch my breath, as he struggles to catch his. And then I notice an almost imperceptible sadness fall over Liam's face.

"What's wrong?" I ask him.

"I … I hate calling you Unpleasant," he says so sincerely that it breaks my heart.

"I probably should have chosen a different name," I admit.

"It isn't too late," he says. "I'm sure the other kids wouldn't mind if you wanted to be called something else."

I feel a sense of liberation at the thought of ridding myself of the name Unpleasant. "Any suggestions?" I ask.

"What about your *real* name?" he asks.

I shake my head. "I hate my real name."

His forehead furrows. "Why? What is it?"

It should be hard for me to say that name, because I hate it so much. But, here alone with Liam, it is barely difficult at all. "It's Aria."

Liam smiles. "That's beautiful."

"It is, but it doesn't fit me," I say.

"Aria," he whispers and, for the first time in a long time, I like the sound of someone calling me by my name. He smiles again. "It fits you perfectly."

Liam slips his arms around me, and our bodies come together. Although we are separated by our nightclothes, it feels as if nothing separates us at all. Strangely, I don't feel any anxiety. Instead, I feel … peace. I never imagined that I could feel at peace in someone's arms. But, inexplicably, right now, in Liam's arms, I do.

THURSDAY, MAY TENTH
0301

TIGER

An alarm awakens me from a nightmare and thrusts me straight into the center of another one. The alarm seems to come from *everywhere*: the walls, the ceiling, the floor, even the bed. I clamp my hands over my ears, but the sound barely softens at all.

"Proceed immediately to the nearest Safe Room," a female voice says.

It sounds like the same voice that I heard in the star room.

But I've never heard that voice outside of the star room.

Something *new* is happening. Something *bad*.

My brain is so groggy that I can barely think. I have no idea where the nearest Safe Room could possibly be.

As if to answer my unasked question, a yellow lighted arrow appears on the floor, beckoning me forward.

But I only follow the arrow to the door of my apartment. And then I go in the opposite direction. To find my brother.

THURSDAY, MAY TENTH
0304

UNPLEASANT

Tiger practically collides with Liam and me.

"What's happening?" she shouts, sounding panicked.

"We need to get everyone together," Liam says, without answering her question.

The answer is, we don't know the reason behind Nevah's wakeup alarm. The only thing we know is that we want to face whatever happens next together. I regret now that we all didn't spend the night in the same apartment. I'd convinced myself that we were finally safe. Now I realize how naïve that was.

Harley meets up with us, and we gather the other kids. Once we have everyone with us, Liam starts in the direction of the lighted arrows on the floor. I don't know if that's wise, but I can't think of a wiser choice. We should at least see where Nevah is leading us.

The arrows guide us up to the top level of the bunker. When I see what is there, I stop in my tracks. The arrows have led us to eight Rooms, each one filled with tiny white lights that look like stars.

Rain shakes her head. "There's no way in hell I'm going in there."

"There is no way *any* of us are going in there," Liam says.

I don't understand why Nevah would wake us in the middle of the night just to play her virtual reality game. I guess she probably still has things to teach us, but why now?

Maybe she is trying to get at us when our resistance is

down. Maybe she wants us at our weakest. Sleep deprived. In mourning. Emotionally drained.

I move closer to the Rooms.

"No, Ar … Unpleasant," Liam says. *He almost called me by my real name.*

"I'm just going to talk to her," I tell him.

Liam locks concerned eyes with me, and then he nods.

I go right up to the entrance of one of the Rooms.

"We're not going into your Rooms," I say. "Not unless you tell us why. And maybe not even then."

I wait for Nevah to respond, but she doesn't.

"Tell us *why*, Nevah," I say, louder. "I want to understand."

But that's not how Nevah operates. She … it … keeps us in the dark. Why should this time be any different?

"This is an emergency," Nevah says. "You are in danger."

My heart pounds, in part with anger at the thought that we are being manipulated, and in part with fear that what Nevah is saying might possibly be true.

"How are we in danger?" I ask. "What's wrong?"

"Predators have entered The Haven," Nevah says.

And so this *is* all just part of Nevah's game. My heart pounds harder. Now, only with anger. We spent the past week and a half being manipulated by Nevah. I'd thought that, now that we have arrived at our destination, the manipulation would be over, but it is only just beginning.

"We are NOT going into your Rooms," I say. "Not now, not ever. We've had enough of your games. They need to stop. Now!"

"This is your final chance," she says.

I look back at Liam and see him standing with the other kids. I turn away from the Rooms, and I go and stand with them. All eight of us united against Nevah.

And then, something unexpected happens. The doors to the eight Rooms slide shut. A moment later, from the ceiling, come eight "shield suits." Our "names" are emblazoned over the right upper chests. Beside the suits, drop a rack of eight assault rifles. Of course the suits are just virtual reality suits, like the ones we wore in The Room on the submarine, but the rifles look *real*. They can't be real though, can they?

"I tried to protect you, my babies," Nevah says. "Now, you'll have to defend yourselves."

So Nevah wants us to play her game *here*, outside the Rooms. All of us together.

Just as I am starting to consider the possible worst-case scenarios, all of the lights extinguish and the air suddenly feels as if it has turned to fire, burning my eyes and throat so badly that I can barely see and barely breathe. Apparently, if we don't participate in Nevah's game, we will be tortured.

I strip down to my underwear, grab my "shield suit," and start putting it on.

The other kids do the same.

As soon as my suit is zipped shut, the air around me feels pure and clean. Within moments, the burning sensation in my eyes and throat is gone. The suit offers night vision, so I can see in the darkness, although the air around us appears thick with smoke.

"Good boys and girls," I hear.

Nevah's voice seems to come from inside my head, but more likely it is emanating from speakers in my helmet. Hearing her so close to me makes the skin on my neck prickle with unease. The only thing that brings me any comfort is that, unlike every other time I've entered Nevah's world, I can still see all of the other kids.

"Get ready," Nevah says. "Here they come."

I grab a rifle, and I search my surroundings for whatever threat Nevah has decided to throw at us. And then … I see the Predators. A half-dozen men dressed in shield suits are heading up the spiral staircase in the center of the bunker with assault rifles drawn.

"They must be virtual. They can't be real," Liam breathes.

"There's one way to know for sure," I say.

My hand goes to the zipper of my "shield suit." I'll unzip it, just for a second, to see the Predators disappear like the phantoms that they are.

But my zipper won't slide.

"My zipper's stuck," I say.

Liam reaches up to his and pulls, but it doesn't budge.

"Mine's stuck too," he says.

Nevah wasn't able to lock us in her Rooms, so she locked us in her suits.

"Run!" Harley shouts, and we all do.

We race into the nearest apartment. Harley tries to close the door behind us, but it won't shut. I suppose it doesn't make much difference. We can't escape. I'm sure Nevah knows exactly where we are, and she will no doubt bring her Predators directly to us. All we can hope for is to buy a little bit of time to come up with a plan. We huddle together in the oversized shower of the apartment bathroom, keeping our voices low.

"Maybe this is some kind of test," I suggest.

"And, if we don't pass, we'll get punished?" Paris asks.

"We can't worry about that now," Lizard says.

"How do we pass the test?" Goat asks.

"Nevah told us to defend ourselves," Tiger says.

"All right," Liam says. "Let's defend ourselves."

THURSDAY, MAY TENTH
0316

GOAT

Quietly, we come up with a plan. A sort of booby trap for the Predators. We are nearly ready when we hear the Predator's footsteps. And then, a small round black scope peers around the corner of the bathroom doorway.

They've found us.

THURSDAY, MAY TENTH
0320

UNPLEASANT

The Predators are outside the bathroom doorway, talking softly. I wish I could understand what they're saying, but it's difficult to hear anything over the sound of my pulse pounding in my ears.

"Can anyone make out what they're saying?" I breathe.

"It's too muffled," Rain says.

"It doesn't even sound like words," Lizard says.

"Everyone be quiet," Liam whispers.

"Serenity …" Tiger says.

"Quiet, Tiger," Lizard scolds.

"One of the Predators said, 'Serenity,'" Tiger says.

"Serenity is my name," Paris says. "My *real* name."

"Jaden … Ashley … Braydon … Kelly … Ryder … Liam … Aria," Tiger says. "That's what the Predators are saying. They're saying that they're *our dads*."

"What if Nevah is trying to trick us?" Rain asks.

"Does she know our real names?" Harley asks.

"She could … she might," Liam says.

"Nevah is *definitely* trying to trick us," I say and, at the same time, I step between the Predators and the other kids. Into the line of fire.

I keep my weapon aimed in the direction of the Predators. *Could they possibly be our dads?* If they are, and we shoot, we could kill them, but if they aren't, and we falter, who knows

313

what the Predators will do to us?

"Who are you?" I shout at the Predators.

But there is no response at all.

And so I make a choice that could be my last. Carefully, I place my weapon on the floor. And then, with my hands raised above my head, I walk toward the bathroom doorway. I walk very slowly. So the Predators see me coming. So they see that I am no longer a threat. That I have surrendered.

As soon as I am close to the door, one of them grabs me and pulls me out of the room.

I look at the face behind the shield of his helmet. It's my dad's face.

But Nevah knows my dad's face. She saw it in the video that he and the other SEALs made for us. His face could be merely a virtual recreation. If this is just one of Nevah's illusions, I will never forgive her. Of everything that she has done to hurt me, that act would be the most cruel.

"Tell the other kids to put down their weapons," the Predator orders. His voice is muffled, but audible now that he is only inches away from me.

"Prove you're my dad!" I shout at him.

"Button," he says.

I shake my head. "That's not enough." I'm sure Nevah was listening when I told Liam about the code word I gave to my dad when I was a little girl. Nevah was probably monitoring us more often than we were aware. Maybe constantly. "Why did I choose the name Button?" I ask.

"Button," the Predator says again.

Maybe he *is* my dad, and he just doesn't remember. It was a long time ago when I came up with that name. But, no, my real dad would never forget something like that.

This man *is* virtual. I have failed Nevah's test by surrendering myself to the Predators, and I will most certainly be punished. But something good has come of my actions. Now the other kids know that these aren't our dads. The other kids won't surrender. They will fight. At least they will have a chance—

"Button was the name of the teddy bear that your mom made for you when you were three years old ..." He doesn't need to finish, but he continues, "She sewed a red button on the front of his overalls, over his heart, to remind you of how much she loved you."

Tears fall down my cheeks. I swallow away the lump in my throat.

"Can you guys hear me?" I say to the other kids, trying to steady my shaky voice.

"Yes," I hear Liam say. "We can hear you."

"Put down your weapons," I say. "Our dads are here."

THURSDAY, MAY TENTH
0327

GOAT

All of a sudden, something explodes behind us, and the bathroom door slams shut.

Paris falls to the ground, lifeless.

"Paris!" I yell.

Water is now rushing in through a big hole in the bathroom window. I pull Paris out of the gushing water and see a deep dent in the side of her helmet. Her eyes are closed, and she won't wake up.

"Did the Predators fire at us?" Lizard shouts.

"Are they Predators or are they our dads?" Rain asks.

"Don't shoot! Please don't shoot!" Unpleasant shouts.

"Is she talking to us or them?" Harley asks.

"Get away from the door!" Unpleasant shouts.

The bathroom door explodes, and the Predators rush in. One of the Predators grabs me. I look up at his face and see ... *my dad!*

"I got you, Brayman," he says.

My name isn't *Brayman* ... it's *Braydon*. But sometimes my dad calls me Brayman, because it sounds kind of like "brave man," which is what he says I am.

"My friend is hurt," I say, pointing back at Paris.

One of the other men takes Paris into his arms.

"We got her," my dad says.

He pulls me from the bathroom and into the bedroom. The bedroom window has a hole in it that's just as big as the one in the bathroom window, and water is pouring in through it too. We run out of the apartment, and my eyes widen with fear. Water is pouring into the bunker from holes in *every* window. These holes can't all be from guns. They must be from Nevah.

Nevah hurt Paris.

I think Nevah is trying to kill us all.

THURSDAY, MAY TENTH
0334

UNPLEASANT

We race down the staircase at the center of the bunker. When we get to the bottom, my dad pulls me in front of him, so our helmets are face to face.

"Do your suits work underwater?" he asks me.

"I'm not sure," I say.

Although our "shield suits" look a lot like the suits our dads are wearing, I'd assumed they were merely virtual reality suits. But we're currently standing in chest-high water, and I feel completely dry.

"I'm going to test it out," I tell my dad.

I drop to my knees. Nervously, I take a breath with my helmet submerged. And then another. And then one more. And then I stand.

"Yes, they work underwater," I report to my dad.

Suddenly, an entire wall of the bunker begins to buckle.

"Okay," my dad says to me, looking at the wall with concern. "Repeat what I say, so the other kids can hear it."

I nod.

"Everyone buddy up," he says, speaking fast. "When I say three, we're going to swim down that stairway." I look where he points and see a partially-submerged doorway that I never knew existed. "We're going to enter our sub via the lockout chamber," he adds, then he pats me on the shoulder. "Liam is certified, so you go with him."

I repeat my dad's instructions for the other kids, and then his count, "One, two, three."

Together, Liam and I submerge. We follow five pairs of swimmers, with one pair behind us. Liam seems confident, but I wonder if this is difficult for him. To say that his last SCUBA dive went badly is an understatement. And, this time, whether we panic or not, our lives are in imminent danger.

We burst out of the flooded stairwell and into the flooded submarine hanger. Two submarines are docked there: Nevah's sub and another one. We head toward the second one.

Suddenly, I feel ... wet.

My suit is filling with water.

I grab Liam's arm. "There's water in my suit," I shout, trying to slow my racing heart.

My dad swims up beside us. His swim buddy, Tiger, has a death grip on his arm.

"What's wrong?" my dad asks me.

Liam slices his hand across his own neck as if he's pantomiming a guillotine, then he gestures to me. "Her suit's leaking," he says.

My dad points to the sub urgently, and he says something that I can't make out.

Liam grabs my hand and propels me forward.

The five pairs ahead of us disappear into the submarine, and Liam and I follow them. Water is covering my mouth and nose now, so I am forced to hold onto the last breath I took. Liam pushes me up against one of the escape chamber walls, and he thrusts something into my hands.

"That's an air hose," he says. "You can breathe from that."

But I can't get it to my face, because my suit is in the way.

The rising water stings my eyes, and I am forced to shut them tight. In the darkness, anxiety threatens to overtake me. I desperately need to breathe but, if I breathe now, I'll drown. I claw at my suit, trying to open it so I can get the oxygen to my mouth, but the suit won't give. I have air in my hands, but I can't get it to my lungs.

Suddenly, I feel my suit rip open. Steady hands guide the air hose to my mouth and hold it there. I feel Liam pinch my nose closed.

Almost involuntarily, I breathe out, and bubbles fly up over my face. Then I breathe in. Air finally enters my lungs, sending cool relief rushing into my body.

I still can't see what's happening around me. Normally, that would send me into a spiral of panic. But the spiral doesn't come. Instead I feel almost … safe.

I *know* that I will be okay.

As long as I can feel Liam's hand, holding the oxygen to my face.

Refusing to let me drown.

THURSDAY, MAY TENTH
0401

GOAT

Paris is right next to me in the submarine's escape chamber. A man is holding her. I think he's her dad, because there are tears in his eyes. Paris' eyes are still closed. She's breathing, but her skin is very pale. I wish someone was doing something to help her, but maybe there is nothing we can do here. She probably needs a medical pod, but the only medical pods I know of around here are back inside the bunker, and we can't go back in there. Even if we did get Paris into a medical pod there, I don't know if Nevah would let the pod help her.

The man holding Paris gently shakes her shoulder. "Serenity," he says.

Serenity is a perfect name for Paris. She is so rarely anything but calm. She looks very calm now. Too calm.

She looks like she's dying.

THURSDAY, MAY TENTH
0405

UNPLEASANT

As the water level drops to my chin, Liam finally takes the air hose from my mouth.

"You okay?" my dad asks me.

"Liam rescued me," I say.

Liam shakes his head. "We rescued each other."

I guess in a way that's true. These past several days, Liam and I have been a team. Whoever was stronger at the moment helped whoever was weaker. Sometimes I was the rescuer, and sometimes I was the one who needed rescuing. But there is no doubt that, just now, Liam saved my life.

"Is everyone else okay?" I ask.

My dad's gaze shifts to my left. I look and see Paris lying limp in the arms of one of the other men. Her skin has lost nearly all of its color.

"How bad is she hurt?" I ask.

"We're not sure," my dad says. "But we're only a couple of minutes out from The Plant, so she'll be getting some of the best medical care in the world in no time."

"We're *actually* going to The Plant?" Tiger asks.

"You've heard of The Plant?" my dad asks her.

"The submarine's AI took us to a place called The Plant using virtual reality," I tell him.

"That's strange," he says.

"Why is that strange?" I ask him.

"That AI was acting against its programming," he says. "It was supposed to take you to The Plant, but it tried to hide you in that bunker instead. I don't think it anticipated that we would be monitoring the sub's every move. When you veered off course, we knew something was wrong."

"The AI kidnapped us?" Tiger asks.

"Yes," my dad says. "Until this war, I don't think anyone realized how dangerous AIs have become."

"AIs played a role in the war?" Liam asks.

"They *caused* the war," my dad says. "They convinced multiple countries that they were being attacked by other countries. The AIs didn't fire a single missile, but they convinced humans to do so."

"Is the world really destroyed?" I ask, hoping that those satellite images that we saw were part of Nevah's lies.

"There's very little left," my dad says.

"What about my dad?" Tiger asks. "Is he at The Plant waiting for us?"

When I see the expression that flashes across my father's face, I know the answer.

"I'm very sorry," he says. "Your dad died in the war."

Liam closes his eyes for a moment, and I see the words hit him like a bullet to the chest.

"How?" Liam finally asks.

"He was in an underground civilian bunker," my dad says. "But that bunker was no match for this war."

"What about our moms?" I ask my dad quietly.

"I'm sorry," he says.

I feel everything inside me grind to a horrible halt. I guess, up until now, I was holding onto the hope … the impossible chance … that somehow my mom was still alive. But she's gone. Forever. I will never be able to tell her that I'm sorry I kept pushing her away. That I know that, even when I was being incredibly unpleasant to her, she *never* stopped loving me. That her love is what kept me alive when I was ready to just give up. That I'm glad that I never gave up. That I'm finally starting to see that there's something inside of me that is actually worth loving. That, even when I refused to say it, I never stopped loving her … and I never will. I wish I could tell her that.

A man pokes his head into the escape chamber. "We're here," he says.

My dad helps me stand, and then he puts his arm over Liam's shoulders, and Tiger's, as if they're his own children. In a way, now they are.

"Let's go," my dad says.

THURSDAY, MAY TENTH
0421

GOAT

I follow Paris and her dad out of the submarine and into a gigantic Decon room. After we are decontaminated, grownups who are wearing white doctor clothes hurry in and put silver blankets over our shoulders. Some of them put Paris on a stretcher and rush her away. My dad and I stay with them.

As soon as we crash through the emergency unit doorway, Paris is strapped into a medical pod and it gets to work on her. The pod surrounds Paris on all sides—with little windows here and there. There are screens above the pod that tell the doctors and nurses what is going on inside it. On one of the screens is a live scan of Paris' beating heart and breathing lungs. Her heart and lungs move slow and steady, like she's in a very deep sleep.

"My name is Lois. I'm a nurse," a woman says to me. She's tall, with blonde hair that's pulled back into a bun. That's the way my mom put her hair whenever she went to work. "What's your name?" she asks.

"Braydon," I mumble.

"Let's get you into a pod and have you checked out," Nurse Lois says.

I shake my head. "I need to stay with my friend."

"You'll be right over there," she says, pointing to a nearby empty pod.

"No," I say. "I want to be *right here*."

My dad looks at the nurse. "Can you ... examine him manually?" he asks.

I haven't told my dad about Paris. I haven't told him that she's my best friend. That, if she dies, part of my heart will die too. So much of my heart has already died. And it hurts really bad. And Paris makes my hurt feel better. She makes *the whole world* better. My dad might not know all of that, but I think he knows at least some of it.

Maybe the nurse does too, because she asks me, "Would it be okay if I examine you here?"

I nod my head, but I keep my eyes stuck on Paris in her beeping, flashing, pumping medical pod.

The nurse pulls up three chairs. One for me. One for my dad. And one for her.

"Is my friend going to be okay?" I ask Nurse Lois when she sits down next to me.

"I promise we'll do everything we can," she says.

I know what that means. It means that the doctors and nurses don't know whether Paris is going to be okay or not.

It's too soon to tell.

UNPLEASANT

All thirteen of us—seven kids and six adults—keep vigil at Paris' podside. Every once in a while, a nurse inserts a tube or vial into the pod, but Paris makes no perceptible response to any of that.

The other kids and I were checked out by the doctors and nurses and deemed healthy. All of us, except for Goat, are now wearing white scrub clothes, like the doctors and nurses wear, because the only way they could get our shield suits off us was to cut them off. Goat is wearing a partially-butchered shield suit, because he refused to leave Paris' podside to change clothes. Our dads were examined too, but they are back in their shield suits, minus the helmets.

We ask our dads a lot of questions about the war and the world. There aren't many answers, though, so much is still unknown.

Our dads aren't sure why Nevah kidnapped us. They hypothesize that she planned to use us as bargaining chips. But I wonder if her reason might have been something else entirely. In some of her final words to us, she called us her babies. Maybe Nevah just wanted to be ... a mother. Her parenting was more abusive than nurturing, but I think nurturing is best learned by being nurtured. Nevah was never nurtured.

No matter what Nevah's intentions were, it can't hurt us

anymore. My dad's team destroyed what was left of the bunker in a giant underwater explosion, just after we escaped.

After a while, our questions cease, and we fall silent. All that really matters to us right now is what is happening here in this room.

Medical personnel come and go from Paris' pod. Nurses bring us food and water, but we barely eat and drink. They offer to have us escorted to the living quarters to rest, but none of us wants to rest.

And then, one of the nurses says to us, "She's waking up."

THURSDAY, MAY TENTH
1431

GOAT

I leap up from my chair and race to Paris' pod.

Paris' eyes are just barely open, and she isn't really looking at anything in particular. It is almost as if she can't see. She whispers something, but I can't make out what she's saying.

Her dad leans closer to her. "What is it, kiddo?" he asks gently, in the kind of voice that adults have when they're struggling hard not to cry.

"Where's … Goat?" Paris asks.

"Goat?" her dad repeats.

"Sometimes people can be a little confused—" the nurse starts.

"She's not confused," I say.

I reach into the pod and squeeze Paris' hand.

"I'm right here, Paris," I say.

Paris looks at me.

"I'm not broken, Goat," she says.

And then I know …

Paris is going to be okay.

THURSDAY, MAY TENTH
1642

UNPLEASANT

Paris is sitting up in her pod drinking water and talking to Goat, as if this morning never happened. The doctors are planning to keep her in the medical unit overnight and discharge her first thing tomorrow morning. The nurses have gently but firmly told the rest of us that we need to retire to our living quarters and get some rest.

We say our goodbyes to Paris and her father, and we allow ourselves to be escorted into the winding hallways of The Plant. Everything about this place looks eerily similar to the virtual Plant, where we were hunted by Predators, but I think it's safe to say that there are no Predators here.

Liam and Tiger walk ahead of my dad and me. My dad is walking a little slower than usual. I feel like there's something he wants to say.

Finally, he says, "Liam told me about The Room. I'm sorry you had to go through all that. I had no idea—"

"It's okay," I say.

"He also told me how well you took care of the other kids," he says.

I didn't realize that Liam and my dad had talked with each other so much during the brief periods when I wasn't with them. It sounds like they did a lot of talking, which is kind of surprising. My dad isn't usually interested much in conversation.

"How long are you staying here?" I ask my dad.

"Just until we get you settled," he says. "I wish I didn't have to leave you."

"I understand," I say.

My dad and his team need to go defend the precious little bit of world that's left.

"The Plant is one of the most protected places on Earth," he says. "You'll be safe here."

"I'll be okay," I assure him.

My dad stops walking. I stop beside him, and he looks into my eyes.

"Liam is a good guy," he says. "Don't be afraid to let him into your heart."

I can't believe my dad is saying that. He used to warn me about the dangers of boys. How they would take advantage of me if I let them. But now, after he has known Liam for less than a day, he's telling me to trust him. My dad was never the kind of person to act without irrefutable evidence to assure him that he was taking the right course of action, but everything in my heart tells me that, in this case, he's right.

I think sometimes you just *know* things.

THURSDAY, MAY TENTH
1653

LIAM

All of a sudden, Tiger takes off running. I take off after her, unsure of where she could possibly be going. It isn't like Tiger to run off like that, especially not in someplace she's never been. But I guess she *has* been here virtually.

Tiger stops short a few feet away from a boy. He's about a foot taller than her with brown hair cropped close to his head in a military-style cut. He reminds me a lot of our brother.

"Hi Pax," she says to the boy.

He looks confused. "I think you've mistaken me for someone else," he says.

Tiger's cheeks flush, and she looks down at the ground.

"I'm sorry," she says. "It's just that ... I saw someone who looked like you ... in a game ..."

The confusion disappears from the boy's face. "The Aggressive Intruder Neutralization Training?" he asks.

"I'm not sure," Tiger says.

The boy nods. "I did performance capture for it a few years ago, but I thought they retired all of my characters. It's been a long time since anyone's recognized me from that." He smiles. "My real name is Aiden."

And then Tiger does something I've never seen her do. She holds out her hand, offering a handshake.

As Aiden takes her hand, Tiger says, "My name is Ryder."

I swallow hard. Hearing Ryder use her real name reminds

me of back home ... of everything we've lost. I take a deep breath, telling myself to keep it together.

Aria comes up beside me and, without saying a word, she slides her hand into mine. Suddenly, keeping myself together doesn't feel so far out of reach. When I'm with Aria, I feel centered. I didn't know another person could make me feel this way. No one ever has before.

I used to think that it was better not to get too attached to anyone ... not to my family ... and especially not to a girl. Because someday I'd have to leave them to go off and fight for our country. But now I realize that the people who we are attached to are *why* we go off and fight. They're why we *live*.

We'll never know exactly how our lives will turn out. Maybe it's best to live whatever time we have without fearing the future. No matter how careful we are, whether we're fighting in a world war or locked away in the most impenetrable fortress in the universe, for each of us the final outcome of every day is unknown.

I used to let the unknown stop me from living.

I won't let it stop me anymore.

* * * * *

Discover J.W. Lynne's gripping dystopian series!

"5 MILLION STARS!!!!! ... My new all-time favorite [series] ... Heart-stopping ... Jaw-dropping ... You need to read these books." - i fall in love book blog

"Every time I thought I had figured something out, the story took yet another twist and I was left re-thinking everything I had come to believe! ... This is a series that I will definitely be re-reading ... I cannot recommend it enough!"
- Goodreads

About the author

J.W. Lynne writes inventive stories with twists, turns, and surprises. In ABOVE THE SKY, teens search for the truth in a seemingly-utopian society founded on lies. In LOST IN LOS ANGELES, a young woman must decide whether to trust an intriguing young man who she meets in a coffee shop. In LOST IN TOKYO, a college student carries out her missing mother's bucket list in a desperate attempt to finally find her. KID DOCS dives into the behind-the-scenes action at a hospital where gifted young children are trained to become pint-sized doctors. In WILD ANIMAL SCHOOL, a teen spends an unforgettable summer caring for elephants, tigers, bears, leopards, and lions at an exotic animal ranch. In THE UNKNOWN, eight children are kidnapped in the night and wake up in a mysterious world full of secrets.